DESTINY

DESTINY

PAUL COX

THORNDIKE PRESS
A part of Gale, Cengage Learning

Published in 2020 by arrangement with Paul Colt

Printed in Mexico
Print Number: 01   Print Year: 2020

DESTINY

PROLOGUE

Late Spring 1916
Communication:
General Esteban Fierros, commander Fierros Brigade
To: General Pablo Gonzales, commander Army Corps of the East
"Most of the cavalry have crossed in to Texas to penetrate the interior of the State, disguised as vaqueros, and to date we have had no difficulty in crossing in parties of 25 to 30 men, dividing them into bands of 20 in different directions, designating Kennedy, Texas, as the assembly point. The Coup should break out tonight after midnight. I expect we will soon have very good news to communicate to you. I leave Monday to put myself at the head of my troops, depending on the orders that General Fortunato gives me. I send a strong abrazo. Expecting you to telegraph me the latest on the International situation."

7

Communication:
General Frederick Funston, commander U.S. Army Southern Department
To: General John J. Pershing, commander Punitive Expedition

"War with de facto government almost inevitable. You are liable to be attacked at any time by large force reaching Chihuahua by train from central Mexico as well as Sonora troops. Your line is too long and troops scattered too much. For a time, we cannot support you. Fall back along your line of communications with view to general concentration of entire force at Colonia Dublan. Such action imperative. No question of prestige can be entertained as military considerations must govern. If attacked do not allow any preliminary success to induce you to advance too far as danger meeting overwhelming force and having your line of communication cut is too great. Acknowledge and report daily."

Excerpt from *The Plan de San Diego*, Harris and Sadler, page 398:

"Precisely how the decision was reached remains unclear . . . Accordingly, what took place on June 10 was not an invasion (of

8

the U.S.) but the frantic postponement of the operation."

CHAPTER 1

Before we proceed with our narrative it is imperative that I introduce myself and in doing so divulge a bit of my family history. My name is William Cabott Weston III and Carnegie Hill has been my home since birth.

The Hill, as the residents genially refer to it, is located in New York City and is home to some of the wealthiest families in the nation. Those that reside on the Hill are what the public rather loosely refers to as "high society." However, it may come as a surprise to the uniformed that to be genuinely accepted in our circles one must not only possess considerable wealth but also the proper bloodlines.

Recently, for instance, it has become disturbingly apparent that the mere possession of wealth qualifies anyone, and I do mean anyone, to take up residence in the Upper East Side of Manhattan. However, none of these nouveau riche would even think of approaching Carnegie Hill without a verifiable pedigree.

We Westons, for example, are in the shipping industry and have been since the Middle Ages. We trace our ancestry back through generations of the most prestigious aristocracies of Europe, and as one might expect, have more than our fair share of royal corpuscles pulsing through our veins. Needless to say, over the centuries that blue blood has, no doubt, contributed significantly to our family's financial success and innumerable accomplishments.

For those of us on the Hill, it is understood that the genesis of our vaunted stature lies not in the clumsy use of brute strength such as that championed by the crusaders or invading barbarians. No, our elevated existence is clearly the result of natural selection if you will. High society is, as Mr. Darwin so brilliantly postulated, simply a prime example of human evolution.

Those on Carnegie Hill and others of our standing have long accepted the unique and historic role we play in shaping and controlling world events, and yet, we readily admit that our influence and power is solely the result of natural laws. We are, and will continue to be, simply the "fittest" of our species. And though we exist in the same murky environment in which the world flounders aimlessly, we not only survive, we inevitably excel.

And since we do excel, we take pride in knowing that over the centuries it has been our discoveries and our innate talents that have sculpted the cornerstones of history and determined the fate of mankind. We recognize that man's destiny is, and always has been, forged by those occupying the zenith of human existence.

Or so I thought until the spring of 1916.

That was the year I graduated from Harvard. It was the beginning of the twentieth century and I was twenty years old. As any man my age, I was full of vim and vigor and cocksure of myself. I was ready to spread my wings and conquer the world. And, I was determined, despite my father's objections, to do it on my own terms. I would, using my own plan, seek fame and fortune and in short order attain both without the assistance or the interference of family.

And after years of monotonous study behind ivy-covered walls, my ambition was inexorably coupled with a thirst for adventure. I was determined, if need be, to travel the world in search of it, but not as a shipping consultant as preordained by my father. No, I was going to be a news reporter. My plan being that after a few years of reporting I would become an editor. I would continue to advance in the news industry and by the time I was thirty would own my own newspaper, commanding the respect of like-minded men such as William Randolph Hearst.

The day I revealed my plans to Father, his voice rose to levels that I had never before heard. It was dreadful. At the time, I thought his behavior quite unbecoming for a gentleman.

Though I was hoping for Mother's support that day, she and father wholeheartedly agreed that news reporting was a shameful occupation. Even if it was just a passing phase, my mother had said, it was a degrading occupation, especially for a Weston.

Father was beside himself for hours but Mother, as usual, proved to be more level-headed. She eventually relented. She then convinced Father to allow me the freedom to purge such foolishness from my system. Then, she explained, I would return a humble and wiser man and gratefully assume my proper role in the company.

She was right to think as she did. But as it turned out, she was only half-right.

Anxious to exert my independence, I packed hastily that same evening and early the next morning; taking only a small suitcase and a leather satchel full of pencils and notepads, I moved into a hotel on Fifth Avenue.

Having secretly taken several journalism classes at school, I was confident the *New York Times* would hire me based solely on my merits. So certain was I that I decided to apply for work, not as William Cabott Weston III but as William Cabott. I would show Mummy and dear old Dad that not only could I succeed on my own, I could do so without employing the Weston name. After all, I reasoned, when I mentioned my Harvard degree, I would have no need of family influence.

However, I quickly learned that my reasoning had its limitations.

For my interview with the *Times* editor, I wore my best suit by Mitchell the Tailor of Midtown Manhattan. I was beaming with pride and expecting something akin to a coronation but all I received was the cold shoulder. I got it from the *Times* but also from the *New York Tribune* and the *Sun.* In fact, the only newspaper in the entire northeast that finally offered to give me a chance was the *Chicago Tribune.*

On the day of my interview, the *Tribune* editor consented to hire me but only under two conditions.

One, if I agreed to go on assignment as subordinate of a seasoned reporter named Floyd Gibbons; and two, if I would be willing to travel to a remote desert region and live there for an indefinite period of time.

Thinking of the Sahara, Egypt, or even India, I jumped at the chance. "Sure," I told him, not realizing at the time what a fool I was. And yet, as you will see, that fateful decision was a life-changing one and the best I ever made.

The evening after my interview found me standing on a crowded train platform waiting for, I was told, one of the *Tribune*'s finest reporters. It was there I first glimpsed Floyd Gibbons.

Working his way toward me was a man in his mid-thirties, tall, thin, and sporting a straw boater hat and tawdry pinstripe suit. His nose was aquiline and his jaw narrow and angular. His lips were thin and between them hung a half-smoked cigarette.

Floyd Gibbons approached me with a smile and we shook hands. Standing next to my small traveling case and with my leather satchel over my shoulder, I introduced myself as William Cabott.

Floyd Gibbons's ill-bred response was, "Bill Cabott, huh. Or is it Billy? Well, either way glad to meet ya, kid. Glad to meet ya."

Our train was nowhere in sight and yet Gibbons spoke to me as if he were late for an appointment of some sort. His words, choppy and quick, rattled past his cigarette, dislodging ashes that dropped to the platform.

Before the vulgar moniker of "Billy" fully registered in my mind, Gibbons handed me a forty-pound suitcase.

"Here, kid," he chirped. "Take good care of this. Our cameras are in there. Gotta have photographs these days. Sketches are a thing of the past. We need photographs! Photographs and lots of 'em."

My mouth may have hung open. I don't recall. But I have not forgotten the weight of that suitcase.

I am what some might describe as "bookish." At Harvard I was highly ranked on our chess team but I didn't quite make the grade in polo. I did, however, qualify for second alternate on the rowing team. But that was the full extent of my athletic career.

In height, I have to stretch to measure five foot seven inches and I scarcely tip the scales at one hundred thirty pounds, and that after a hearty meal. Nevertheless, I accepted the suitcase and the assignment of caring for it without complaint.

After we boarded the train and got settled, I worked up the courage to ask Gibbons where we were going and what we were going to be reporting.

He lit a fresh cigarette, shaking the flame off the match as he answered, "Columbus. We're off to Columbus."

I nodded, searching my brain for some intelligent response. Watching him suck on the cigarette, I asked in all seriousness, "South America?"

"I wish," scoffed Gibbons and then blew smoke out of his nostrils. "I wish. Columbus, New Mexico. You know the Mexican thing. Pershing's going after that murdering Pancho Villa."

I was twenty years old and just out of college. I'd never heard of Pancho Villa. Neither did I have any idea who Pershing might be, but William Cabott Weston III was not about to admit his ignorance, at least not to the likes of Floyd Gibbons.

However, being distracted by my predicament, I was unaware of the blank look displayed on my face.

Gibbons glanced at me and then his eyes roamed over the leather satchel still hanging from my shoulder. He laughed and the tone of his laugh was laced with ridicule. I felt blood rush to my face. Never had I been scorned in that manner. And this man was a mere employee of a newspaper. And a Chicago newspaper at that!

"President 'watchful waiting' Wilson," explained Gibbons, "is finally going to do something about our border with Mexico. The damn pacifist has no choice now."

I was helpless. I had no idea what Gibbons was talking about. For the first time in my life, I chose to swallow my pride. I still remember the rancid taste of it.

I coughed a little as Gibbons's smoke encircled my head. "Please forgive me, Mr. Gibbons. I'm not up on the latest news. I'm fresh out of college. My studies, you understand, were rather consuming. What's happened?"

I remember how Gibbons grinned that night. His eyes narrowed and then darted back and forth as if he were watching a moving picture. Sly is what he was, like a fox. And treacherous.

"Well," began Gibbons, "I'm sure you've been following the war in Europe. Some say we're going to get in it and fight against the Germans. I don't know about that. President Wilson's trying to stay out of the whole mess.

"But most people don't give a hoot about Mexico. That country's been in civil war for the last six years or so. Anyway, who cares how long it's been? Unless you live down along the border, that is. They care plenty down there but nobody pays much attention to them. Not enough votes.

"A few Americans getting murdered by Mexican bandits once in a while hardly makes the papers up here. But last January, eighteen American businessmen were murdered down in Mexico by what are called 'Villistas.' They're called that because they're Pancho Villa's men. Get it? Villistas.

"His real name is Francisco Villa but that's beside the point."

I started to ask a question but Gibbons barely took a breath before he continued. "This Pancho Villa is nothing more than a bandit turned politician. He fancies himself as some sort of general.

"Wilson used to favor him because he was kind of a Robin Hood. We even sold him guns and ammunition early on in his revolution. But then Wilson switched sides and favored the more respectable Venustiano Carranza and then put an embargo on arms sales to Villa.

"Villa got sore, so he brought a small army and attacked the town of Columbus in the

20

black of night. His men killed ten soldiers, murdered eight civilians, and wounded eight more soldiers.

"He used his army and invaded the United States that night. That invasion's what got the country up in arms now. It's a matter of national pride . . . for those that know what happened, that is."

The last comment stung. I felt suddenly ashamed of myself. All I could muster was a weak, "Well, there were finals at school. I'm afraid I studied so intently I lost touch with current events."

Gibbons grinned as if he were a cat playing with a mouse. "I see, Kid. That must've been rough on you."

I shrugged and started to speak. I knew I should say something but drew a blank.

If Gibbons would have had a tail, it would have been twitching at that moment. With his eyes locked on me, he grinned again and then inhaled more smoke.

"Anyway, now you're up to speed. Columbus was two days ago. Wilson approved military action yesterday. General Pershing is to head it up. The paper's pulling some strings. We may get to go along with the general. We'd be the official national correspondents for the expedition. And as far as reporters are concerned, that's the brass

21

ring, Billy.

"We've got competition, though. The *New York Tribune* is trying to horn in. We gotta beat them to Columbus and convince Pershing that we're the ones that should do the reporting."

Slowly, my mind was beginning to focus. The words *killed, murdered,* and *wounded* were starting to soak in.

I remember lowering my voice. I wanted to sound like a serious reporter, or at least what I thought one should sound like. "So we're going to war with Mexico? We're going to report on the war, then?"

"It might come to that," answered Gibbons. "War, I mean. What we're covering, though, is called a 'punitive expedition.' It's based on the old idea of 'hot pursuit' that was used by both us and the Mexicans in the Geronimo days. And both sides have used 'hot pursuit' since then, chasing bandits back and forth across the border.

"That 'hot pursuit' must be in some old treaty somewhere because that's what we're using to justify going after Pancho Villa. But the Mexicans, holy cow, how they hate us down there.

"You ever hear of the Plan of San Diego?"

I merely shook my head.

"Well, a year ago last January, the authori-

22

ties down in Texas arrested a Mexican named Ramos. He had this revolutionary manifesto on him. It said that starting February twentieth there was to be an uprising all along the southwest. Mexicans, blacks, and Japanese were supposed to rise up and kill every white male over the age of sixteen. An all-out race war is what they had planned."

Dumbfounded, I glared at Gibbons. What he was saying was preposterous. "That is hard to believe. Are you certain?"

"Sure am. The Mexicans said it was 'Yankee tyranny' that stole the southwest from them back in 1848. They were out to get back Texas, New Mexico, Arizona, California, and Colorado. Can you imagine?"

The year of 1848 triggered a memory, something I had learned in school. I felt a flood of relief rush over me. I finally had something intelligent to say.

"But we had an all-out war with Mexico in '48. We won, but then we paid them millions of dollars for the land."

Gibbons chuckled as he leaned his head back and blew smoke rings into the ceiling of the passenger car. "Mexicans have a short memory, I suppose. But some of them can hold a grudge a long time. Hell, that was seventy years ago.

"Anyway, February twentieth came and went and nothing happened. So we just laughed off the whole thing. But then in July of last year, Mexican raiders started crossing the border and killing Americans. Down in Texas it got so bad the army was called in to help the Rangers restore order.

"It didn't get much news coverage then, but those raiders were called 'seditionists.' They were actually trying to instigate the San Diego plan, to start a race war.

"But guess who was behind those raids? Guess who was in charge of killing our innocent farmers and ranchers down in south Texas?"

I took a wild guess. "That Pancho Villa fella?"

"Not hardly," sneered Gibbons. "Villa is a straight-up bandit. The one behind those raids is a slippery snake. In fact, he's commanding the Federal troops fighting against Villa."

"Venustiano Carranza? The one President Wilson favors over Villa?" I asked.

"Yep. The one our illustrious, pacifist president not only favors over Villa but also the one he officially recognized as the legitimate president of Mexico. Wilson switched from favoring Villa to Carranza

24

because Carranza was properly elected by the people, or something like that. And then Wilson slaps an arms embargo on Villa. On top of that, Wilson, who claims to be neutral in the whole affair, lets Carranza's troops ride our trains on our side of the border to launch a surprise attack on Villa in Mexico.

"That's why a lot of us think Villa invaded the U.S. and murdered those people in Columbus. He wanted to get back at Wilson for betraying him."

I tried to make sense of what I was hearing. I had never paid attention to politics. I recalled my father repeatedly referring to politicians as tools, mere puppets of industry. But politicians were never associated with barbarity.

"But if Carranza is behind the raids in Texas," I said, "that means both Carranza and Villa have invaded us."

"Right. But Carranza always denied he was behind the raids even though we knew good and well he was calling the shots. You see, Villa made no bones about the fact it was him that invaded Columbus. And that's the difference between the two of them . . . if there is any."

I thought for several seconds and then said, "But if we're after Villa and this Carranza is fighting Villa, aren't we allies with

Carranza? Why should we fear war with Mexico?"

Gibbons forked his fingers and took the cigarette from his lips. He leaned forward. "Politics, my friend. The same stuff that sells newspapers. Politics. Carranza is playing both ends against the middle. If he can use the U.S. to get rid of Villa, that's good for him but his presidency would still be shaky. If he starts a war with us and takes back some of the land Mexico lost in '48, he could make himself a damn emperor and nobody would care."

The rest of the conversation and train ride was inconsequential. Except, that is, for our stop in Kansas City. It was there while waiting for the next train to El Paso that Gibbons said he needed to send a telegram. I was directed to stay with luggage until he returned.

It wasn't until we reached the Columbus train depot that I discovered to whom the telegram had been sent.

Minutes after Gibbons returned from sending the telegram we boarded the Southwestern bound for El Paso. That night we slept sitting up but I didn't open my eyes until sunrise. I noticed then that the train was heading west and realized both Gibbons and I had slept through the brief stop in El Paso. I dozed off again and awoke two hours later as we pulled into the station at Columbus. It was early morning but the temperature outside was already eighty degrees.

Growing up in eastern cities as I did, I had never visited a small town. In fact, I'd never seen one. Nor had I ever been in a desert. Columbus, New Mexico, was a dismal combination of both. It consisted of a scattering of wooden buildings nestled in the middle of nowhere and surrounded by thousands of square miles of sunbaked sand and half-dead brush.

Looking out the north side of the passenger car, I could see that every street of Columbus, all half-dozen of them, was paved with dirt. The paint on the few structures that had been painted was blistered and peeling. Any exposed wood was cracked and bleached white by the heat and wind. There were, however, three city lots next to the train tracks that contained piles of burnt timber and scorched bricks, no doubt the results of Pancho Villa's raid.

The town, however, was full of activity. Clouds of dust rose everywhere as men, horses, and wagons dodged and weaved through the streets.

When the train jerked and came to full

stop, I looked out the windows to the south. Through a haze of dust, I could make out a sprawling army camp. Hundreds of tents of varying shapes and sizes were being erected in rows that reflected adherence to strict military precision. Stacks of hay bales and wooden crates were everywhere. Most of the larger crates were being loaded onto wagons while the smaller ones were being drug or carried by men in uniform.

The soldiers wore flat-brimmed campaign hats with a Montana peak. And even in the heat, they were decked out in long-sleeved khaki shirts. Their matching pants were baggy in the seat but from the knee down to the shoe top they wore snug-fitting canvas or leather leggings. Some wore neckties, many wore pistols. All were drenched with sweat.

Gibbons rested a hand on my shoulder as he leaned and looked out the window. "Hell of a place, eh Kid? What ya bet the shirts those boys are wearing are made of wool?"

Before I could answer, Gibbons snatched his small suitcase and snickered, "That's the army for you. Wool shirts in the desert."

Clumsily grabbing my suitcase and the heavy camera bag, I followed Gibbons. I stumbled as I stepped down from the train and onto the hollow-sounding planks of the bustling loading platform.

I glanced around at the confusion and raised my voice. "What now?"

Gibbons didn't answer. Being much taller than I, he could better see what was going on around us but seemed to be looking in only one direction. He rocked up on his tiptoes for a better look and then waved vigorously.

Without a word, he started working his way through the crowd. Like a well-trained dog, I followed on his heels as best I could.

Near the end of the platform, Gibbons reached out his right hand. Another civilian, somewhat shorter than Gibbons but just as wiry looking, shook Gibbons's hand.

I was behind Gibbons so I leaned to one side to see what was going on. I heard Gibbons bellow, "Robert, you son of a gun, how are you?"

The only substantive difference I could see between the two men was that the one called Robert sported a mustache and had a cigar dangling from his lips instead of a cigarette. At first, I thought they might be related.

"Did you get us a room?" asked Gibbons, having to speak over the racket. "This place looks packed!"

"One hotel room, one bed," replied Robert. "We'll have to share the bed but it's better than the floor. It was the last room in the entire town."

Gibbons slapped Robert on the shoulder. "Just like old times."

Robert glanced down at me. He took the cigar from his mouth and pointed at me with it. "Who's that?"

I believe, for the moment, Gibbons had forgotten me. He stepped aside, grinning as I'd seen him do for the entire trip. "Oh. This is Billy. Billy . . . what was it, Kid?"

"Cabott," I said, setting down the heavy camera case and extending my hand. "William Cabott."

The man switched his cigar to his left hand and shook mine. "Robert Dunn. *New York Tribune.*"

"That's right," agreed Gibbons. "Robert and I go way back."

I smiled and nodded even though I had noticed that Robert Dunn was referred to as Robert. Not Bob, and certainly not Bobby.

I should have known what was coming next. In my defense, I will say that I did at least feel uncomfortable. I was just beginning to digest what Dunn had said about the hotel accommodations when his next words broke into my thoughts.

"Well, Billy," offered Dunn, "there are empty cots down with the freight wagons. Almost all the drivers over there are civilians. They look like soldiers because they're part of the expedition. But they don't have any patches on their shirts. That's how you tell them apart from the real soldiers. Anyway, look them up. That's the only place left to sleep."

"Where would those freight wagons be?" I asked Dunn, shouting over the noise.

Dunn waved a hand for us to follow and we shoved our way through to the steps and then down alongside the tracks next to the depot.

"That building over there is the Custom House," said Dunn, pointing to a sturdy-looking white building just across a road a few yards to the west of us. "Behind it you'll find the cots and a place to eat, too."

Without so much as a blink or a nod, Gibbons took the camera case from my grasp. "Go get settled, Kid. We'll be at the hotel."

Stunned and speechless, I watched the two men turn their backs and start walking away. Somehow, I had the presence of mind to call out, "Which hotel?"

Dunn half turned and yelled over his shoulder, "The Hoover. Ask around. You'll find it."

And with that abrupt admonition, the two reporters disappeared into the dusty chaos that was Columbus, New Mexico, on that March day of 1916. It was the day I was baptized into hell. Or so I thought at the time.

I don't know how long I stood there. I do remember the sudden quiet. That's what happens when the mind goes blank.

But then someone bumped into me, knocking me sideways. The blow restored my senses and I began weaving my way through the soldiers toward the Custom House. As I did so it dawned on me that I had purposely been given the brush-off by Gibbons and Dunn. Worse, I had been taken for a fool and treated with utter disrespect.

My blood began to boil.

At that moment, I was ready to march after Gibbons and Dunn and properly introduce myself. I was going to set them straight and, with only slight exaggeration, tell them that my father, William Weston II, could buy both their measly newspapers if he so desired. Or, more realistically, I was going to tell them that all I needed to do was say the word and both of them would be fired immediately. Once I revealed my true identity, I was going to relish watching the arrogant grins disappear from their ill-bred faces.

But as I worked my way toward the Custom House, I began to calm down. For whatever reason, on that particular day, amidst all the confusion and frustration, I chose to remain Billy Cabott.

Just to the rear of the Custom House I spotted the teamsters and their wagons. I found the drivers to be far more hospitable than Gibbons and Dunn and by noon a gruff-looking army quartermaster was issuing me a cot, two blankets, and some free advice.

"Be sure," said the quartermaster, "to not let the edge of your blankets hang down onto the sand. If you do, you might wake up with a scorpion or tarantula as a bunkmate."

"Thanks for the warning," I said, feeling a chill run up my spine.

"If you're hungry," the quartermaster offered, thumbing over his shoulder, "there's a mess tent down that way."

I shook my head. "I'm not hungry. I think the heat or perhaps the dryness has taken away my appetite."

"It's neither," grumbled the quartermaster. "It's the damn air itself. Take a whiff."

Inhaling deeply, I could indeed smell

something peculiar. At first, I assumed it was a combination of sweaty men and horse manure. "It is a bit peculiar," I said.

"A mess of Villistas were killed in the raid. They're burning some of the bodies. That's what you smell."

Blocking that repugnant thought from my mind, I located the sleeping area. After fumbling for a half-hour, I finally managed to assemble my cot and then, with a few choice curse words, slid my suitcase under it. Having no desire to eat and no inclination to seek out Gibbons and Dunn, I chose to familiarize myself with the situation in Columbus.

Staying out of the way of the hustle and bustle but asking questions everywhere I went, I learned that the military establishment adjacent to Columbus was called Camp Furlong and that its ranks would soon swell to more than five thousand men. And as soon as the companies were organized, General Pershing and the United States Cavalry would plunge into the heart of Mexico in pursuit of Pancho Villa.

Radios and field telegraphs were to be used as much as possible for communications, but some claimed that Pershing might even, for the first time in military history, consider the use of airplanes. They said the general planned to stay in touch in the rougher terrain by dropping dispatches from the planes as the pilots flew over the soldiers on the ground.

There were also rumors that Carranza was not going to allow Pershing the use of Mexico's railway system for transporting supplies. But rumors were running rampant in Columbus. That particular rumor, though, made no sense to me since Carranza, the de facto president, had granted permission for our military to enter Mexico and also wanted Villa killed.

All day I asked questions and took prolific notes with a pencil and pad of paper. Finally, just before sundown, I glimpsed Gibbons and Dunn walking through Camp Furlong. I suppose it was my pride but I made no effort to follow them. After all, I reasoned, I was a Weston. I would forge my own destiny with or without them. And for now at least, I would keep what I had written in my notes to myself.

Such was my attitude the first day.

By the morning of the second day, the stench of burning bodies had dissipated somewhat and my stomach was growling. At the mess tent, I managed to swallow some scrambled eggs but with the funeral pyres still smoldering, fried bacon was out of the question. Equally unappetizing were thoughts of Gibbons and Dunn. My ill feelings toward them had simmered throughout the night. I awoke with the conviction that hell would freeze over before William Cabott Weston III would go hat in hand to search for Floyd Gibbons. If anything, Gibbons could come looking for me.

Later that afternoon, as I was meandering about town, an automobile came barreling down a side street and then slid to a stop just inches from my shins. When the dust cleared, I saw Dunn sitting behind the steering wheel and Gibbons sitting next to him.

"Hey, Billy," called Gibbons, coming to his feet and peering over the cracked windshield of a broken-down Model T Ford. "Where have you been? I've got news for you."

I brushed some dust from my shirtsleeves. "I've been around. Asking questions. Quite busy, actually."

Gibbons nodded. "Good! You keep it up. Pershing's leaving tomorrow on horseback. Me and Robert are going to be allowed to follow his cavalry column in this."

I tried not to act surprised. "Where'd you get the automobile?"

Waving a hand majestically over the car, Gibbons replied, "This fine specimen was purchased by Robert. He wrote out an I.O.U. on a scrap of paper. It was the only crate with four wheels left for sale in the entire county."

Dunn leaned his head to the side looking around the dirty windshield. "Sorry, Kid. This wreck is only a two-seater. With our baggage and all . . . well, you know how it is."

For the second time in two days I felt like I'd been slapped in the face. But somehow, I managed to maintain my dignity.

"How about the other reporters?" I asked evenly.

"As far as we know," answered Gibbons, "Robert and I are the only two with an automobile. And Pershing wants newsmen along that can keep up. So I guess it's just me and Robert for now. Robert and I will be leaving for Culberson Ranch in the morning. That's about sixty miles west of here. From there, Pershing and his entire western column will cross the border. The rest of you reporters will be allowed to come along later, I suppose."

"Well then," I quipped, forcing a smile, "I shall find you somewhere in Mexico."

Gibbons flashed his usual grin as I stepped out of the way. "That's the spirit, Kid. See ya south of the border."

And with that farewell, Gibbons and Dunn roared off toward Camp Furlong. I, on the other hand, made a beeline for the two-story Hoover Hotel.

Walking past the bullet holes recently blown into the hotel walls, I went straight to the clerk. My guess was correct. Gibbons and Dunn must have just found out about Pershing's plans to cross the border, for the clerk knew nothing about them leaving. I was able to secure their room for myself. Paying for the next week in advance, I took satisfaction in knowing that if I was going to be left behind, I would at least have decent accommodations.

The next morning, I was waiting in the lobby when Gibbons and Dunn came down the stairs with their luggage and camera equipment.

Dunn saw me first. He set his bags down in front of the front desk and then turned toward me. "You're learning fast, Kid."

Gibbons craned his neck around, his narrow face registering surprise. "I'll be damned," he snorted. "You get our room?"

It was my turn to grin and it felt good. "Paid for it yesterday."

"Smart," grunted Gibbons, and then turned and paid his bill.

When Gibbons and Dunn were finished

at the front desk, they hefted their bags and walked out of the hotel without so much as a goodbye. I was offended by such rudeness and yet, I had to admit, that only seconds before both men had paid me a genuine compliment. Later, I was to learn that such behavior was not uncommon. In fact, it was quite normal.

Minutes after I moved into my room, General Pershing's western column, consisting of three thousand men and four thousand horses and mules, left Columbus for Culberson Ranch. However, since Carranza had refused the use of Mexican trains to transport American supplies, Columbus was far from lifeless. Pershing had been forced to make other arrangements to maintain his supply lines and, as a consequence, I spent the next week observing the arrival of hundreds of gasoline-powered motor wagons of every make imaginable.

Arriving first by special train, for instance, were two companies of motor wagons, or trucks as they were being called. There were thirty vehicles in each company. Among them were Packards, Whites, Pierce-Arrows, Dodges, and other makes I'd never heard of, much less seen.

The trucks were off-loaded and then rolled down the streets of Columbus and into Camp Furlong where mechanics made adjustments and added some final touches.

Not only trucks but eight airplanes, half-assembled JN3s, arrived on the trains. These so called "Jennys" were to compose Pershing's 1st Aero Squadron and I watched them closely. I knew that if Pershing chose to make flight an instrument of war it would make headlines from coast to coast.

By the end of the week, Camp Furlong was filled with motorized vehicles, and I suddenly realized that I was witnessing history in the making. Whether the army wanted to admit it or not, it was easy to see this expedition was going to mark the end of an era. The valiant and noble warhorse, used for centuries, would soon become obsolete, replaced forever by grotesque gasoline-powered machines.

With that in mind and with army clearance, I telephoned my observations in to the *Tribune,* my first "angle" as the jargon goes. The editor said he liked my ideas and would blend my "old army–new army" angle into Gibbons's next column on the expedition. But then the editor explained that my contribution would be anonymous, meaning Gibbons would receive credit for my reporting.

Hanging up the phone that day, I was

beginning to think my father had been right about becoming a reporter. And yet deep down I knew that if his prediction indeed turned out to be correct, it would have been correct for all the wrong reasons.

I had chosen my career assuming my innate abilities and talents would open doors for me and lead to my inevitable success. Now, without family influence, those doors were slamming in my face on a daily basis. That, neither my father nor I had anticipated.

After phoning the paper, I dejectedly sat down in the shade of a small shed. For an hour, I considered my predicament and then promised myself I would wait a few more days, no more than a week, before I made a final decision. Then, if things did not take a turn for the better I would admit defeat and head for home.

Lacking the courage of my convictions, though, the next week came and went with me still in Columbus. During that time, I observed an extraordinary influx of civilians. Demand for services was such that the house across from the hotel was converted into a restaurant. It was there I began taking my meals, and at breakfast one day in early April my life took an abrupt turn. However, that fateful detour was but one of

41

many I was about to take.

That morning I was sharing a table with a captain named Ross who was in charge of organizing a truck convoy bound for Colonia Dublan, Mexico. Discovering I worked for the *Tribune,* he spoke freely.

Colonia Dublan, Ross told me, was a Mormon settlement. Mormons, that is, of the polygamist variety. Near that town, Pershing was to establish his headquarters for the campaign.

According to Captain Ross, the first week in Mexico had gone badly for Pershing. Due to faulty information provided by both the Mexican peons and Carrancista soldiers, Pershing found himself chasing his own tail. Not only was the state of Chihuahua immense and virtually unmapped, Pershing soon discovered that most of the peons living there were sympathetic to Villa. There were some opposed to Villa but those few Mexicans despised the Americans more than they did Villa, considering the Americans to be invaders. As a result, it was all but impossible for Pershing to find guides.

The few guides the general did manage to hire deliberately misled him, and the Federal Carrancista officers, often as not, did the same. In less than two weeks, Pershing had come to the realization that no Mexican could be trusted in matters of war.

Ross also informed me that a hapless news reporter learned of the problems Pershing was having with the Mexicans. Yesterday the reporter had called in his story without clearing it with the general first. The reporter's name was Van Camp and Pershing had just had him arrested. That was to send a message to all us reporters that we had better get army clearance before reporting anything. The army referred to that regulation as "censoring."

But whether it was reported or not, the captain made it clear that trouble with the Mexicans was the reason General Pershing had decided to bring in Apache scouts.

"Apache scouts," I said, almost choking on a piece of bacon. "This is the twentieth century. We have motor trucks, auto cars, airplanes, radios . . . we have all that and yet we send for Indian scouts! That makes my head spin!"

Ross laughed. "Mine too. I didn't think there still was any such thing. But both General Pershing and Colonel Dodd were in the Geronimo campaign when they were fresh out of West Point. Both of them worked with Apache scouts back then."

"Where will Pershing find any in this day and age? I mean, do they even exist?"

"Come to find out," Ross admitted, "we've had Apache scouts in the army ever since the days of Geronimo. There's two dozen of them. And of all places, they're up at . . . Fort Apache. And get this. They claim two of those scouts helped chase after old Geronimo back in '86!"

I shook my head in disbelief. "They'd be close to sixty years old!"

Ross nodded. "It does make you wonder, don't it? But keep in mind Pershing is over sixty and so is Dodd. And I wouldn't want to cross either one of them."

I agreed and thinking out loud I said, "But with all these marvelous motor wagons, auto cars, and even airplanes . . . fantastic machines . . . we still have to rely on stone-age skills."

Grinning slyly, Ross said, "Well, we're making some progress. General Pershing gave up his horse when he got to Colonia Dublan. From then on, he's been riding his 'gasoline steed,' a sleek black Dodge touring car!"

CHAPTER 2

After obtaining the required army clearance, I once again telephoned my story in to the *Tribune,* this time about the Apache scouts. The editor liked it and said he would run it as a solo article under my name. He also said he was working on a way to get me across the border so that I could link up with Gibbons as a backup war correspondent.

Hearing that good news caused the blood to rush to my head. But then the editor asked if there was anything else I'd learned in Columbus. In my excitement, like a fool, I answered without thinking.

I hurriedly explained that several wounded Villistas were being taken to Deming for a trial. And that trivial bit of information sealed my fate.

The country was thirsty for revenge, the editor explained with a burst of excitement. A trial of some of the invaders would, in his opinion, go a long way in satisfying the public. And news coverage of the proceedings would undoubtedly boost circulation.

My life turned on that tarnished little dime. I went from becoming a dashing war correspondent to lowly court reporter in a matter of seconds. A court reporter, I might add, that had nothing to do for the next several days. Nothing, that is, but confer with the other half-dozen reporters that shared the same dismal fate.

Columbus had its first sandstorm a few days later. That morning was the first time I'd seen paint blasted off metal by the wind. Even in the hotel, waves of sand drifted across the floors while a fog of dust filled every room. Grit was in my eyes, my ears, and my mouth. The fine desert silt even penetrated the fibers of my clothing. In the stifling heat the silt mixed with sweat and for a day and a half my skin was coated with a layer of sticky slime.

A couple of more days passed and then some of the Villista prisoners died of their wounds and the trial was postponed. Meanwhile in Columbus, trains arrived day and night to unload tons of military supplies, which kept the town in a state of constant turmoil. For us reporters the whole operation was a vivid display of organized chaos.

But that was an angle that none of us dared to report.

Army censors made certain our proud country was only to read that we had been attacked, we were sending in the cavalry, and our armed forces were going to teach the Mexicans a lesson they would never forget. However, any fool could see that our cavalry, infantry, and equipment, in fact our entire army, was woefully unprepared for an invasion.

It was especially unsettling since I had, for the first time, begun to educate myself on world events. From the other reporters, I learned that two weeks earlier the Germans had torpedoed the *Sussex* in the English Channel with twenty-five Americans on board. And that in the last twenty-four hours the Germans had announced "unrestricted submarine warfare" in those same waters.

Rumor had it that we were on a collision course with Germany and might indeed become embroiled in the World War going on in Europe. And yet our army was having trouble mounting an invasion into neighboring Mexico. What chance, I asked myself, did we have in trying to fight the war-hardened Germans on another continent thousands of miles across an ocean?

And to emphasize our country's predicament, the next morning in Columbus, two dozen Apaches stepped off the train. Indian scouts the United States Army needed just to find the enemy.

But as fate would have it, at the very same moment I was enduring the sandstorm in Columbus, New Mexico, another army scout named Monte Segundo was standing alone, knee deep in mountain snow sixty miles from the Canadian border.

Monte Segundo preferred to be alone. By all accounts he was a hard man to get along with and his friends were few and far between. However, though he and I were polar opposites, I am proud to say that I eventually became one of those few friends. And, in time, so did Rosa. Rosa del Carmen Fernandez Bustamonte, to be precise.

When I first met Monte Segundo he hardly spoke a word to anyone, including me. However, as events began to unfold, events destined to alter the trajectory of all our lives, Monte gradually changed. In the end, he spoke more freely about himself and his life. And it was a godsend that Rosa del Carmen Fernandez Bustamonte and I were there to listen.

That is how I know with certainty what happened to Monte Segundo in the Rocky

Mountains of North Idaho on that cold day in the spring of 1916.

He was hunting that morning and had seen a flicker of movement. He eased a hand inside the grimy wool coat that stretched tight across his thick shoulders. His palm came to rest on the worn wooden grips of a Colt pistol. Forty paces up the mountainside, a windfall had wedged in a stand of pine saplings. Above the snag a gray ear had twitched.

Slowly pulling the pistol from its holster, Monte shifted his weight. The ear flicked again but the body of the white-tailed deer was masked by tangled brush and the fading light.

It was late afternoon. Earlier that morning the sky had been blue but by noon turned slate gray. Now storm clouds were beginning to churn. Monte stood motionless, listening to the eerie, muffled silence that he understood always preceded a heavy snow.

He knew that when the snow began to fall the deer would become careless. He had learned that and much more during the time he lived with the Kootenai Indians.

Monte was nine years old when he joined the band. He was with them only six years but had worked hard during that time and learned quickly.

In the beginning, the Indians that some-times lived on the mudflats near Sandpoint only taught him how to catch squawfish and dry them on willow frames. It was squaws' work but Monte did what he was told and caused no trouble so the Kootenais began to teach him other skills. And they eventually let him hunt using his only possession, a Colt single-action pistol.

Even if they had asked, which they never did, Monte Segundo could not have told the Kootenais how he had come to possess such a weapon. As far back as he could remember the pistol had always been his. Not even Ned Carpenter had tried to take it from him. Nor had the townspeople that hanged Ned Carpenter.

In 1888 Sandpoint, Idaho, was a railroad town, a cesspool of humanity, and one of the roughest settlements remaining in the West. What justice there was came swiftly and enthusiastically at the end of a rope. Several times men had been hanged in pairs or three at a time in what were referred to as "hanging bees." The record number for Sandpoint, nicknamed "Hangtown," was six men hanged in six minutes.

Ned Carpenter was among the half-dozen souls "jerked to Jesus" that record-setting day. And little Monte Segundo was in the crowd. He watched the man everyone assumed was his father kick and jerk for a full minute before he finally stopped and swung gracefully back and forth.

If anyone had cared to notice, they would have seen that Monte did not shed a tear. But no one noticed.

How he had come to live with Ned Carpenter was another thing Monte could not recall. In fact, there was a lot about his early childhood Monte Segundo could not remember. But somehow Monte always knew Ned was not his real father and that Segundo was an Italian name.

For a short time, there had been a woman living with Monte and Ned Carpenter but she had disappeared long before Sandpoint.

Back then, Monte assumed the woman left because Ned routinely got drunk and threw her cats against the barn. But that was only a guess. Monte always figured the woman must have liked those cats. Mainly, he thought that because she didn't make a habit of smacking them across the face or yanking their hair out by the roots. No, she petted those cats just about every day.

Large flakes of snow, like so many chicken feathers, began floating down. The silence deepened, the heavy flakes walling off the

51

outside world and blanketing the mountain with a disarming sense of calm.

Monte eased his pistol out into the cold. It was a forty-five caliber, enough to down a deer at close range. And Monte always got close. The Kootenais had taught him well.

As the deer stepped out into the open, Monte eased back the hammer. Although the antlers had been shed, it was easy to see this was a nice buck.

Waiting until the buck looked the other way, Monte raised the pistol and fired. The deer collapsed where it stood with a bullet hole neatly through its heart.

Perhaps it was at that moment Monte Segundo began his fateful journey, a journey that I was privileged to witness almost from the beginning to the end.

Holstering his pistol, Monte unsheathed his hunting knife. He swallowed hard. That day he was determined to do what he'd never been able to do, what he'd never admitted to anyone that he could not do.

Trudging through the snow, Monte began to sweat. His stomach began to roll. Dropping to his knees next to the buck he fought back the urge to vomit.

Grabbing a back leg, Monte rolled the deer on its back exposing its white underbelly. He brought the knife closer to the deer but, as usual, his hand began to shake. But, as he had done on numerous other occasions, he forced the blade closer, his fingers clamping like a vice around the handle of the knife.

Gritting his teeth, he tried to stop his hand from quivering. He swore as the shaking worsened. He continued to swear. He swore until the shaking became uncontrollable.

Suddenly raising the knife high overhead, Monte screamed and then slammed the blade deep into the snow.

Monte had killed big game since he was a boy. But not once in his life, not one time in thirty-one years, had he ever been able to field-dress an animal, to cut it open and pull out the steaming tangle of entrails.

For years, he had been a logger and, since he enjoyed hunting, was also a major supplier of camp meat for the crews. He told everyone that he didn't dress out a deer because he wanted to keep the meat clean, that dragging a gutted deer through the woods tended to foul some of the best cuts.

When he downed moose, elk, or bear he simply went back to camp and rounded up a few men and a packhorse. When it came time to clean the animal, Monte was always busy doing something else.

No one ever questioned him about bringing his deer into camp with fifty pounds of innards still inside. Partly, it was because Monte Segundo had a thick black beard, menacing brown eyes, and a hair-trigger temper. But it was also due to the fact that he was five-foot-ten inches tall, tipped the scales at two hundred pounds, and was extraordinarily strong. Everyone in the mountains and in town understood that Monte Segundo was a "bull of the woods." So that fifty extra pounds he chose to drag into camp was nothing to him.

That evening, after dragging the buck to the cook shed for butchering, Monte went to the bunkhouse. It was near dark and the snow was still falling. Kerosene lanterns filled the building's windows with an inviting amber glow but when Monte stepped inside, the bunkhouse was empty. Word had spread through camp that there was to be a dance in town and the lumberjacks had already left for Sandpoint.

Monte shook the snow from his coat and hung it on a peg. Going to a cedar footlocker next to his bunk, he opened the lid and grabbed a folded khaki shirt and matching pair of pants. Setting those clothes aside, he took out a gun cleaning kit and then ejected the empty brass casing along with the four live rounds from his pistol.

The khaki clothes were only used one weekend a month. That was when Monte and several of the loggers drilled with the state militia. Close to sixty men, in and around Sandpoint, made up Company A. They were officially attached to the Idaho second regiment.

Monte didn't care what his company was called or who they were attached to. And he could care less for the weekend drills. The only thing about the militia he took seriously was that Company A might someday be called on to fight. Just who they would fight didn't matter to Monte. Whether in a bar, in a logging camp, or with the militia, fighting of any kind came naturally to Monte Segundo. But if the altercation was for a good cause, it was all the better.

Most of the loggers in camp were newcomers to the area. They had no idea Sandpoint had once been known as Hangtown or that until the turn of the century the town was a wide open, hell-roaring boomtown.

When the century rolled over, Monte was fifteen years old. The Kootenais had recently moved farther north and Monte had been living with the whites for the last few months. He had just started learning the logging trade when his foreman, one of the few men Monte happened to like, was shot in Sandpoint while playing poker with a card-shark gambler.

Monte was at the camp when he got the news. Without a word, he strapped on his pistol and jumped on a bareback wagon mule. It was five miles to Sandpoint and by the time he got there the gambler had already hightailed it out of town but with a posse hot on his trail.

When Monte caught up with the posse, they were meandering near the southern bank of the Kootenai River.

The men said they had lost the trail and were ready to head back to town. Monte, almost full grown and broad in the shoulders, rode up close to the men and demanded to know exactly where they had lost the trail.

A rider to Monte's right snickered and said, "You think a Dago whelp can . . ."

A roundhouse backhand smashed into the speaker's jaw, knocking him out of his saddle and onto the ground.

Resting a hand on his pistol, Monte glared down at the man, daring him to get up.

"Now, you damn sons of bitches," Monte roared, "where'd you fools lose the trail?"

Every man in the posse froze. The man on the ground wiped blood from his mouth.

He swallowed hard, grunted something unintelligible, and then pointed to a sparse stand of alder.

Riding to the trees Monte slid off his mule. In less than a minute he had remounted and was leading the posse at a fast trot. A half-hour later the gambler was cornered in some rocks with his back to the river. After a few shots were fired back and forth the murderer offered to give himself up in hopes of talking his way out of a noose.

The shooting stopped but before anyone could react, Monte Segundo walked into the open and closed to within ten feet of the rocks. Apparently thinking he had made a deal, the gambler showed himself. When he did, Monte shot him dead.

After that, Monte Segundo was a talked-about man. A few years later, the town tried to get him to be their sheriff but Monte laughed at the idea of wearing a badge and flatly refused. Instead, the very next Saturday night he showed the town of Sandpoint what he could do with his fists, taking on three railroad toughs in his first barroom brawl. And that night he wasn't even drunk.

In those days, Monte Segundo was half-wild and hell on wheels. Yet, whenever a posse was formed, Monte was called on to lead it. But he only agreed if it concerned murder or harm to a woman. He would have nothing to do with chasing thieves or robbers.

After a few more years of no-quarter frontier justice, the lawless elements melted away and Sandpoint became a respectable town, a quiet town. Even bar fights were frowned on.

And that was about the time, perhaps out of sheer boredom, Monte Segundo decided to join the Idaho Militia.

After cleaning the black powder residue from his pistol, Monte stowed it and the rest of his gear in the footlocker and headed for town.

Walking through the double doors of a large log building that served as the community hall, Monte paused and glanced around. The dance was crowded, with men outnumbering women three to one, so he worked his way around the edge of the room and made his way to the bar. He ordered a beer and as the bartender was setting the mug down a man wearing an overcoat and derby hat came up beside Monte. The man in the derby rested his right palm on the bar. In his left hand, he held a rolled-up newspaper.

Glancing at Monte the man said, "Nice

dance. Nice dance."

Monte nodded and took a sip of beer.

The man extended his hand. "Gunderson's the name. Pete Gunderson. Just came down from Canada."

Monte shook his hand but said nothing.

"Just got in on the train," chirped Gunderson. "Dandy little town you have here. By the way, what's the name of that big lake out there?"

"Ponderay," muttered Monte.

"Ponderay, eh? Well it's just paradise down here. That's what I'd say. No worries about current events around here, eh?"

After taking another sip of beer, Monte asked, "What current events?"

"You know, Mexico's attack on Columbus, New Mexico; your army marching into Mexico to catch the murderers and all the while those Mexicans in the middle of another one of their revolutions. It's pure chaos down there. Chaos."

"Somebody was murdered?" Monte asked.

"Ten civilians. One was a woman. A woman with child, no less. Altogether, eighteen dead counting the soldiers. Two of them had their throats cut. All in the black of night. A sneak attack."

Gunderson unrolled a *New York Times* on top of the bar. He pointed to the headlines

59

and then a front-page photo. The headline read, "Twenty Apaches to be Scouts." The photo was of two long-haired men in army uniform.

Monte could barely read so he paid little attention to the newspaper and continued drinking his beer.

"Your army's already in Mexico," continued the Canadian, "but they're stretched thin. So thin in fact, they're hiring hundreds of civilians to drive army wagons and auto trucks to supply the troops. The situation is so critical the civilians must be armed and ready to fight. Can you imagine, you sign up as a civilian and then discover you're practically part of the military? There's even talk of having to activate your National Guard."

It was then Monte set his beer down and slid the paper over to take a closer look at the headlines.

"Not only that," the Canadian added, "as you can see the army is even sending for two dozen Apache scouts!"

When Monte heard the word *Apache,* the muscles in his neck tightened involuntarily. His eyes dropped to the photo. "I only see two."

The Canadian laughed and shook his head. "Those two are celebrities you might say. Thirty years ago, they actually helped chase your famed Geronimo throughout northern Mexico. Those two know the country."

Leaning low, Monte studied the photo more closely. One scout was noticeably taller than the other and Monte's gaze went to him first. When he slid his eyes to the second Apache he stared at it for a full minute.

Monte straightened up. Feeling a sudden stiffness in his neck and shoulders, he shoved the paper back to the Canadian and sneered, "Ugly sons a bitches. Hope they remember how to follow a trail."

"They'll need to," agreed the Canadian. "Pancho Villa is apparently very good at hiding his tracks."

The Canadian had pronounced "Villa" as one would "village" and without a thought, Monte corrected him.

"It's not Villa. Them two L's makes it Vee-yah."

"Oh, that's right," said the Canadian. "I did hear that but I keep forgetting. So, do you speak Spanish?"

"Nope," answered Monte, then took a gulp of beer. "Just picked that up somewhere."

The Canadian folded the newspaper and

set it down in front of Monte. Tapping the paper with his finger, he said, "Keep the paper if you want. It's a week old. I've read every word."

Monte nodded, folded the paper a second time, and then stuck it in his back pocket.

The rest of that evening was uneventful, and Monte considered the growing stiffness in his neck and back was due to dragging the deer. On his return to camp he began to wonder where Columbus, New Mexico, was, but other than that he gave the news of the raid little thought.

He went to sleep that night like most other nights. He slept soundly for several hours as he usually did. But then he had one of his nightmares.

In the all too familiar dream, Monte was on fire, his skin was burning. Flames surrounded him but he could not move. If he tried to cry out, the searing pain became worse. Then, out of the crimson flames the shadowy bulk of a man's face appeared, looming over him. The devilish eyes were mere slits, the lips thin and wide. There was hair, lots of it, black and wild.

Then there were arms. Reaching for him. Arms grabbing him and then shoving him deeper and deeper into the flames.

When Monte opened his eyes, he could

see the bunkhouse ceiling. The moonlight was coming through the frosted window next to him. He heard one of the men snoring peacefully. The air bathing his sweating face was crisp, almost cold.

Throwing off his blanket, Monte inhaled deeply. There was no pain now. No flames. No arms shoving him into a scorching fire.

Monte wiped a sheet of clammy sweat from his forehead. He'd had the same nightmare many times before but this time it was more vivid, the excruciating pain all too real.

In the darkness, Monte's eyes narrowed. Words spoken by the Canadian began to echo in his clouded thoughts. "Columbus. Army. New Mexico. Murder. Woman. Columbus. Apache. Columbus. Ten dead. Army. Dead. Columbus. Murder . . ."

Sitting up, Monte shook his head and blinked his eyes to clear his mind. It took a moment. He breathed the invigorating night air for several seconds. The logger that had been snoring rolled over and then the bunkhouse became serenely quiet.

Monte leaned forward and looked out the window. The moon was full and bright. Ice was crystalized on the glass panes. All was as it should be and yet something seemed strangely out of place.

Lighting a candle, Monte reached for his pants and fingered the folded newspaper from the hip pocket. Slipping it out, he quietly unfolded it. He stared at the photo of the Apaches for a half-hour and then tore off the photo of the Apaches, folded it, and tucked it into the pocket. After blowing out the candle he finally drifted into a dreamless sleep.

The following morning was routine, up at dawn, finished at dark, to bed by nine. But that night the same nightmare woke him again. The next day, he was uneasy. The third night, the dream returned but with even more intensity. His uneasiness became irritability. After a week of nightmares, Monte was ready to erupt. Every logger in camp could see it and everyone did their best to give him a wide berth.

Monte was working one end of a double-handled crosscut saw when a thought flooded his consciousness.

His mind, that afternoon, was blank from fatigue and lack of sleep when the idea of going to New Mexico came to him out of nowhere. Then, as the notion took root, he decided that he would volunteer as a member of the Idaho Militia and sign up to be an army scout. Then, he reasoned, he would join the Apaches and help track down

Pancho Villa.

For the first time in days, Monte felt relieved. When he slept through the following night without a nightmare he was convinced he had made the right decision.

Now you have to understand that Monte was always a bit different, not to mention impulsive, so when he announced his intentions the next day to leave for New Mexico, there was no great effort to change his mind.

CHAPTER 3

The day the Apache Scouts of Company A arrived in Columbus I was in Deming with a dozen other reporters waiting for the trial of the Villista prisoners to finally begin. Instead of opening statements for our high-profile trial, we received notification the proceedings would once again be postponed.

I can't say I was disappointed with another delay. What intrigued me far more than the trial was the imminent arrival of the Apache scouts, especially the two veterans of the Geronimo campaign.

After receiving the news about the trial all of us reporters loaded back onto the military truck that had brought us to Deming, a Jeffery Quad. It was called that, I came to find out, because the four solid rubber wheels of the one and a half-ton truck were engaged all of the time. The civilian driver said the truck could go through mud, water, and deep sand with no problem. And on the return trip, over my personal objections the driver proved the truck could attain a speed of fifty miles per hour.

Happy to have survived that reckless demonstration, I was first to hop down off the wagon box when we reached Columbus. I went straight to the train station, made a few inquiries regarding the Apaches, and was directed across the road to the Custom House.

I don't remember exactly what I was expecting, certainly braided hair, beads, moccasins, and perhaps a few eagle feathers. But the lone Apache I saw standing by the Custom House had none of that.

He was in military dress from his campaign hat down to his knees. From there down, I did see that he at least wore moccasins. But there were no silky braids or eagle feathers. Under his campaign hat, I saw nothing but a crop of long bushy hair.

This scout, I was told, was Hell-yet-suey. He was hereditary chief of the White Mountain Apaches and over fifty years old.

From a short distance, I watched him for a moment. He spoke to several of the soldiers as they walked past him, but I could not make out what was being said.

Hereditary chief was an impressive title

and Hell-yet-suey was a vicious-sounding name, but as I moved closer I heard what sounded like begging.

However, as I listened more closely to the guttural tone of his broken English I realized he was not actually begging. On the contrary, he was almost demanding, without success I might add, to be given sand goggles, sweaters, or electric flashlights.

Thinking of an Apache wearing sand goggles and holding a flashlight caused me to chuckle. Still smiling, I approached the not-so-wild Hell-yet-suey until we were face to face. When he made eye contact with me I explained that I was a news reporter and had a few questions I wished to ask.

The Apache grunted what sounded like approval but before I could take a breath, his craggy, sun-beaten face seemed to turn to stone. He turned south and waved a sweeping brown hand toward Mexico.

"Heap Mexicans," he said with black eyes full of hate. "Kill 'em all!"

In that instant, the old man that had been asking for sand goggles transformed into a cold-blooded Apache warrior. Instinctively, I knew this Apache had been in battle and had killed men. Lots of them.

A chill ran down my back. I nodded solemnly as if I understood, which of course

I didn't. I thanked the Indian and then excused myself. Walking away from the awesome presence of the Apache war chief, I remember feeling so very frail, as if everything I had ever accomplished was utterly insignificant.

Hell-yet-suey, on the other hand, was undoubtedly a fearless warrior. He had faced death in battle and had taken the lives of other human beings. In doing so, he had stolen their most precious possession. And that barbarous act, I suddenly realized, was the epitome of raw power, of ultimate power. And that power had nothing whatsoever to do with wealth, bloodlines, or Carnegie Hill.

My confidence was shaken. Confidence in what, exactly, I didn't know but that jolt of reality reached down into the core of my soul and gave me a kick in the gut.

I milled about town for close to an hour before I felt normal again. Only, I didn't quite realize my "normal" was in the process of being shaken off its foundation.

Asking more questions about the scouts, I was finally introduced to a white lieutenant named Shannon. He was in command of the scouts, willing to talk and full of information.

He told me of Charly Shipp, who spoke

excellent English and was good-natured. There was Nakay, the oldest at sixty-three, and his brothers, Sergeant Chow Big. Nonotolth, who spoke fair English and was also known as First Sergeant Pony. And then he mentioned Norroso and Ask-elde-linney also called Major. The latter two, Shannon explained, were the two army scouts who participated in the Geronimo campaign.

I asked the lieutenant if I could interview the scouts and, to my surprise, was refused permission. Lieutenant Shannon confided in me he had just met them himself but was warned that the Apaches did not allow whites into their midst, that the Indians were extremely exclusive.

I then asked Shannon if the Apaches would accept him as commanding officer. He leaned close to my ear and whispered.

"Do not print this. But I have no idea what they will do. I have absolutely no experience working with Indians. To say the least, I am ill at ease."

And with that dead end, my heart sank. It sank even farther the following day when the scouts left for Colonia Dublan. With the trial on hold and the Apache scouts gone, Columbus was nothing more than a supply depot. Now, all the news worth reporting was coming from south of the border. Meanwhile, I was three miles north of Mexico, which meant I was stuck squarely in the middle of nowhere with absolutely nothing to report.

Disgusted and finally willing to admit defeat, I packed my bags and went to the train station. Approaching the ticket window, I happened to glance at my reflection in one of the windows.

What caught my eye was the leather satchel hanging from my shoulder. I thought of the half-filled notepad inside and suddenly felt sick to my stomach. I realized that I, William Cabott Weston III, was quitting, allowing my dream to wither and die.

The dejected image in that reflection rattled me. I started to have second thoughts. Though it seemed much longer, I had only been in New Mexico for less than a month. After such a short time, was I truly ready to accept that I had failed?

Stopping where I was, I sat down on my suitcase to think things through one last time. It was during that soul-searching that the train rolled in from the west. I had only a few more minutes to make my final decision but inexplicably I was distracted by the disembarking passengers.

Most were civilians the army was hiring as

mechanics or drivers, but others were business people coming to make money off the financial boom the army had brought to Columbus.

That fateful afternoon, only one man stepped off the train in an army uniform. With my chin in the palm of my hand, I didn't notice him at first. In fact, I didn't notice him at all until he walked up to me.

I heard him ask, "Do you know where I can find headquarters?"

Lethargically lifting my head, I half-heartedly glanced up. Monte Segundo had shaved off the logger's beard and so what I saw at first was just another clean-shaven soldier.

"Yes, I do," I said, reluctantly coming to my feet.

As I stood, I happened to notice the pistol Monte was wearing on his left hip. It was not the standard army issue and it was backwards. My eyes shifted and I was even more surprised to see, on the opposite hip, a staghorn-gripped hunting knife encased in a beautifully beaded scabbard.

Fully erect, I took a closer look at Monte. He was several inches taller than me and twice my width. His cheekbones were high, his jaws square and his eyes dark and penetrating. All in all, his features gave me the impression Monte Segundo had been carved from granite.

What I said next, I attribute to what seasoned reporters refer to as a "hunch." Something told me this man, like the war chief Hell-yet-suey, was no ordinary soldier.

"It would be easier if I showed you," I said. "I've got the time."

"Appreciate it," replied Monte.

I started off down the train platform half thinking Monte would follow behind me but he stepped alongside me as we walked.

"Captain Peters is in charge of Camp Furlong," I offered. "His tent's a little hard to find."

Monte said nothing but as we went down the stairs and turned south toward the camp, I couldn't help but notice that other civilians as well as soldiers took one glance at us and then stepped out of the way. And I knew very well they weren't doing it on account of me.

Walking down several rows of dusty, brown wall tents, we stopped at one with a wooden sign staked in the ground near the open flap. The sign said "Officer of the Day."

The tent flaps were tied open. I stayed outside, watching as Monte stepped in.

Inside the tent, I saw piles of paper-filled boxes, a desk, and an officer at work behind it. Monte walked directly up to the desk and saluted.

"My name is Monte Segundo. I'm here to volunteer, sir."

The soldier behind the desk looked up and snapped off an abbreviated salute. He had lieutenant's bars on his shoulders and irritation stamped on his face.

The lieutenant looked Monte over briefly, then his eyes locked onto Monte's cross-draw pistol.

"Hell, I thought Georgie Patton was our only Sears and Roebuck cowboy. Now, look at you."

The lieutenant shook his head and then went back to his paperwork. Scribbling on a piece of paper, he asked, "You a driver or mechanic?"

"I'm a tracker," Monte said. "I want to join up with the Apache scouts."

"No," answered the lieutenant, not bothering to lift his head. "The general already tried civilian scouts. They weren't any good. That's why he got Indians."

"I can track as good as any Indian," Monte said matter-of-factly, "and I'm not a civilian."

Tossing his pencil down on the desk the lieutenant stood up. He glared at Monte and then looked him over again.

"What the hell are you, then?"

"I'm Idaho Militia. Company A, second regiment."

A disbelieving scowl furrowed the lieutenant's face. He laughed. "You mean National Guard, don't ya! Hell, you're one of those damn weekend soldiers?"

I couldn't see Monte's face but I heard the change in his voice when he said, "Something funny about that?"

The lieutenant laughed some more. "Yeah, there's a whole lot funny about that. Compared to regular army the National Guard's a joke. I'd sooner sign up a bunch of Boy Scouts as the likes of you."

Monte's punch came from his hip and landed on the point of the lieutenant's chin, sending him over backwards and almost out the back of the tent.

Turning on his heels, Monte whipped out his hunting knife and casually cut both canvas ties as he left the tent. As the tent flaps unfurled he sheathed his knife.

"Which way's Mexico?" Monte asked as casually as if he were looking for an ice cream parlor.

I'd never seen anything like what had just happened. Monte had knocked out an army officer in the middle of an army camp teeming with soldiers and didn't seem to have a care in the world.

I must say that I am actually quite proud of what I did next. Fully aware that my suitcase still sat at the train station and all I had with me was my leather satchel, I said boldly, "It's easier if I show you."

"Appreciate it," said Monte.

"I heard you tell that lieutenant your name is Monte Segundo," I said, then hesitated. Under the circumstances, William somehow seemed inadequate. "My name is Billy Cabott."

And just like that, Monte Segundo and Billy Cabott started for Mexico. We walked west down a row of tents and soon came to the dirt road that led to Las Palomas. A quick look over our shoulders told us we weren't being pursued so, wasting no time, we headed south.

In minutes, we were past the edge of camp and crossing an expanse of sand that was devoid of anything but a few scattered mesquite and creosote bushes. In the distance, we could see a cluster of white adobes glimmering through rippling heat waves.

"That Mexico?" asked Monte.

"It is. That little town out there is Las Palomas. It's only a couple of miles."

"Well then, I won't get lost," said Monte.

I knew what Monte meant but I was swept

up in the moment. Monte Segundo's sudden appearance was the most exciting thing that had happened since I arrived in Columbus. So I said, "If it's all the same to you, I'll come along. I'm a reporter. I work for the *Chicago Tribune.*"

Monte glanced down, his dark eyes sweeping over me. "Suit yourself."

A half-hour later we were at the border crossing. Two American soldiers with rifles slung over their shoulders stood in front of a twenty-foot opening in a barbed wire fence, a fence stretching as far as could be seen to the east and west. A red and white pole that hinged on one end served as a gate. A few feet from the two guards a lone Mexican soldier guarded the Mexican border with his green and white pole. One hundred feet behind the Mexican was the town of Las Palomas.

Both American soldiers were privates. One asked, "Where do you think you're going?"

"Mexico," answered Monte, as we stopped a few feet in front of the privates.

"No soldiers in Palomas," said the private. "Thanks to that bunch that got drunk and tore up the place last week. General's orders. Ruined it for everybody. And now the whole damn camp is dry."

Not knowing what Monte might do next,

I said, "We're civilians. I'm a reporter for the *Chicago Tribune.* This man is with me. Neither of us has any connection with the army."

Indicating Monte with a flick of my head, I added, "He's strictly National Guard. He's helping me with a story about Las Palomas."

The privates glanced uncertainly at each other. Seeing their hesitation, I played a hunch.

"We'll bring you back something. Something to drink perhaps?"

Both privates looked over Monte's uniform. Seeing no military insignia, they agreed to my proposition and let us pass. We took five steps and then stopped again. The Mexican guard eyed us for a moment but when Monte dropped a fifty-cent piece into his palm, he too allowed us to pass.

"Where to now?" I asked, as my eyes darted over Las Palomas.

"The nearest bar," said Monte. "Somebody there will know something."

Las Palomas was almost the mirror image of Columbus. But instead of weathered wooden buildings, there was a haphazard array of drab flat-roofed adobes and a sprinkling of brush huts. And the streets, instead of being cluttered with horses, trucks, and wagons, held a menagerie of chickens, dogs, and a pair of wandering burros.

We saw a few Mexican men, very old, squatting in the shade of the adobes. Their eyes, shaded by large straw sombreros, followed us as we passed but their weather-beaten faces displayed no emotion. Even the dogs we encountered did not bother to bark. Instead, they continued to lie in the dirt, merely lifting their noses to sniff the parched desert air.

In minutes, Monte pointed to one of the larger adobes. The sandblasted word *Cantina* was barely legible on the outer wall.

"That's a bar, there."

"Cantina?" I said and then took a pencil and tablet from my satchel and wrote the word down.

Tucking the pencil in my shirt pocket, I followed Monte into the cantina. I was somewhat surprised how cool it was inside but I was shocked when I discovered the floor was nothing but packed dirt.

As my eyes adjusted to the darkness inside, I saw that the bar was made of nothing more than heavy, rough-cut planks. A handful of crude tables and chairs were scattered around the floor and the only person in the cantina was a short, fat

Mexican. He stood behind the bar and was already placing two shot glasses down next to a bottle.

"Welcome, señores. Tequila?"

Monte walked to the bar. "What's tequila?"

"Good whiskey, *amigo*. Is like good whiskey."

"Yea? How much for the bottle, then?"

The bartender held the bottle up and studied it. "Is only half a bottle. Six bits."

Monte slapped the coins on the bar and scooped up both glasses and the bottle. He then went to the back wall farthest from the open front door and took a table in the darkest corner.

Sitting with his back against the wall, Monte tasted the tequila.

After smacking his lips, he licked them from corner to corner. "Not bad. Smoother than whiskey, though."

I took a drink. Actually, it was more like a sip. Even so, I felt that taste of tequila burn all the way down my throat, through my chest cavity, and then drip into the pit of my stomach.

I managed to nod without choking. I tried to lick my lips but I think my tongue was already numb.

That was one of the few times I saw

Monte Segundo crack a smile. It was faint but it was there. And it made me feel good, as if I had earned his approval.

"Which way did the American army go, *amigo*?" Monte asked the bartender. "My young friend here is a news reporter."

The bartender only shrugged.

"Ask him," I said in a half-whisper, "how to get to Colonia Dublan. That's where the army has its headquarters."

Monte nodded. "How about Colonia Dublan? Can you tell us how to get there?"

Again, the bartender shrugged but this time his head swayed back and forth in indecision. He was about to speak but suddenly froze.

Voices were heard coming from outside the cantina. Men were singing and coming closer.

Grabbing two bottles, the bartender slammed them down on the bar. Then he scooped up a double handful of shot glasses and nervously began arranging them in a neat line.

With his eyes flared wide, the Mexican glared at us. "Carrancistas!" he warned, and then turned toward the door and began to smile.

The singing grew annoyingly loud until a grimy Mexican officer, armed with only a

81

pistol, lumbered into the cantina. He was followed by three more equally filthy soldiers with rifles hanging from their shoulders.

The singing stopped and the officer spoke to the bartender. All the Mexicans laughed and then all eyes shifted to the open door. The officer called to someone out of sight.

A moment later a fifth soldier came through the door with a rifle in one hand and a rope in the other. The rope, stretched tight, was anchored to something outside the door.

Again, the men laughed but this time it was a hideous laugh.

The fifth soldier gave the rope a yank and a Mexican woman tied at the wrists flew through the door and fell on her knees.

Her hair, raven black and tangled, covered her face. Her cotton blouse had been ripped at the neckline and hung loose, exposing a bare shoulder and part of her back. Her dress was soiled and she wore sandals on her feet.

Not noticing us in the corner of the cantina, the officer continued to bellow as the woman slowly raised her head.

She spoke then. Whatever she said was laced with venom and full of defiance.

The soldiers roared with more laughter.

And then the fifth soldier looked our way. He spoke and all eyes, including the woman's, locked on us. You could have cut the silence with a knife.

I was so frightened, I couldn't move. But I could sense Monte next to me and somehow, and I can't begin to tell you how, I knew he was as calm as a cucumber.

"Hello, boys," offered Monte.

A rumble of muted voices went through the men. I could only make out the word *gringos.* I at least knew what that meant.

The officer relaxed somewhat. *"Buenas tardes, amigos."*

"Don't speak Spanish," returned Monte, all the while watching the officer's hands. "You speak English? My friend here works for a newspaper."

The officer spoke and the bartender filled the waiting glasses. Without taking his eyes off us, the officer took a glass and threw back a shot of tequila.

"I speak pretty good," smiled the officer. "What are you doing in Las Palomas?"

Now, at this point I expected anything but what Monte said next. But as it turned out, that was his way. You never knew what Monte Segundo was thinking or what he was about to do.

"I'm looking for Apaches. But right now, I

think I want that woman."

His eyes narrowing, the officer held his hand out and the bartender refilled his glass. "We might be done with her . . . if you pay enough. How much do you offer?"

Monte stood easily and finished his glass of tequila. He grabbed the bottle. "Let me take a good look at her."

The officer barked out an order and two soldiers grabbed the woman by her arms and forced her to her feet. Monte took a swig from the bottle as he approached the woman.

Stopping in front of her, he reached out to pull her hair away from her face. The woman lunged at his hand. Her jaws open wide, she snapped at Monte's fingers as he jerked back.

The soldiers burst into hysterical, rolling laughter.

Before anyone could even blink, Monte's tequila bottle shattered across the fifth soldier's skull and a left fist plowed into the next soldier's face. Like ducks in a row, a powerful right flattened the third.

The officer at the end of the bar struggled to get his pistol out of its holster.

Monte stepped past the remaining soldier, whose feeble blows were bouncing off him as if he were made of oak.

Grabbing the officer's pistol hand, Monte slung the Mexican like a rag doll and slammed him into the wall of the cantina.

Monte drew his own pistol and wheeled back around. He expected the remaining Mexican to try for his rifle but he was running out the door.

It was over in seconds and four unconscious and bleeding men lay sprawled on the dirt floor.

Holstering his pistol and taking out his hunting knife, Monte went toward the woman. She jerked back and growled like a cornered beast.

Monte paused. He held the knife still until the woman calmed. He then pointed at the rope tied around her wrists.

"Tell her I won't hurt her," Monte said to the bartender who had not moved since the tequila bottle had shattered.

The bartender muttered some words. The woman seemed to relax. She raised her tied hands and brushed her hair to one side. Then she spit into Monte's face.

Without wiping away the spit, Monte clutched a fist full of the woman's hair with his left hand and lifted her completely off the floor.

She dangled motionless for a few seconds and then Monte brought her close. "Don't do that," he said evenly and then eased her back down.

Without another word or any more resistance from the woman, Monte cut the ropes that bound her hands.

"Tell her she can go," Monte said.

"He will tell me nothing," snarled the woman. Bristling with fury she added, "I will go when I want. No one tells Rosa del Carmen Fernandez Bustamonte when or where to go."

Monte squinted at Rosa. "Well, I'm Monte and I don't give a damn what you do."

The bartender gasped and hurriedly made the sign of the cross over his chest. "You must all go, señor," he insisted. "More soldiers will come. And she is a Villista, a *soldadera*!"

Monte glanced at me. I was still glued to my seat. He motioned me over and then slid a rifle off one of the soldiers and then jerked off a belt of cartridges.

Handing the rifle and belt to me, he asked, "You ever shoot a bolt action?"

"No."

"Well then," Monte said handing me the rifle and belt, "you can just carry these for now."

With her eyes locked on Monte, the woman slowly crouched down and took a rifle and cartridge belt from another soldier.

Rising slowly and careful not to point the rifle toward Monte, the woman buckled the cartridge belt and slung it over her head and across her shoulder.

"They will come for all of us. We go to the horses now!"

"Hold on," Monte said and then quickly took the pistol and leather belt from the officer. Offering both to the woman he added, "Looks like these'll fit you pretty good."

Still simmering, the woman snatched the rig. When she had buckled it around her waist she spun on her heels and hurried out the door.

Monte looked at me. I must have been a sight. He chuckled and snatched a cap off of one of the soldiers. "Take this," he said offering me the hat. "We better do as she says."

Without questioning the reason for the hat, I slid it on my head and said, "Fine with me."

We sprinted out the door and barely caught up to the woman before coming to a corral that held seven saddled horses. The woman went to a small paint and swung into the saddle as if she was born to it.

Monte grabbed a bay and turned to see

how I was doing. "You do ride?"

I lied, having never been on a horse. "Not much," I said, throwing the rifle and cartridge belt over my shoulder.

"Watch and learn, then," grunted Monte as he grabbed a handful of the bay's mane with one hand and the saddle horn with the other. "Grab something and hang on tight."

Stepping into the saddle, Monte went to the gate as I latched onto a roan. I managed to get my left foot in the stirrup and then hopped a few times. Pulling myself up, I threw my right leg over the rear of the horse and thankfully landed in the saddle facing the right direction.

A shot rang out from the shadows down the street. Monte threw the gate open. The woman kicked her horse into a run. My horse lunged after hers, almost flipping me over backwards. I felt Monte's hand push me forward and I regained my balance.

It was a stampede as the three of us along with the remaining horses raced breakneck speed out of town. And if there were any more shots I did not hear them. It seems abject fear tends to dull the senses.

As we had bolted past the last adobe of Las Palomas Rosa snatched the reins of one of the riderless horses but the other three gradually fell behind and stopped running.

We had covered at least five miles before slowing to a walk.

Eventually, with no one following, we dismounted to adjust our stirrups and tighten the cinches. After that, we continued on. It was then I discovered that I could stay on a walking horse without too much trouble and eased both hands off the saddle horn and, for the first time, took up the reins.

We rode that afternoon until it was almost dark. We hadn't eaten in hours and I was sore from head to toe. It was also getting cold so I was more than relieved when Rosa, who had been in the lead the entire time, veered off the road and stopped in front of a squat one-room adobe.

There was no light coming through the gaps in the plank-board door or from the window. The rude hut looked abandoned but still it was a welcome sight. That evening, it was painfully obvious that anything would be more comfortable than the leather brick I had been straddling for an eternity.

When I stepped down off the horse, my knees buckled and my rifle banged into the side of my head. "Where are we?" I asked, steadying myself but beyond caring if anyone noticed my legs wobble.

"This was my Tio Juan's home before the

Carrancistas came. He lives far away now."

Monte glanced around. "Any firewood?"

"There is wood," Rosa answered. "You have matches?"

Digging into his shirt pocket, Monte handed two matches to Rosa.

"Wood is behind the adobe," said Rosa, adjusting the rifle on her shoulder. "If not, there is a fence for the chickens that we can burn."

Rosa stepped inside the adobe and Monte went around the back. I stayed right where I was and stole the opportunity to vigorously massage my aching buttocks.

Having found a stub of a candle, Rosa lit it. A welcome glow bathed the inside of the old adobe and I limped inside.

Again, the floor was only dirt but I didn't care. Except for a couple of pots in one corner and a fireplace built into the middle of one wall, the house was completely empty.

Rosa was holding the candle. Her entire face was smudged with dirt. With her hair pointing in every possible direction, she was the consummate portrait of a witch.

"Go to the horse I was leading," she ordered. "Bring the saddlebags to me."

I gazed at her blankly. "The saddlebags?"

Rosa took a step toward me. Holding the

candle up close to my face, she glared at me for a full count of ten. "Bring the leather bags that are tied to the back of the saddle. *Cabrón*."

At the time, I didn't know what saddlebags were but I did correctly surmise that *cabrón* was not a term of endearment.

In the dark, it took me a while to untie the bags and when I returned to the adobe a fire was blazing in the fireplace. Rosa, with her rifle on her shoulder, was standing to one side and Monte on the other. Six feet apart, they faced each other.

I stepped directly in front of the fireplace and between the two of them. I offered the saddlebags to Rosa. "This what you wanted?"

Without taking her eyes off Monte, Rosa snatched the bags from my hand. She flipped open one pouch. First, she took out a pair of binoculars but then put them back. Next, she brought out a thick piece of what looked like cardboard. She bit off a piece, hesitated, and then handed the saddlebags back to me.

"I think she just invited you to dinner, Billy," Monte said.

Reaching inside the saddlebags, I had no idea what to expect. Feeling nothing but hard flakes of some sort, I brought out a sheet. It felt like a piece of the saddle I'd been straddling.

I anchored my teeth into the leather and snapped off a corner. To my surprise, it tasted good. "What is it," I asked as I chewed.

"Goat," Rosa answered.

Deliberately using his left hand and keeping his eyes on Rosa, Monte reached inside the saddlebags and took a piece. "Back in the cantina," he said, "you spouted off a wagonload of Mexican names. Which one do we use to get your attention?"

Rosa raised her chin. "You," she began defiantly, "you can call me Captain Bustamonte. That is what the men under my command call me."

Chomping off a large piece of jerky, Monte ground it between his jaws for a moment. "Well, them back at the cantina didn't seem to be following your orders none too much."

Rosa exploded with a blistering string of Spanish that needed no literal translation.

Amidst the tongue-lashing, Monte continued chewing, his expression that of complete indifference.

When Rosa paused to take a breath, I tried to intervene. "How are we going to sleep?"

Monte's eyes then dropped to Rosa's torn

blouse and bare shoulder. Not missing a thing, Rosa immediately began tying the frayed edges together.

"Been wondering about that myself," Monte said. "I don't trust her and she sure as hell don't trust us."

I looked around the bare floor for a solution, but a shadowy bit of movement caught my attention. I strained my eyes and they focused on an ungodly creature crawling inches from my feet.

"What is that?" I yelped, jumping to one side.

Monte instantly raised his leg and slammed the heel of his boot on the intruder, smashing it into the dirt.

"Scorpion," Monte said simply.

"Are there more?" I asked, my skin erupting with goose pimples.

"Likely," replied Monte.

I shuddered. "Do they have those where you come from?"

For a moment, Monte didn't answer. He looked perplexed. "No. No they don't. I've never seen one before."

I looked to Rosa for some insight. She was scowling at Monte but then her eyes suddenly narrowed with suspicion.

"Do they bite?" I asked.

"That one does not," snipped Rosa. "But

there are others."

Thoughts of Carnegie Hill and silk sheets flashed through my mind but I quickly blocked them out. I had made an impulsive choice and there was nothing to do but stay the course I was on.

"Are they poisonous?" I asked.

"That was a big one," Rosa said. "They are not the bad ones."

Rosa paused as a sinister smile brightened her dirty face. She glared at Monte. "It is the small ones, they are the ones that will kill you."

Reaching down, Monte took a piece of wood and tossed it into the flames. "So . . . Captain Rosa, who were those soldiers back at the cantina?"

Some of the tension drained from Rosa's shoulders. "They were Carrancistas."

"And what are you?"

"I am Villista. I am with General Pancho Villa, the man you Americans hunt but will never catch."

Monte slowly shook his head. "I'm not particularly looking for Pancho Villa. As a matter of fact, if the United States Army got hold of me, they'd arrest me. I'm not army. I'm Idaho Militia, some call us National Guard."

"It does not matter what you are," scoffed

94

Rosa. "Now, the Carrancistas will arrest you. Or kill you. And if the Villistas catch you they will only kill you. So why are you two *gringos* here? Do you want so much to die in Mexico?"

Recovering from the scorpion scare, I offered what little I could. "I am a news reporter. I work for the *Chicago Tribune.* I'm not fighting anyone."

Rosa squinted at me as if I were a fool. "And what are you reporting?"

There she had me. I answered honestly, "I don't know, yet."

Monte's mood suddenly darkened. "I'm here . . ." he said staring into the flames, "to find the Apache scouts that are with Pershing's army."

Rosa's eyes held on Monte. "Why?"

Monte didn't answer for several seconds and then said gruffly, "That's my business."

Rosa well understood the Mexicans hated and feared the Apache and had for hundreds of years. However, Rosa also understood military tactics. And she knew how to read men.

She had heard the Apache scouts were coming for Villa and knew they would eventually find him. Anything or anyone that interfered with the Apaches would only aid the general. And that night Rosa could see that the man standing before her, the man that had defeated five Carrancistas with his bare hands, very likely had a score to settle with the Apaches. And if that were the case, Monte Segundo could be of use to the revolution.

"The Carrancistas," offered Rosa, "are searching for me. And now they are searching for you. We should work together to get what we want, me back to my army and you to your scouts. But first we must get past the Carrancistas."

"A truce, then," I said. "We call a truce for now. Then we can all get some sleep."

Monte grinned at Rosa but there was no humor in it. "Trust in the Lord and keep your powder dry, eh?"

I blinked. "What? Is that a Bible verse?"

"No," Monte said, "It's just something folks used to say. Kind of like, 'sleep with one eye open.' Isn't that right, Captain Rosa?"

Chewing on her jerky, Rosa smirked. "I will sleep well. It is the two of you that will not."

"Sure enough," returned Monte. "Me and Billy are civilized men and sleeping next to you'll be a challenge. Why, just the sight of you would scare a vulture off a gut wagon."

Rosa's eyes flared. For a moment, she

stopped chewing. I expected more venomous Spanish but strangely there was none. Instead, Rosa stole a glance at Monte and then turned and went to the pots that were piled in the corner.

"There is a well in the back," Rosa said. Picking up one of the pots along with the candle she adjusted her rifle sling. Quite unexpectedly she said, "I will get water."

Monte and I watched her go out the door. We looked at each other, both wondering the same thing.

"Think she'll come back?" I asked.

"Beats me. Can't say I'd blame her if she didn't. Especially after what she's been through with those Mexican soldiers."

I suppose I hadn't allowed myself to dwell on the unthinkable. Somehow it seemed indecent to even formulate certain thoughts but now Monte was forcing me to face an ugly reality.

"You mean . . . those men . . . they violated her?"

I remember how Monte looked at me then. It was if he was seeing me for the first time. He thought for a moment before he answered.

"Yeah. They did, Billy. But she's tough. Not like the women you're used to. Or me either for that matter."

In shocked disbelief, I rubbed my forehead, trying to clear my head. The pain of doing so sobered me instantly. I winced.

"Quite a sunburn you got there," Monte said.

"Just walking from Columbus to Las Palomas?"

"It's the desert. The sand reflects the sun. It'll fry you quick."

I took my hat off and looked at it. "So that's why you gave me the Mexican's hat?"

"By the time we got to the cantina, you were already bordering on medium rare."

Replacing my hat, I turned toward the door. "I am terribly thirsty. Do you think it'll be safe to drink the water if she brings any back?"

"I think she'd shoot us easy enough but I doubt she'd poison us. But you never know. One way or the other I need to find out how to get to the Apache scouts. My guess is, she knows where they are."

"It was no secret they were coming," I said. "It was in the papers and there are plenty of Mexicans hanging around Columbus. No doubt some are spies for Pancho Villa . . . and some for the Carrancistas."

The fire popped and a red-hot coal arced out of the flames and onto the dirt floor. Monte kicked it back into the fireplace. "I thought the Carrancistas were on our side."

"Pershing is trying to keep it a secret, but President Carranza doesn't want us in his country at all. In fact, our presence might even start a civil war in Mexico."

Still gazing into the fire, Monte said, "Sounds like a damn mess down here."

"Then you should go back where you came from," said Rosa, stepping through the door.

Monte and I turned. Neither of us moved another inch or said a word. Rosa had untangled her hair and worked it into two long braids that neatly hung down in front of her shoulders. Her face was spotless and the amber glow of the candle she held highlighted one of the most exquisite beauties I had ever seen.

Knowingly, Rosa paused. She looked at me first and then at Monte. Her eyes held on him as she slyly held out the pot of water.

"Thirsty?" Rosa asked with a sultry undercurrent in her voice.

Without taking his eyes off Rosa, Monte took the pot and drank it half empty. He wiped his mouth with the back of his sleeve and then handed me the water.

"I'll go tend to the horses," Monte said, flatly, and then stepped around Rosa and out the door.

I saw Rosa smile. Her eyes, focused on nothing in particular, filled with a reptilian glimmer. In a near panic, I looked away and started gulping water as if I were dying of thirst.

"You are a shy one," taunted Rosa.

I finished the water, gasped for air, and then shrugged. "I'm just a reporter, ma'am. Just an observer."

"How long have you known him?" asked Rosa.

"Monte? I just met him today."

"And you followed him into Mexico?"

"It seemed like a good idea at the time."

"And now?"

Finally gaining a few ounces of courage, I glanced at Rosa.

"I sensed something different about him the minute I saw him. He was a man on a mission of some sort and whatever it was, I wanted to be a part of it. I have a hunch his story's going to be worth the trouble."

"And for that you risk your life?"

Frowning, I admitted, "I hadn't counted on that part. But it's too late to turn back now."

"You are both fools," snipped Rosa. "I fight for freedom. That is worth dying for, not a story written on paper."

"You say you fight for freedom," I said.

"Freedom from what, exactly?"

"Freedom from the rich, the *haciendados*. They have all the land, all the money, all the cattle. We will take all they own and give it to the poor. The *haciendados* are Spanish. They deserve nothing. Except maybe to be shot."

Thoughts of the French Revolution raced through my mind. I recalled the illustrations of beheadings, the street gutters flowing crimson with the blue blood of the French aristocracy . . . some of whom were my ancestors.

"It is a common struggle," I said feebly.

Rosa huffed. "You know nothing."

I stiffened a bit. "I'm learning."

"In the revolution, you learn quick or die quick."

"Yes, ma'am."

Monte returned with two saddles under one arm and four blankets under the other. He dropped the entire load in front of the fireplace and went back outside.

Reaching down, Rosa took her saddle by the horn and positioned it to one side of the fire. She grabbed two of the blankets and held them close to the flames.

"Getting them warm?" I asked stupidly.

Rosa shook her head. "People sweat. Horses sweat. These will be our blankets tonight."

Feeling all but useless, I picked up the other two blankets and started drying them. It was then I realized that nothing I had ever learned or experienced had in any way prepared me for a life of hardship. Watching the steam rise from the blankets, I began to realize how I had been pampered my whole life, how blind I was to a way of life so many were forced to endure day after day.

And there was Rosa, a woman no less, courageously fighting in a revolution, struggling to break the bonds of poverty or die trying.

At that point, to say I felt profoundly inadequate would be an understatement.

Monte came in with the last two saddles and bridles. "The horses are watered. I found a little corral and put them inside."

"You found the corral in the dark?" asked Rosa, unable to hide her surprise.

Setting the saddles down, Monte said, "I see better'n most in the dark. Always have."

"*Gato,*" mumbled Rosa.

"Yeah," replied Monte as he hung the bridles on an iron peg protruding from the wall. "Yeah. Like a cat."

Rosa's eyes narrowed. "I said, *gato.*"

Monte came back to the fire. "Thought you said cat."

102

"Gato," said Rosa, watching Monte closely, "means cat."

Squatting and warming his hands, Monte said, "Sounded like cat to me."

I yawned. "What's the word for bed?"

Rosa ignored my question but Monte said, "Ask Captain Rosa what kind of sleeping arrangements she wants. It'll be too cold away from the fire with just these horse blankets so we're gonna be real cozy."

"Ma'am?" I asked. "What would you prefer?"

Without hesitation, Rosa said, "You in the middle. You between me and *El Gato.*"

Monte stood. "Looks like it's gonna be a long night. I'll get more wood."

Rosa's eyes followed Monte until he was out of sight. "He is a strange one."

After moving one of the saddles to the middle of the dirt floor, I continued drying the blankets. "He's different alright."

"Why did he rescue me?"

Squinting at Rosa, I said, "Why, ma'am, you were . . . you were being mistreated. I only wish I was as strong and brave as Monte. He did what any gentleman should have."

"Just because I am a woman?" scoffed Rosa.

"Certainly, ma'am. We aren't barbarians."

"Not what?"

"Hooligans. Bad men."

Rosa thought for a moment. "You, maybe. I am not sure about *El Gato.*"

"An army officer in Columbus insulted him," I said. "Monte did to that officer pretty much the same thing he did to the soldiers in the cantina. He seems to live by a code, a code that disappeared long ago."

Nodding her approval, Rosa said, "General Villa is much the same. A code. Yes, the general lives by this code, too."

What Rosa said struck me as odd. If what she told us about herself was true, she was fighting in a war, carrying a gun, and risking her life. No American woman would even think of doing such a thing.

"Does General Villa allow women to go to war, to fight against men? Is that part of his code?"

Rosa flinched ever so slightly and dropped her eyes. "He does not respect women soldiers. Not like General Zapata to the south. But some of the *soldaderas* do more than cook for their men. We fight. It is our choice."

"What do you mean 'the *soldaderas* cook for their men'? You mean they pack food and send it with the soldiers?"

"No. Most *soldaderas* carry food and

water and blankets for their men. They walk with them to war. How else do you think the men eat? When they stop walking the women cook and then sleep with their men."

I was incredulous. "The wives go with their husbands to war?"

Rosa shrugged. "Mostly they are wives. Many times, a woman just picks a man. Or then he gets killed and she picks another. It is not so important. We are all in the revolution together."

"But where do they sleep?" I asked, still grappling with what I was hearing.

"Sleep? Where do you think we sleep? In the trees?"

"No. Of course not. But in tents, maybe?"

"We have no tents. Only blankets. But if there is an adobe or hacienda nearby the general will take it. Sometimes we get the barns."

At that juncture, I wondered what Rosa was thinking about me. I was sunburned, saddle sore, and afraid of scorpions. I could only imagine how she would react if she discovered that I had never in my life slept on the ground.

There and then, I made up my mind to keep my mouth shut as much as possible, to reveal as little of my ignorance and inexperience as I could. And I vowed to make myself useful at doing something, anything.

Monte returned with an armload of wood and began stacking it next to the fireplace. "We need to talk, Captain Rosa. About tomorrow."

"I have thought of it already," said Rosa and then paused. "What do I call you, *gringo*?"

"My name's Monte Dell Segundo. But nobody calls me Dell. And neither will you. The Kootenais called me *Kahlssa*. Means three. Because the first time I fished with them I caught three fish and the first time I hunted with them I killed three deer."

"Kootenais?" I said.

"Indian tribe up north. I lived with them for a while."

"So that's why you told that sergeant in Columbus you could track as good as the Apaches?"

Rosa smirked, her eyes locked on Monte. "Maybe I will call you Kootenai. I like that."

Monte stopped stacking and turned. "Monte will do just fine. And I'm gonna demote you from captain. I'll just call you Rosa."

Turning her brown eyes on me, Rosa asked, "And you?"

I hesitated. "Billy. Billy Cabott."

Standing, Monte brushed his hands on his shirt. "So, Rosa, what do you think about tomorrow?"

Rosa stared into the fire before she answered. "You freed me from the soldiers. So, I will take you to Colonia Dublan. That is where the Apaches were taken. And then my debt to you is paid."

"Deal," agreed Monte. "How far is it to this Colonia place?"

"One day's ride. Maybe two. We go first through the village of Boca Grande. It is not far from here. Then we pass through La Ascensión. But if there are Carrancistas in those villages, we go around."

I thought for a moment, recalling that Colonia Dublan was Pershing's headquarters. I knew the army was in the process of laying telegraph wire and that it would reach all the way back to Camp Furlong in Columbus. Those in Colonia Dublan might know, in fact probably did know, about Monte Segundo and the lieutenant he slugged. They also might know what happened in the cantina in Las Palomas.

"Monte, Colonia Dublan and Columbus might be connected by telegraph. They're most likely looking for you. How are you going to find the Apaches without being recognized and arrested?"

"I'll go in at night, ask a few questions. I don't know. I'll figure it out when we get there."

I glanced at Rosa. "And how far will you be from General Villa once we get to Colonia Dublan?"

"I was captured in Namiquipa. General Villa defeated the Carrancistas there. He will be nearby. Namiquipa is seventy miles below Dublan."

"But Villa is steadily heading south," I protested. "I've seen the reports. There'll be nothing but Carrancista soldiers north of Namiquipa. You would try and make it all that way by yourself?"

Rosa stepped around me and shoved her saddle closer to the fire. "You think too much," she said, laying out one blanket and then her pistol within easy reach. "Tomorrow will take care of itself."

Monte positioned his saddle and blanket as Rosa lay down and draped her second blanket over her shoulders.

I was left standing between them and asking myself what I'd gotten myself into. Looking down at Rosa and Monte, I was certain of nothing save the sinking realization that, on my own, I would not survive one single day in Mexico.

"Well then," I said trying to sound cheery,

"we'll cross the bridges as we come to them."

Attempting to seem like an old hand at what I was doing, I laid out my blanket just as Monte had done. And I used the saddle as a pillow just like Monte and Rosa. But unlike them I was asleep in minutes.

Rosa didn't trust Monte and that kept her awake that night. But what kept Monte awake was worry, worry that he would have another nightmare. As he had done on the long train ride from north Idaho, he vainly searched for any clue that would help him understand why his dreams, nightmares that used to be few and far between, had become almost nightly occurrences.

With his head propped on the saddle, Monte studied the dancing flames. He thought of the fire in his nightmares and of the searing pain as the flames consumed his flesh. For hours, he considered the shadowy outline that loomed over him, wondering to whom or what it might belong.

Finally, with his eyes growing heavy, he resigned himself to the fact that the face might belong to no one at all, that it could be a total fabrication. But as he was drifting off to sleep, a woman's voice was whispering to him, telling him the face in his dream was that of an Apache.

Rosa had pretended to sleep but from time to time peered at Monte. She watched him for hours and saw him finally close his eyes.

She was about to fall asleep herself when she heard a word spoken softly.

"Corra."

Instantly awake, Rosa reached for her pistol. Feeling the wooden grip, she wrapped her hand around it and waited.

She heard it again but this time the word was louder and more urgent.

"Corra!"

Sitting up, Rosa looked at me, then at Monte.

Suddenly, Monte jerked in his sleep and yelled. "Corra!"

That woke me. I blinked, trying to focus, and rolled my head left and right.

Monte's eyes were open and Rosa was sitting up. "What was that?" I asked, half awake. "Who is Cora?"

Monte rubbed his eyes and sat up. "What's going on?"

"You dreamed," said Rosa.

Monte focused his eyes. He sat up, leaned forward, and then tossed several sticks into the fireplace. "I don't remember any dream."

"You said 'Corra' many times," Rosa said.

"Then you yelled it."

"Cora," grumbled Monte. "I don't know any Cora."

With my head still on the saddle, I glanced from Monte to Rosa. "I have an Aunt Cora."

"When you wake from a dream, it is remembered," said Rosa.

"Not this one."

Rosa's eyes narrowed. "*Corra* means only one thing to me."

"What's that," I asked.

"In Spanish, it means . . . run!"

CHAPTER 4

A chill woke me before sunrise. I stirred and tried to roll over. My face puckered with pain. Everything but my hair seemed raw or bruised. For a few seconds, I had no idea where I was or what kind of terrible accident I had been in. But then, lying still, my head cleared and I pulled myself together.

I heard Monte sit up and then Rosa. Clenching my teeth, I did the same. For a moment, I was convinced that during the night a huge scorpion had crawled down my shirt and sunk its venomous fangs deep into my flesh. But then, remembering the long jolting ride from Las Palomas and the hard dirt floor beneath me, I understood the source of my misery.

I tried to speak but had to clear my throat first. "Looks like we'll get an early start."

Monte and Rosa stood at almost the same instant. They exchanged an unfriendly glance. I managed to get my legs under me and stand without my lips quivering from the pain.

"Any chance of getting something to eat in Boca Grande?" Monte asked.

"If there are no soldiers, yes maybe."

"Do you think they'll know about us so soon?" I asked.

"*¿Quién sabe?* Who knows."

"What side are they on, the people in town?" Monte asked.

Rosa shrugged indifferently. "Many villages take no side. They know if they take any side of this war, they will pay. Sometimes the men are taken away and forced to fight. Sometimes the women . . . they are taken, too . . . or used and left behind. Sometimes the men, old and young, are killed. And then there are the bandits that come to rob and rape. The villagers just try to stay alive."

Monte peered at Rosa. "Hell of a war you got down here."

Jerking her saddle off the floor, Rosa snapped, "You know nothing about our revolution. Nothing!"

Hefting his own saddle, Monte started for the door, "At least I know right from wrong." Kicking the door wide open he said, "And I think you do, too."

Rosa followed Monte, lugging the saddle as she went. At the door, she stopped. The sun was just rising.

Monte was several steps in front of Rosa when he turned to say something. Instead, he was distracted by the sun's rays reflecting off the braids of her hair, the glimmer of her eyes, and the golden hue of her skin.

What happened in that instant is difficult to explain. To Rosa and I it truly was only an instant and yet to Monte, it was much, much longer.

In Monte's mind, a rifle butt came out of nowhere and smashed into Rosa's skull. He heard a thwack like the sound of a boiled egg being thrown against a tree trunk. Blood gushed over Rosa's face. He saw bits of her hair and skin fall to the ground.

In his throat, he felt a scream that could not escape, and for the first time in his life, he felt terror.

And then it was over. Nothing had happened. Rosa was standing in the sunrise glaring back at him.

"You are a damn *gringo*," she bellowed. "You will never understand."

Monte didn't hear a word Rosa said. The scene of her skull being smashed flashed through his mind in a fraction of a second and then was gone. But it left him stunned.

Monte realized his heart was pounding and recalled an old man he had found wandering in the mountains of Idaho. It had been a long, miserable winter and then a cold spring brought more snow. Trapped alone in his cabin, the old man had barely clung to his sanity during the winter months, but the lingering spring snows had turned him into a lunatic.

Monte began to wonder if he too was losing his mind. The dreams of being burned alive were becoming more frequent and more intense and now he had envisioned crushing a woman's skull with a rifle butt.

Rosa walked on past Monte to the horses. When I came out of the adobe, Monte was standing motionless with the rising sun at his back.

I didn't see the expression on his face until I was a step away.

I froze. "What's wrong?"

Monte blinked several times. He shook his head and then rubbed a hand over his face. "Nothing," he muttered and again started for the horses.

I had no doubt that something was bothering Monte but I naturally assumed it had something to do with Rosa. But for the life of me, I couldn't fathom what she could have done or said that would embed such a morbid look in his eyes.

Thankfully, Monte saddled my horse without saying a word. Watching Rosa effortlessly saddle her own horse, I felt like a fool standing there. But it would have been much worse had I actually tried to do it myself.

I watched closely, trying to memorize everything Monte was doing, but I could feel the disgust in Rosa's glances. My face flushed and I felt the stinging heat of humiliation.

Monte tightened the latigo strap and then buckled the headstall. "Got it?" he asked.

"Yes."

"Watch and learn. Can't ask more'n that."

Rosa huffed. "Reporters!" she snorted and then with her rifle strapped over her shoulders, she stepped into her saddle and grabbed the reins of the extra horse. How she did it so gracefully and in a skirt, I'll never know. I think even Monte was impressed.

"I will lead," Rosa said testily. "You follow."

Monte waited until I got settled and had a firm grip on the reins before he mounted. I expected a sarcastic retort to Rosa's orders, but instead, Monte merely studied the empty desert.

116

When Rosa was twenty yards ahead, Monte and I rode away from the adobe, thankfully at an easy walk. In minutes, we were heading south, following a road that was little more than a goat path threading its way through a forest of thorny mesquite. In less than an hour we were riding into Boca Grande, a village identical to Las Palomas but half its size.

A handful of barefooted children were playing in the dusty street but when they noticed us approaching they stopped what they were doing. Some called out what to me sounded like a warning.

Several adults hurried from the adobes, shading their eyes to see us better.

With Rosa still out in front, we rode past the first adobe.

A small girl stood suddenly and shouted, *"Bandidos!"*

One of the larger boys grabbed the girl as the rest of the children scurried toward the adobes.

Rosa reined in. She called to the children and then to an old woman who had stepped boldly into the street. After the woman nodded and shook her head, Rosa continued riding.

We rode on in silence. Midway through the clustered villagers, a young woman pointed at Monte. *"El Muerte,"* she said softly. *"Es el Muerte!"*

Rosa turned and leered back at the woman and then glanced curiously at Monte.

From the other side of the street a medley of hushed voices echoed the words, *"El Muerte. Ayi, es El Muerte!"*

Another woman pointed at Rosa. *"Ella es la mujer capitan!"*

"Friendly bunch," muttered Monte, speaking for the first time since leaving the old adobe.

"I guess they don't see many Americans," I said. "But it sounds like they know Captain Rosa. Did you hear that woman say *'capitan'*?"

Monte nodded but by then we were out of the village. The three of us rode on for about a mile when Rosa suddenly spun her horse around.

"They know what happened at the cantina. If they know at Boca Grande they will also know in La Ascensión. There may be Carrancistas there waiting for us."

"What do you mean they know," I asked. "How could they?"

Rosa tossed her braids behind her shoulders and pointed at Monte. "Him they know. They call him *El Muerte.*"

I sighed. "I don't get it."

"Gringos!" sneered Rosa. "In the cantina," continued Rosa, again pointing at Monte, "he spoke his name. When the bartender heard it, he made the sign of the cross. Now I know why. It is because the bartender heard *'Muerte'* not Monte."

"So what?" said Monte.

"And maybe, too, you killed some of the Carrancista soldiers in the cantina."

I was flabbergasted. "That's crazy."

"What do you know, reporter?" Rosa said. "I know my people, my customs. At least one of the soldiers is dead. Maybe more. That is why they now call him *'El Muerte.'* Death."

Thinking of how Monte had lifted Rosa with one hand and how he had demolished the line of Mexican soldiers, I began to wonder. Could Monte be so powerful? Could he kill a man bare-handed and with so little effort?

"They deserved what they got," Monte said, simply. "If they're dead, they're dead."

Hearing such a cold-blooded comment sent a jolt of fear through my body. It finally dawned on me that I had wandered into something way over my head. I was barely out of college. Only weeks before I was at home atop Carnegie Hill discussing my future plans with two loving parents. Now, I was trapped in a godforsaken country in the middle of a war and very possibly traveling with two heartless killers.

Thinking of being arrested by the Mexican government, I fought down a wave of panic. I told myself that Rosa was jumping to conclusions, that there must have been some misunderstanding at the cantina, that she was mistaken about everything.

I tried to console myself with the knowledge that Monte and I were, after all, United States citizens. He was not part of the army and I was only a reporter. We were neutrals, not killers. And deep down, I must admit, I was taking refuge in the fact that I was a Weston, a family not to be taken lightly.

Before my heart had a chance to stop pounding, my comforting thoughts were shattered.

"And you," Rosa said to me, "the Carrancistas will be hunting you along with *El Muerte.* Now the two of you are no better than *bandidos,* no better than me."

"Hunt me?" I exclaimed in a tone far too shrill. "No, this is all a mistake. Once I explain . . ."

Rosa burst out laughing. She laughed so hysterically I thought she had lost her mind.

"What," I said and then raised my voice

over her laughter. "What is so damn funny?"

Slowly, Rosa regained her composure and wiped the tears from her eyes. "No one explains in this revolution. No one. Not even priests and nuns are safe. Not until it is over. There is only the firing squad, *ley fuga.* You will explain nothing!"

"We need food," Monte said, seemingly paying no attention to my fright. "Can we get supplies in Ascensión?"

"We can try," answered Rosa. "But many American wagons and motor trucks go through that village. We will ride just east of Ascensión to Ojo Federico, instead."

Glancing at me, Monte said matter-of-factly, "You can ride north, road or no road, and be back in the states in a day or two. You can make it without food or water if you leave now.

"Likely you'll run into our army somewhere along the way. You got a good chance to make it. It's your choice, Billy."

There was nothing profound in what Monte said. It was how he said, "It's your choice, Billy," that got to me. That simple statement was enough to rip the yellow streak off my back. That and, for the lack of a better word, the burgeoning charisma of Monte Segundo.

Inexplicably, the fear left me. More than

that, however, I sensed that I was standing on a precipice about to witness something of vital importance. I felt a surge of confidence, an epiphany if you will.

Then and there I knew if I were to ever become a renowned reporter, or to accomplish anything worthwhile, my present circumstance would test the strength of my character once and for all time.

"I'm staying," I said.

Monte nodded his approval. I even detected a glint of admiration in Rosa's eyes. Feeling as though I had earned a modicum of respect, I felt six feet tall. Without a doubt, I knew I had experienced my first taste of manhood.

"In that case," said Rosa, suddenly dismounting, "I will show you how to use your rifle."

I stepped down and took the rifle off my shoulder, knowing nothing more about the weapon than to keep the barrel pointed up.

Rosa came up beside me with her rifle in hand. "These are German Mausers," she said and then jerked a five-bullet clip from her bandolier.

Sliding the bolt back, she shoved the clip down into the rifle and then slammed the bolt shut. "You do it," she ordered.

I did as I was told. Using my own rifle

122

and clips, I was surprised how easy it was. "Now what?"

"Venga," she said and took a few steps away from the horses. "Come!"

After showing me the safety and how to line up the front and rear sights she pointed to a rock at the base of a mesquite tree. "Shoot the stone."

The target was fifty paces away, which at the time seemed quite a long shot for a first lesson. I slowly raised the rifle but Rosa stopped me.

"Like this," she growled and slapped the rifle into her shoulder. "Tight on your shoulder. Be quick."

Rosa's rifle roared, her bullet hitting dead center of the rock.

"Quick, then," I repeated and threw the rifle to my shoulder, found the sights, and fired.

I felt the jolt of the recoil and saw an explosion of sand six inches from the rock. "I missed."

"Close enough," Rosa said. "Now you are trained as good as any Mexican peon. And we cannot waste our bullets. Now you are a soldier."

Watching Rosa eject her empty casing and then set the safety, I did the same. She looped her rifle over her head and shoulder but I hesitated. I found myself enjoying the feel of the Mauser in my hands and how the sun glimmered off the polished wood and machined steel. But there was something else. As I stood there admiring the weapon a strange euphoria engulfed me, a sensation I had never experienced. It was the sense that I now possessed power, incredible power. And I liked it.

Rosa led the way to Ojo Federico but no longer rode so far in the lead. A quarter mile from the village we stopped alongside each other under a blistering midday sun. The village looked the same as the previous two and, like them, looked to have at most two hundred inhabitants.

Sliding her rifle from her shoulder, Rosa laid it across her lap. I started to follow suit but she held her hand up. "We don't want to look like bandits. We will ride in easy.

"If there is trouble, we scatter and meet back where we shot the Mausers."

Monte drew his Colt and opened the loading gate. "Fine with me," he said, shoving a sixth cartridge into an empty cylinder.

"Can you hit anything with that?" Rosa asked.

Monte holstered his pistol. "I don't shoot at 'anything.' Never have."

Rosa thought for a moment and then huffed. She looked again at Monte. "You have black hair and brown eyes."

"They tell me that comes with being Italian."

"If there are Carrancistas, they will be looking for two *gringos.* One wearing an American uniform. But with a sombrero and serape you could pass for Mexican."

I rubbed a finger down my sunburned cheek. "Well, I sure can't."

"Do you speak any German?" Rosa asked.

"Yes," I answered. "And French and some Latin."

Rosa thoughtfully squinted her eyes. "There are many Germans here on the side of Carranza. If you are caught by the Carrancistas, speak only German."

"Do the villagers of Ojo Federico like the Carrancistas?" Monte asked.

"Maybe yes, maybe no. Some they hate. Some Carrancistas are worse than the bandits."

"I got a few American dollars," Monte said. "How much would a sombrero and a poncho cost?"

Rosa paused ever so slightly before answering. "We will trade the extra saddle. There is a *tienda,* in Federico but it will be empty. If there are any goods to trade they will have been hidden.

"I will go in alone and trade with the villagers."

"No," Monte said as if the word itself was cast in iron.

I expected Rosa to object but she didn't make a sound. Where I expected to see hostility, I detected an unmistakable softening in her eyes.

"We'll go in together. We'll go slow and easy. And I'll take the lead. If there's a need, I can shoot faster than the two of you combined."

Rosa's eyes dropped to Monte's belted pistol. For the first time, she noticed the worn grips. A number of old *gringo* gunfighters still lived in Mexico. She recalled having seen many of them as a child and some of the most dangerous wore their *pistolas* in the same cross draw.

"Then I will take the rear," Rosa said.

"If there are soldiers there," I asked, "how many would you expect?"

"There would be a *jefe de armas,* a commandant, and five or six men. Like there was in Las Palomas. Farther south there would be more men, maybe fifty."

With a quick nod, Monte nudged his horse past Rosa and we started into an easy walk. In seconds, we spotted a man on the

126

road. He was leading a burro out of the village and ambling toward us.

As the distance closed between us, I could see the Mexican was bent and old. He paid us little mind until we were a few feet apart and then he stopped.

Wrinkled, expressionless eyes peered at us from under a tattered sombrero.

Rosa greeted him. They spoke for a full minute before the Mexican trudged on past us.

Glaring at the village, Rosa said, "Six soldiers and a commandant. They have taken all the food for themselves. And any of the women they want. Now is a good time for us to enter. It is siesta."

"What's that?" I asked.

"They will be sleeping," answered Rosa, "or almost asleep. After the midday meal, a siesta is customary in Mexico."

"Good," Monte said and off we went with my heart in my throat.

The town looked deserted but as we passed the first adobe a dog barked and then three children ran out of a nearby alley.

Rosa halted and spoke to them. The eldest, a boy of eight or nine, spun on his bare heels and ran across the street and through the doorway of an adobe.

In less than a minute, two elderly women emerged and then hobbled over to us. Rosa began speaking, first holding up two fingers and then holding up one. She pointed to the saddle on our extra horse.

My eyes swept the street ahead. I looked from building to building, peering into the black shadows of the open doors and windows. I saw no movement and, except for the three women haggling, I heard no sound.

Finally, it was settled. One woman went back into the adobe she had come out of and the other disappeared into the alley the children had come from.

Rosa dismounted, holding the reins of her horses.

"How'd we do?" Monte asked.

"Wait and see."

Shortly the women returned, one carrying two sombreros, the other a serape and a bulging cotton sack tied at the top with a leather thong.

One of the sombreros was quite large. Rosa handed that one and the serape to Monte. Taking the smaller sombrero, she shoved it down on her head and quickly looped the sack over her saddle horn. She then handed the reins of the spare horse to one of the old women.

"You traded a horse and saddle for a couple of hats and a poncho?" Monte asked as he took off his hat and slipped the serape over his shoulders.

"And food. These people are almost starving. Food is worth more than gold here. It was a fair trade. And they know who you are."

Swinging up into her saddle Rosa added, "We have what we need. We should get off of this street. We can ride behind the adobes and be on our way."

"Suits me," agreed Monte, looping his campaign hat on his saddle horn and donning the sombrero.

We rode east down the first alley, then turned south down another. Even though the main street was less than fifty feet away we were relatively hidden from view.

If we had chosen a slightly different route out of Ojo Federico we would never have seen the boy. But we did.

He was small. His hair was shaggy and his clothes ragged and soiled. He sat against a wall with his knees folded up to his chest. His face was buried in tiny hands and he was weeping.

Monte drew up suddenly. Curiously, he stared down at the boy for several seconds and then turned back to Rosa. "What's wrong with him?"

At the time, I couldn't fathom why Monte would do such a thing. It was a child and children cried all the time. With Carrancistas nearby, there was no time to stop and ask such a question.

"*¿Que pasó?*" asked Rosa.

When the boy raised his head, his dirty face was streaked with tears, tears that reflected the rays of the sun.

When the boy looked up, Monte did not see the child in front of him. What flashed before his eyes was the image of another boy, similar in appearance and yet different. The boy Monte saw, however, was looking up but the tears that streaked his face were mixed with blood. Monte heard a distant voice, a vaguely familiar voice yelling, "Run!"

Monte shook his head. Fighting off yet another hallucination, he looked away from the boy in the alley.

The boy spoke to Rosa.

"The Carrancistas took his mother," Rosa said. "He has not seen her in two days."

Hearing those words ignited something vicious inside Monte Segundo. His eyes suddenly blazed with fury.

"Where?" Monte demanded.

"*¿Donde?*" Rosa asked.

130

The boy wiped away his tears and stood. With the three of us following, he walked down an alley toward the main street. He stopped and pointed at a large adobe. *"Ahi."*

Without waiting for an interpretation, Monte tossed his sombrero and serape on the ground. He dismounted and then put on his campaign hat.

I knew something bad was about to happen even though I couldn't imagine what was coming. Before I could say a word, Monte drew his pistol and started across the street toward the large adobe.

Equally as bizarre, Rosa, without a word of protest, hopped down and swung her rifle off her shoulder. Gathering the reins of Monte's horse and then her own, she handed them to me and then took a position at the corner of an adobe facing the one across the street.

She kneeled and took aim.

At first, I thought she was going to shoot Monte but then I realized she was covering him. The thought crossed my mind that they had done all this before, that they were a team. But I knew that was absurd. And yet they seemed to move as one.

Monte walked through the open door and was instantly out of sight. A few breaths later a muffled shot rang out. Then a second.

Two more shots in rapid succession followed. There was a fifth shot and moments later a sixth.

I heard the sound of glass shattering and then a bloodcurdling scream.

Seconds passed and then a soldier staggered into the sunlight clutching his bleeding throat with both hands.

He collapsed in the middle of the street. And then there was absolute silence.

Next to appear from the darkened doorway was a young woman. The boy sprang to his feet and ran to her.

Rosa held her position, ready to shoot. But the next person to emerge was not a Carrancista. It was Monte and he was using a strip of cloth to wipe blood off his hunting knife.

Rosa stood. *"Madre de Dios,"* she said.

I seconded her sentiments with, "Holy Jesus!"

Sheathing his knife, Monte stood in the doorway and started ejecting the empties from his Colt. He had fired six times and then bloodied his knife. I was incredulous.

The old man said there were seven soldiers. And Monte was taking his time reloading. Had he killed all seven? Seven men in less than a minute?

The villagers began to appear from nowhere. They gathered around the young woman and her son, comforting them both.

Monte started for us. He walked easily, his eyes fixed on nothing in particular.

Rosa waited until he was close. "You are not wounded?"

"No."

"They are all dead. All seven?"

"All seven were bad men," said Monte, hanging his military hat on his saddle horn and again donning the serape and sombrero.

Monte and Rosa mounted at the same time, as if their movements had been choreographed. In unison, we rode down the main street.

Rosa veered a few steps closer to the dead Carrancista but I stayed away. Except for my grandfather's funeral, I had never seen a dead man and this one, covered in glistening red blood, had died right in front of my eyes. I could not bring myself to look directly at him, but kept him in the corner of my eye as I rode past.

Rosa, on the other hand, paused next to the body. She then leaned to one side and spit on the dead soldier. After wiping her lips with the back of her hand she nudged her horse into a trot to catch up. "Another day and we reach the *colonia*," she said, "but only if there are not so many *gringos* on the road."

Monte rode several feet in the lead and Rosa settled in next to me. Passing the growing crowd of villagers, we could see every eye was riveted on Monte.

We were just beyond the last adobe when we heard a woman's quivering voice. *"Viva El Muerte!"*

Then a child shouted at the top of his lungs, *"Viva El Muerte! Viva El Muerte."*

Dozens of villagers then joined in voicing the same chant, their voices echoing off the adobe walls until we were well out of hearing range.

Rosa seemed anxious to speak to me. We slowed our pace and let Monte get farther out in front.

"I have been with the revolution for two years," Rosa said softly. "I have never seen anything like that!"

I was still reeling from it all, almost in a state of shock. "If he did kill a soldier in Las Palomas," I mumbled half to myself, "it was unintentional. But this was . . . this was different. He went in there with the intent to kill them. And he had no idea who or what was inside that adobe. It doesn't make any sense. None of it makes any sense. Seven men are dead!"

"Does he feel so strongly about protecting

women?" Rosa asked.

The calm in Rosa's voice rattled me even more. She was behaving as if the deaths of the men were utterly insignificant.

I glared at Rosa but she seemed to be daydreaming.

"I think . . ." she mused, "I think it was the boy that caused it. But why would Monte stop for that *niño*? Just because he was crying? There was no reason for him to do such a thing. We could have kept on riding and none of this would have happened. It was . . . it was as if he risked his life because of the boy, not for the woman."

Rosa paused and thought for a moment. "He is a brave man, *muy macho.*"

I shook my head. "He has no fear. None. I don't know if that's the same thing as being brave."

Little did I know how wrong I was that afternoon. Ahead of us, Monte Segundo was grappling with the realization that he'd had another hallucination, one that had enraged him and sent him into the Carrancista headquarters. It was the second inexplicable episode in one day and at that moment Monte was growing more and more fearful he might be losing his mind.

For some reason, seeing the boy sitting against the adobe had startled him. Or was it the crying? Either way, Monte recalled a storm of anxiety had instantly engulfed him.

The hallucination of the bloody face came next. It occurred after the boy had raised his head. From then on, all Monte felt was rage. But unlike what he felt in the cantina in Las Palomas, he knew this rage was not triggered by concern for a helpless woman. No, what Monte Segundo experienced, what baffled him, was his burning desire to avenge the boy.

But even more disturbing than the boy was the vision he had of crushing Rosa's skull. That had nothing to do with rage. What he felt at that moment was horror, horror that he could even possess such an insane thought.

I pointed at Monte as Rosa and I rode behind him. "He hasn't even looked back to see if we're back here."

"He knows," Rosa said flatly.

We rode on in silence for a moment. "Another thing," I said. "How did the villagers know he was *El Muerte*? How could word have gotten to them before we even got there?"

Rosa pondered my question before she answered. "Mexicans are poor people. So, we value simple things. Music, dancing, and stories cost us nothing. Stories like that of

El Muerte travel quickly. There are trains out of Columbus and telegraphs in Agua Prieta. The Tarahumara Indians can run one hundred and fifty miles in the mountains without stopping. We have our ways. The news of *El Muerte* will spread like wildfire now. Nothing will stop it. And that is very dangerous for us."

"You mean, until we get to Colonia Dublan," I objected. "Then we can straighten all this out."

Rosa glanced at me out of the corners of her eyes. "But what if you cannot? And if the Apache scouts Monte seeks are not there and have gone farther south? What will you do then, Billy?"

CHAPTER 5

We had to leave the road twice to hide from long caravans of motor trucks on their way to Colonia Dublan. Sitting astride our horses in the dense mesquite, we watched the mechanical monstrosities rattle by in billowing clouds of dust.

Some trucks carried bales of hay, some tanks of water, others wooden crates of various sizes. Everything and everyone was covered in a dense patina of gritty desert sand.

After they passed, we followed the tire tracks until sundown and then swung west of the town, which was located near the Casas Grandes River.

Following the river and staying in the cottonwoods along the bank, we were able to ride within a half-mile of the army camp undetected. At dusk we dismounted, tied our horses, and crept up the riverbank to take a closer look.

Inside a new barbed wire fence, precise rows of crisp olive-drab tents blanketed forty acres of a small prairie. Several sentries armed with rifles were patrolling the perimeter.

A short distance north of the camp both Monte and I were astonished to see an array of neat two-story brick houses and white picket fences.

"What kind of place is Colonia Dublan, anyway?" I asked. "That looks like a town you'd see in the states."

"Mormons," said Rosa. "The men there have many wives. They come here to live. They are *gringos* but even Villa leaves them alone. As do the Carrancistas. They bother no one."

"Polygamists?" I exclaimed. "They came all the way down here?"

Rosa shrugged. "There are other *colonias* in Mexico. This is but one. They all look the same. All are Mormons with many wives."

"They're straitlaced, aren't they?" asked Monte. "No drinking, cussing. That sort."

"Maybe in the *colonias*," said Rosa. "But on the east side of the camp there are saloons going up and whores. Plenty of *putas* for the soldiers."

"Sounds right," snorted Monte. "Nothing ever changes."

"How will you find the Apaches?" Rosa asked.

"Well," Monte said, "I guess I'll wait 'til dark and then go have a look."

It was then I saw my chance. There was something I could do that would surely impress both Rosa and Monte. And I dearly wanted to impress them both, to be useful. Strange to say, I wanted to be a part of them, in some small way to be like the two of them.

"No, Monte," I objected. "They'll very likely be looking for you. They'll have a good description of you by now and you're not easy to miss. I'll go in," I said, laying my rifle aside and adjusting my leather satchel. "As a reporter, I can ask all kinds of questions and no one will think anything of it. I can find out where the scouts are, no problem. I'll go now. There's no reason to wait until dark."

Rosa grunted her approval. "And I will go to the saloons and brothels. My people will be all around the camp. Villa's spies have been watching since the *gringos* got here. His men walk freely around the camp and no one knows who they are."

Monte sighed. "Alright then. I'll see to the horses."

As Rosa and I stood, Monte cleared his

throat. I'll never forget it. It was as if the words struggled to get past his lips. "You be careful, Rosa."

Perplexed, Rosa turned and looked at Monte. She handed him her rifle without saying a word but even in the fading light I saw her blush.

I grinned as Rosa and I walked toward the camp.

Rosa glanced at me. "What are you smiling at?" she demanded.

Looking straight ahead, I replied, "Oh, nothing. Nothing at all."

"Cabrón!" muttered Rosa. *"Hijo de la chingada!"*

Near the entrance to the camp Rosa and I separated. A sentry by the front gate caught sight of me.

"Who goes there?"

"William Cabott. Reporter for the *Chicago Tribune.*"

The sentry nodded. I walked up to him, eyeing the camp. "Have you any idea where the reporters gather?"

The soldier pointed down the perfectly straight rows of tents. "Down about a hundred yards. Big tent on your left. Flaps open. This time of day, should be a half-dozen reporters in there."

Nodding to the guard, I made my way

down the lanes of tents. Soldiers were inside most of them, a surprising number playing cards or shooting dice.

The news tent was much larger than the others and circular in shape. Wooden chairs were haphazardly scattered over a canvas floor. Only two reporters were anywhere to be seen.

Recognizing both reporters from the trial in Deming, I easily started up a conversation. After an hour, I was caught up on all the latest news that reporters were entitled to and some they weren't. It was the news being blacked out by General Pershing that I found most intriguing.

When I got back to Monte it was full dark, and he was camped down on the bank of the Casas Grandes with a small fire going.

Monte was sitting close to the fire leaning against his saddle. He seemed deep in thought but he looked up at me when I stepped into the light.

"You eat in the camp?"

"Forgot to. Too much going on I guess."

Pointing to the sack Rosa had gotten in Boca Grande, Monte said, "There's cheese in there. And more jerky."

I set out my blanket and saddle and took a seat across from Monte. Glancing at him, I reached in the sack and grabbed a wedge of cheese. I could see he was agitated. I assumed it was because of what happened in Ojo Federico.

"What'd you find out?" Monte asked.

"Plenty," I said, taking a bite of cheese. "First off, they're looking for you, sure enough. That officer you slugged remembered your name but there's something fishy going on."

"Like what?"

"They're calling you 'Private Segundo' like you were regular army. But they have to know you're state militia."

"Sure, they do."

"Some are claiming Pershing wants to charge you with treason because you supposedly killed a Carrancista in Las Palomas, an ally. Only a spy or a soldier can be charged with treason."

"I didn't kill anybody in Las Palomas," Monte said. "At least not on purpose."

I shrugged. "That's the story that's going around, anyway."

"So that's why I'm all of a sudden a private?"

"That seems to be the case."

Monte shrugged. "Learn anything else?"

"I heard Pancho Villa is telling everybody that he only wants to kill Americans now,

143

that he doesn't want to kill any more Mexicans."

"Then we best steer clear of him and his men," Monte said. "And the sooner we get rid of Rosa, the better."

"Do you think she would harm us?"

"Not now. She needs us to get past the Carrancistas. But when she's done with us . . . sure."

I heartily disagreed with Monte but chose to keep that opinion to myself.

"I learned, too, that the Apache scouts got here a few days ago. They'll be assigned to Colonel Howze of the Eleventh Cavalry. I'll find out more tomorrow. There's a big news meeting then. All the reporters show up for that.

"Pershing's not in Colonia Dublan any longer. In fact, he's completely out of touch at the moment. He's at least one hundred miles south of us and communicates by airplane. A pilot named Foulois finds him, lands, and then brings back his dispatches.

"The general is chasing Villa with three columns of cavalry. Colonel Brown heads one to the east, Major Tompkins in the middle, and Howze to the west.

"They say Howze gets the Apache scouts because he'll be in the rough terrain of the Sierra Madre Mountains and not out in the desert. That's country some of the scouts are familiar with and where their tracking skills will come into play.

"Another thing I learned is that even though the Carrancistas are trying their best to kill Villa, just like we are, they aren't helping us at all. They're still refusing us the use of the railways. Worse, they're often actually getting in the way on purpose, helping Villa escape."

Monte grunted. "I had a couple of friends when I was a kid, two brothers. One was bigger'n the other by quite a bit. They got to fighting one day and after a while the bigger brother was beating the daylights out of the littler. I figured I'd step in and help out the little one. Then they both turned on me, waling away on me like I was their worst enemy.

"I never forgot that. But I've heard others tell stories just like it. These Mexicans are no different than those brothers, I suppose."

I took another bite of cheese and laughed. "It's all so strange, though. The whole operation. Three huge cavalry columns on who knows how many horses, not to mention all the pack mules they have, and General Pershing driving all over the desert in a Dodge touring car, sending messages by airplane, all the while trying to keep up with the horses. And the general is out there in the middle of nowhere with nothing more than four automobiles, three trucks, and twenty men. No other help for miles and miles in any direction."

I paused for a moment to dig into my satchel and retrieve a notepad.

"On top of that," I continued, as I opened the pad and found my notes, "the general's aide-de-camp is a lieutenant named . . . George Patton. We can't report this but I was told Patton said this about the commander-in-chief, President Wilson, and I quote, *'He has not the soul of a louse nor the mind of a worm. Or the backbone of a jellyfish.'* End quote. Can you believe all this? Crazy is what it is. Plain crazy."

"Yeah," grumbled Monte, "Maybe you're right."

At the time, Monte's comment meant nothing. What I didn't know was that for the last several hours he had been wondering if he himself wasn't crazy, that he was losing his grip on reality.

He had tried to stop the visions from creeping into his mind during the day but they continued to invade his thoughts. Again and again, he kept seeing Rosa's head being crushed, the flames around him, the dark face above him, and, ever since Ojo

Federico, the vision of a small bloody-faced boy looking up at him.

But it was not just the visions or hallucinations that plagued Monte. An ever-increasing mixture of rage and guilt had been gnawing at him for hours.

A twig snapped in the darkness beyond the fire. Like a cat, Monte rolled and sprang to his feet with his pistol cocked and pointed.

"It is me," said Rosa. "I am alone."

Monte eased the hammer down on his Colt and let out a long sigh. "Come on in," he said holstering his pistol.

Everything had happened so fast, I was still trying to take it all in. I had never seen anyone react so quickly. Nor had I ever seen anyone turn deadly as fast as Monte Segundo.

Rosa went to Monte and held out her closed hand. "Here."

Monte hesitated and then extended his hand. When he did, Rosa dropped something into it. She then held her hand out to me and did the same.

It was a hard piece of something. I couldn't tell in the firelight.

Rosa put one of the pieces in her mouth. "It is candy. From the Chinese."

"Chinese?" I exclaimed. "What do you

mean Chinese?"

Rolling the candy around in her mouth, Rosa put her fingers to the corners of her eyes and pulled them back. "*Chinos*. Chinese."

I shook my head. "Chinese? In Mexico?"

"You learn quick, *gringo*."

Rosa picked up her rifle and then sat down by the fire with the Mauser across her lap. "There are many *Chinos* here in Mexico. Mostly men. They want to get into your country but are not allowed in, so they stay here. Some marry Mexicans. Some have joined the Carranza government. Villa wants to kill them all. The *Chinos* help the *gringos* wherever the army goes. They cook, wash, sell cigarettes, candy, soap. You *gringos* came to Mexico but know nothing of how to make a war. You are helpless little children. You need the *Chinos*."

I didn't know how Monte felt but I was growing tired of Rosa's attitude and I found her comments particularly insulting. My anger got the best of me.

"We know plenty about making war," I said indignantly. "We know enough to never fight like the Mexicans."

Rosa sucked on her candy for a moment. "*Gringos* can't fight. General Villa says we could take Washington in six months if he wants."

Feeling the heat rise in my face, I popped the candy into my mouth. "I heard about that tonight and a whole lot more. Villa is a braggart. He can say whatever he wants in Mexico. What bothers me most is what he does to innocent people and calls it war."

"What do you know of war, Billy?" questioned Rosa. "You only fired a rifle one day ago. I have been fighting for two years. I have killed many men. And how many have you killed?"

That really steamed me. I was insulted by Rosa's statements and humiliated by them at the same time.

"In war," I countered, "we in the United States don't murder priests or burn women to death."

Monte held on to his candy. "What are you talking about?"

I relaxed a bit, realizing I may have said too much but I was committed to answer Monte.

"Tonight, at the reporter's tent I learned a great deal about Pancho Villa. For instance, last November he and his men were approaching a small village. The villagers thought Villa's men were bandits so they shot some of his men. When Villa showed up they apologized over and over but Villa didn't care. He lined up all the men in town and was going to execute them.

"The local priest begged and begged Villa not to shoot them. But then Villa shot the priest in the head and went ahead and executed every single man in town."

Rosa stared at me but said nothing.

"And the women?" asked Monte.

"Worse. They were Carrancista women. They had been gathered together in a tight group. One of them had a gun and took a shot at Villa and narrowly missed him.

"Villa demanded to know who fired the shot. No one confessed. So he had them tied into bundles like so much firewood, all ninety of them, soaked them in gasoline, and burned them alive."

When I finished speaking I was sorry I had said a word. There was nothing but silence for a long time as the three of us stared blankly into the dancing amber tongues of the campfire. Finally, I drummed up enough courage to ask a question that had been eating at me, a question I had to have answered. "Rosa, how is it a man like Pancho Villa is followed . . . is admired by so many Mexicans?"

"You do not know Pancho Villa," defended Rosa. "You choose to believe the lies that

Carranza tells. What you say did not happen, not the way you tell it. And even if it did, it was done by *El Carnicero,* not General Villa.

"The general has run the evil Spaniards out of Mexico, he has taken from the wealthy that abuse the peasants and given to the poor. He has built one hundred schools for our children, something the rich would never allow. That is Pancho Villa.

"If bad things happen in the revolution it is only because of men like *El Carnicero,* that damned Rodolfo Fierro. Sometimes men like him are hard to control when the blood is hot."

I considered what Rosa had said for a moment, admitting she could be right. I had not considered that the reports given to the army might have been inaccurate, perhaps even falsehoods. "What does *El Carnicero* mean?" I asked.

Monte, who had seemed not to be listening to us, suddenly said, "It means 'the butcher.' "

My eyes darted to Monte and then to Rosa. For several seconds she stared at Monte, her brow slowly wrinkling with suspicion.

"Is that right?" I asked Rosa. "*Carnicero* is a butcher?"

Ignoring me, Rosa's eyes narrowed into dark slits. "How do you know this?" she demanded.

Staring into the campfire, Monte answered simply, "I got no idea. Must've heard it somewhere."

Even I didn't buy that explanation. Neither did Rosa.

"On the way to Federico," said Rosa, "I said you should have a serape. You remember this?"

"Yeah. So?"

"Later you called it a *poncho*."

"I don't know if I did or didn't. So what if I did?"

"And you knew what a scorpion was but said you never saw one before."

Both Rosa and I waited for an explanation. I remember how the flames reflected in the black pupils of Monte's eyes, eyes that seemed strangely empty.

Rosa grew impatient. "In the adobe last night, in your dream you said *corra* but you spoke it as we speak it. It was not the name of a woman. You were saying 'run!' "

Monte sat up suddenly, his eyes wide. What he was seeing at that moment was a woman, a woman with braided black hair looking back at him. Her face paled with fear and then twisted into a mask of panic.

Startled by Monte's reaction I jerked backward. Rosa latched onto her rifle with both hands, her trigger finger resting on the guard.

At that moment, Rosa was half convinced Monte was more than he pretended, a man that could indeed speak Spanish, a spy perhaps or even an assassin sent to kill Pancho Villa.

"Monte?" I said. "What is it?"

"The dream I had last night," Monte said softly, "I remember now. It was about a woman. I think she was my mother."

"And her name was Cora?" I asked.

Shaking his head, Monte answered, "I never knew my mother. Or my father."

Rosa relaxed her grip on the Mauser. She studied Monte thoughtfully as her finger tapped on the trigger guard. "And what did your mother look like in your dream?"

Monte glanced at Rosa. Once again, in a flash, he saw her skull being crushed by the butt of a rifle, a rifle similar to the one she was holding.

"She looked," Monte said, his eyes holding curiously on Rosa, "an awful lot like you."

"So your mother was Mexican?" I asked, taking in Monte's dark skin and brown eyes.

"Ma and Pa were Italian. Or so I was told."

"Well then, that explains it," I said, sounding and feeling as if I were quite the intellect. "The Italian language is very similar to Spanish. That's why you recognize a few words here and there.

"And your name, Monte Segundo, certainly has an Italian ring to it."

Rosa's trigger finger relaxed. "Segundo sounds Mexican to me."

"Does it mean anything?" asked Monte.

Rosa glared at Monte, searching for any sign of treachery. "Second-in-command," she said, her voice thick with suspicion.

"Likely something similar in Italian," I offered. "Like most western European names, it would likely reflect a profession of your ancestors. Perhaps they were in military service."

I would have continued my enlightened discourse but I happened to notice that both Monte and Rosa were staring at me as if I had two heads.

"Segundo is someone that works on a ranch," Rosa said, clearly dismissing me as an idiot. "He is in charge of the *vaqueros.*"

"What kind of ranch?" Monte asked.

"*Vacas.* Cattle."

Feeling quite the fool, I sheepishly nodded. "That makes sense, too."

Satisfied Monte was not a threat, Rosa sat back and laid the rifle next to her.

Vowing I would someday learn to keep my overeducated opinions to myself, I searched for some means to redeem myself. On impulse, I took a few sticks of wood and then tentatively tossed them on the fire. A few sparks rose but nothing more. No one objected. Rosa didn't sigh nor did she disdainfully shake her head. On the contrary, both Monte and Rosa acted as if nothing had happened.

Having never fueled a campfire, I breathed a sigh of relief that my first attempt had gone smoothly. Encouraged by this acquisition of an outdoor skill, my confidence was somewhat bolstered.

"What did you do at the camp?" I asked Rosa.

"I talked to my people. The women that sell tortillas but especially the *putas* at the sanitary house. Those women know the most. All soldiers talk to them there. But the Mexican men find out things, too."

"By sanitary house, you mean the hospital?" I asked naively.

Rosa rolled her eyes. "The whorehouse. Your General Pershing set it up for the army so they don't go too far away from camp.

Or get sick from bad *putas.*"

I was aghast. "General Pershing set up a bordello?"

"Who else?" Rosa frowned. "He is the general of an army, Billy, not the leader of a priesthood. Pershing's Chinese can do the laundry and even cook sometimes but they cannot do what the Mexican women can do."

"And what do the Mexican men do?" I asked, bracing myself for the answer.

"The men sell smokes to the soldiers. Mexican cigarettes. And sometimes marijuana."

I shrugged. "What's marijuana?"

"It is what we smoke in Mexico. It makes us brave before battle and happy after the battle is over."

"A cigarette does all that," I asked skeptically. "It makes you brave?"

Rosa nodded though unconvincingly. "General Villa says it makes him more *macho.* I believe him."

"Learn anything about the Apaches?" Monte asked.

Tilting her head to the south, Rosa said, "They are gone to join with one named Howze. Gone south. Two days ago. They go to Bachíniva. They are commanded by a young fool named Shannon. Already the

Apaches disobey him. Already the Apaches got drunk and fought with him. Shannon knows nothing about Apaches. He does not believe they left the camp and murdered a Mexican one night. He is a fool."

Monte's eyes narrowed. "The Apaches, the army scouts, murdered someone down here? At Colonia Dublan?"

"The Apaches," Rosa said, "will kill Mexicans as long as they are in Mexico. That is what Apaches do. You *gringos* cannot stop them. You will not even know when they are gone from your camps."

A hidden thought had been gnawing at Monte all evening but as yet it had no form or substance. Try as he might, he could not bring it to mind. All he knew for certain was that his desire to find the Apaches was growing stronger by the hour.

"Then I'm going south in the morning," said Monte. "I came down here to meet up with the Apaches. That's what I intend to do."

"General Villa," said Rosa, "is south as well."

Stiffening my lower lip, I dropped another stick on the fire. "I've come this far," I said somewhat dramatically. "Count me in."

Rosa stood and turned from the firelight. She reached inside her blouse and then faced us. Holding up her hand we could see something in her palm.

"Soap from a *Chino*," she announced. "I go to the river. When I come back I will give you the soap. Then you two go to the river."

Smiling I said, "It would be a pleasure. Thank you, Rosa."

Rosa looked at me oddly, I would say puzzled. She glanced at Monte and then back at me. *"De nada,"* she replied, and then disappeared into the night.

I lowered my voice. "Monte, in a rough sort of way she's quite beautiful, isn't she?"

Monte raised an eyebrow. "Any damn way you look at it, she's downright pretty. But I'm sure she knows that. Her kind always does. Those are the ones you gotta watch out for."

"What do you mean?"

"Women like her can tear a man to pieces. Some of them don't even blink an eye doing it. Most of them are pure poison."

Squinting thoughtfully, I said, "But that's not right. It's not fair. To be so attractive to men and then be so . . . that's not how it's supposed to be."

"That's nature, Billy, like it or not. Men are bigger and stronger but usually don't stand a chance against them. Most times with a man and woman, it's sort of like a war.

"You ever seen a big buck with huge sharp antlers, neck all muscled up for fighting . . . and him chasing after a doe. He runs after her like a damned fool, half the time with his tongue hanging out.

"If a man don't watch out, he'll be doing the same thing as that buck. And that little doe will lead him wherever she wants him to go, too. That's how the big bucks get shot. Chasing tail when they should be looking out for themselves. Like the Good Book says, '*I find more bitter than death the woman whose heart is snares and nets.*' "

Only half listening to Monte, I thought of Rosa wading into the river. I felt a rush of heat. "I'll remember that."

Monte glanced at me and chuckled. "Up in the snow country, the trick to staying warm is to not get too hot. You start sweating and you'll freeze up. That can kill you. When it comes to Rosa, you remember that. Don't get yourself all heated up."

Several minutes passed and I wasn't cooling down. Trying not to think of Rosa bathing naked in the moonlight, I changed the subject. "Mind if I ask about your dream, about your mother?"

For a long count of ten, Monte said nothing. Then he took a deep breath and let it out slowly. "The sun was reflecting off her hair. She wore it in braids just like Rosa. She was raking or hoeing, maybe working in a garden.

"I was up high looking down. Something was wrong, something so bad that I tried to scream at her, to tell her to run. But the words wouldn't come out, no matter how hard I tried. She looked up at me. She was scared. Of what I don't know. But she looked at me . . . so afraid. I can still see the look in her eyes."

"You're sure it wasn't Rosa?" I asked. "You know how crazy dreams can be."

Monte scratched the back of his neck. "Sure. But it was my mother. Don't ask me how I know but it was her."

"Did you ever dream about her before?"

"Never."

I mulled things over for a minute or so. "I'll bet Rosa triggered it. You said they look alike."

"That's what I'm thinking, too."

"Well, that could be good. Maybe being around Rosa will help you remember some more about her. Kind of like reading a diary helps you remember things you've long forgotten."

Monte was about to speak when Rosa

stepped into the firelight. Her hair was straight and wet. She began to run her fingers through it with one hand.

Her blouse was damp. It clung to her breasts. My heart skipped a beat. My face stung with prickly heat.

Handing the soap to me, Rosa smiled faintly, knowingly. "Your turn," she said, and then turned toward Monte. "And yours. You both smell like sour burros."

Accepting the soap, I staggered to my feet, unable to take my eyes off Rosa. I didn't see Monte get to his feet but I did feel his hand on my back giving me a shove toward the river.

"Come on, Billy," he said. "Before you freeze to death."

The moon was nearly full when Monte and I waded into the shallow Casas Grandes. I noticed three things that night. The water was surprisingly warm, Monte was a mass of muscle, and the skin on his back, legs, and arms was covered with small round scars.

Monte submerged himself in the water and then stood up with the water running waist high. He didn't look at me when he spoke.

"To answer your question, they say I had small pox. I don't remember it. Must have

161

been too young."

I felt guilty for having noticed. I didn't want to admit it but I couldn't deny it either. I was trapped.

"Don't worry. Everybody wants to know. I'm used to it."

I had heard of small pox and what it could do to a person but this was the first time I had actually seen a survivor. I could see Monte must have suffered terribly. But there was nothing for me to say, so I lathered up, dunked myself, and then handed him the soap.

"I can remember back to when I was four years old," I said. "Some things, anyway. One Christmas I remember in particular."

Monte started scrubbing with the soap. "I can think back to when I was eight or so. I was passed around from family to family. I guess you can say I was a troublemaker. But I know leather straps and switches weren't of any use because I didn't straighten out 'til I went to live with the Kootenais. I settled down some after that. By then I was fourteen or so."

I dug my toes into the slimy river bottom and felt the mud ooze between my toes. "Did you wear moccasins and hunt with a bow and arrow?"

"I wore moccasins," Monte said, lathering

his hair with soap, "but I hunted with my pistol. Some of the old men still used a bow but I never learned."

Monte leaned back and rinsed his hair. He raised back up. "You think Rosa'll be there when we get back?"

I was taken aback. "Why wouldn't she be?"

Monte ran his fingers through his hair, combing it back. We started back toward the riverbank and then Monte said in a low tone, "I don't trust her. She's a Villista through and through, and we're Americans."

Stepping up onto the sandy bank I said, "But we're getting along now, the three of us. Don't you think so?"

Monte slipped into his shirt. "I don't make it a habit to trust many people, or to depend on them either." I could see Monte smirk as I dried my face with my shirt. "But you, I trust."

Rosa was braiding her hair as we approached the fire. To this day, I have never seen a more stunning example of pure, unpretentious beauty.

She looked up at us and smiled. It stopped me in my tracks but Monte kept walking.

Unable to help myself, I blurted, "Why, you look lovely, Rosa."

"Gracias," she said, ignoring Monte as he sat down across from her.

Taking a step, the toe of my shoe caught on a twig. I stumbled but caught my balance. Monte sighed and shook his head.

Rosa eyed Monte. "Billy is a *caballero,* a gentleman."

Monte glanced up at the stars. "He is that."

"And what are you?" teased Rosa.

I moved closer to the flames to get the dampness from my clothes. To my surprise, instead of warming up to Rosa, Monte's features began to harden.

"What am I?" Monte said. Avoiding eye contact with Rosa, Monte glared at the flames for several seconds before answering. "God only knows."

CHAPTER 6

We would have ridden out of the riverbed before sunrise the following morning but hearing the distant rumbling of engines, we decided to wait. A half-hour later Rosa and I stood by our horses watching as a convoy of southbound trucks slowly disappeared into a glistening dust cloud.

Holding the reins of my horse I pointed at the auto trucks. "They told me a convoy like that averages fourteen miles in an hour. That's the future. Motorization. That's what's coming."

Rosa reached into her saddle pocket and took out our only pair of binoculars. She gazed through them at the trucks. "If there is a road, maybe. Truck wagons go nowhere if there is only a trail to follow. And Mexico is full of trails."

Monte led his horse up from the river and glanced at the tail end of the convoy. "What do you think, Rosa. Should we take the same road as them?"

Rosa lowered the binoculars. "That is one way south to the next town but there is another way to El Valle, a trail through a valley between the mountains. It goes to San Miguel. From there a trail goes east to El Valle if you wish to go there."

Thinking of my sore backside, I asked, "Is San Miguel out of the way? Is it the same distance to El Valle?"

"The same. Only a little slower."

Monte saddled up. "Then let's take the trail."

Rosa replaced the binoculars and stepped easily into her saddle. I managed to settle onto my saddle sores without making a sound. My only consolation was that I inadvertently caught sight of Rosa's right leg as she swung it over her cantle. Realizing she had enlisted the protection of men's pants under her dress, I felt a bit less the sissy, and that minor discovery somewhat eased the pain emanating from my backside.

Rosa took the lead and we headed west, splashing across the Rio Casas Grandes. In minutes, we were threading our way through a brush-choked ravine following a narrow but well-worn trail.

An hour later we veered south and began a steady climb. When we started to see stunted pine trees, Rosa stopped to let the horses catch their breath.

Monte turned in his saddle, studying me. "If it gets rough up ahead, really steep, reach up and grab a handful of mane. Pull yourself forward. It'll help the horse and it'll help keep you in the saddle."

I clutched some mane. "Like this?"

"Closer to the head."

I tried again. "Here?"

"Good. And hang on tight. It won't hurt the horse and he'll thank you for it later."

Rosa turned. Her eyes swept over me and then thoughtfully rested on Monte. "What is it you do, Monte Segundo? How do you live?"

Reaching down Monte checked the tightness in his cinch. "I'm a lumberjack."

"And what is that?" Rosa asked.

"I cut down trees. Big ones."

"But you are a *pistolero.*"

"I do alright. I've done more than cut down trees."

"*Pistolero?*" I questioned.

"Gunfighter," said Rosa. "There are many old ones in Mexico. *Gringos* that came here. I have seen them.

"I have seen them also in the moving pictures. But the real *pistoleros* are not like the ones in the moving pictures."

Surprised, I asked, "Where did you see a picture show?"

"El Paso. There is a theater in Columbus but I have never been there. Only El Paso, across from Juárez.

"But they show moving pictures to the army in Colonia Dublan. Some of the Mexicans there told me they sit with the officers and watch.

"Two years ago, the *gringos* from California made a moving picture with General Villa. They paid him in gold to be in it. The *Californios* took their camera into the battle at Juárez. They almost got shot. They made the moving picture but I never saw it."

I took off my cap and scratched my head. "Say, I remember hearing about that. Actual fighting was shown in the movie. I would like to have seen that."

"I think maybe you will get your chance," Rosa said and then nudged her horse on up the trail.

Wondering what Rosa meant, I held my reins until Monte fell in behind her. An instant later the meaning of Rosa's words hit me. Forty-eight hours earlier, the realization that I might see an actual battle would have been chilling. But the news merely triggered a fleeting wave of anxiety that was replaced with nothing more than a novel curiosity. However, as I started up the trail, I must confess, that novel curiosity gradually degenerated into a macabre desire to observe, firsthand, men at war.

Another hour of riding brought us to a rock-strewn mountainside, which we clattered over for a quarter mile before topping out on a sprawling pine-studded mesa. The horses were lathered and blowing hard so we found some shade and dismounted. There was still an hour of sunlight left. The mesa was two thousand feet above the Casas Grandes River and the air was relatively cool. A whisper of a breeze drifted through the trees.

I was about to ask Rosa how much farther it was to El Valle when we heard a loud noise that sounded as if a drummer were vigorously clapping two heavy sticks together.

At first, the ominous knocking seemed to surround us. We looked everywhere but saw nothing.

A moment later, Rosa pointed up into the top of a dead pine. *"Pitoreal,"* she said.

I followed her eyes and saw an enormous woodpecker, a full two feet in length. Its head was bright crimson, its back an iridescent black. Its massive ivory-colored beak was pounding the tree with amazing force.

I glanced at Monte to make sure he saw the bird. He appeared spellbound but was not looking up at the woodpecker. His eyes were fixed on the horizon locked in a vacant stare.

"Up here, Monte," I said pointing at the bird. "It's a giant woodpecker."

Monte stood stone-still.

Rosa turned toward Monte. She studied him for a moment and then looked at me with a question in her eyes.

I just shrugged.

While Rosa and I were hearing the sharp beak of a *pitoreal* chipping away at a dead tree, Monte was hearing something drastically different.

Monte heard the sound just as we had but instead of looking up to see a *pitoreal* he saw a man who had been lashed spread-eagle to a corral fence. Where his stomach had been, there was a gaping hole. The man's legs were drenched in blood and his entrails were stretched out across the sand. The man was taking his last breaths.

What Monte heard, what had triggered yet another vision, was not the sound of a woodpecker searching for food but a sound that was virtually identical. What Monte Segundo heard was a death rattle.

I stepped closer to Monte and nudged

him. "Monte," I said smiling, "It's a wood-pecker. A huge one."

Monte blinked. His glossy eyes slowly focused on me. "A woodpecker?"

Once again, I pointed.

Monte's head went up. His face darkened as he watched the woodpecker pound on the tree.

Taking a few steps away from Rosa and me, Monte unexpectedly drew his pistol and fired.

Black feathers exploded from the *pitoreal* as the heavy forty-five slug ripped through the bird, jerking it off the tree.

With its wings outstretched, the wood-pecker bounced off several branches on its way down and finally hit the ground with a lifeless thud.

Stunned, I said nothing for several seconds. Trying to make sense of killing such a magnificent bird, I asked the only question that came to mind. "Are those good to eat?"

"The Tarahumara eat them," answered Rosa, seemingly unmoved by the shooting. "They have as much meat as a squirrel."

"A squirrel?" I asked, unaware that anyone would ever eat a rodent.

Before anything more was said, we heard another ominous sound. But this time we all knew what it was. The snap came from behind us and it was the breaking of a twig.

We spun in unison. Expecting to see Carrancistas, Monte brought his pistol up, cocked and ready.

But to our relief, there were no Mexican soldiers.

Not ten paces behind us, however, stood a cadaverous-looking man with long gray hair and beard to match. He wore a tattered cast-off suit that included an unusually long coat that at one time had been black.

"I have salt," said the intruder.

The three of us stared at the man, all wondering where he had come from and how he had gotten behind us.

"Salt," he said again. Cautiously reaching inside his coat, he brought out a small cotton sack that was closed at one end with a drawstring. "For the *pitoreal*?"

The old man spoke English well but had a Mexican accent.

"You want the bird?" I asked finally.

"To share of course. I have salt to offer. That and some fishing line are all I have. All else was stolen by bandits."

"Where are you from?" Rosa demanded. "How did you get here?"

"I am a wanderer. I walk wherever I go."

"You alone?" asked Monte, still holding his Colt.

"Very much. Until I met you."

Monte glanced down at the man's feet and then scanned the woods behind him.

"I'll take a look around," said Monte, and then began backtracking the steps of the old man across a carpet of pine needles.

"The bird must be eaten fresh," Rosa said, to the old man. "I will build the fire. You will clean it and cook it."

"It will be my pleasure."

"What is your name, sir," I asked.

"Call me Marco. And you?"

"I'm Billy. This is Rosa. And the tracker is Monte."

Marco immediately went to find the bird. I waited for him to get some distance between Rosa and I.

"We're stopping to cook?" I asked.

Rosa huffed. "I'm tired of jerky. And the horses are tired. I say we eat and rest.

"You *gringos* can go on if you wish," said Rosa, heading off to gather firewood. "To-night, I will eat *pitoreal* with salt."

Taking my rifle, I started off through the trees in the direction Monte had gone. In minutes, we met up by a fallen log. He was walking toward me.

"He's alone alright," said Monte.

Starting back to the horses, I said, "His name is Marco. I can tell he's an educated

173

man. I wonder what he's doing out here all by himself."

"As long as he's harmless," Monte said, "it's none of my business."

I was a bit uneasy about telling Monte of Rosa's decision to stop and eat but I wanted him to know before Rosa sprang it on him.

"Rosa insists on eating the bird before any more riding."

Monte's only response was, "If she wants to eat a damn woodpecker, she's welcome to it."

Leaving well enough alone, I said nothing more until we were back with the horses.

Just beyond our mounts, a fire was already burning inside a circle of rocks. Several feet beyond it, Marco was plucking black feathers and Rosa was carrying an armload of firewood.

"That's a lot of wood for one scrawny bird," grumbled Monte.

"The trail off the mesa is difficult," returned Rosa. "It will be too late to ride down after we eat. The wood is for tonight."

"What if I told you the old man wasn't alone, that he was with a bunch of bandits. You'd be going to a lot of trouble for nothing."

"But he is alone. I did not have to track him to know that."

174

"Lucky guess," snorted Monte. "You going to share your blanket with that old desert rat? Now that you invited him to dinner he'll want to spend the night, too."

Rosa dropped the firewood near the fire. "He can keep himself warm. We can build two fires. He can sleep between them."

Marco came toward the fire. Holding the plucked woodpecker, he skewered it with a long stick. At that point, the small carcass started to arouse my interest.

"I'd like to try some of that," I said, feeling my mouth begin to water. "What does it taste like?"

"With the salt," answered Marco, as he lowered the bird over the flames, "somewhat like chicken. Better yet, like a rooster.

"And you are welcome to some of it. We will divide our good fortune four ways."

"Three," said Monte, sneering at the plucked bird. "I want nothing to do with the damned thing."

Marco's wrinkled eyes shifted upward toward Monte. He studied him for several seconds and then returned to the bird.

"You are the one they call *El Muerte*?" Marco asked.

Monte glared down at the old man. "What makes you say that?"

"Who else could you be?" asked Marco,

gently rotating the bird. "As it was once said, *'I have laid strength upon one that is mighty; I have exalted one chosen out of the people.'*"

I was impressed. "Is that Shakespeare?"

"No," Marco answered.

Stunning everyone, Monte said, "It's from Psalms."

Marco nodded but his eyes held on the fire. "And how does *El Muerte* know such a thing?"

"I lived with the Kootenai Indians awhile. Jesuit priests visited us a lot."

"Then you have a remarkable memory," observed Marco.

It was the word *memory* that finally yanked the linchpin from the locked-up secrets of Monte's buried childhood. In fractions of a second he saw the inferno that burned him, the dark face of the man who had thrown him, the rifle-fractured skull, his fearful mother, the small boy, and, in vivid clarity, the mutilated and dying man.

But with that kaleidoscope of vision fragments came a welcome revelation. For the first time in weeks Monte Segundo knew he was not losing his mind. In that remarkable instant by the fire, Monte realized his visions, hallucinations, and his nightmares were not signs of impending insanity. They were remnants of memories, memories that had long been forgotten.

"I'll be damned," Monte muttered. "Memory! All this time. I'll be damned. They're memories!"

The three of us watched in silence as Monte slowly walked away from the fire and into the woods.

"Something troubles him," Marco said, as he reached in his pouch and then sprinkled a pinch of salt on the *pitoreal.* "Am I to blame?"

I sat down by the fire. "No. It's not you."

"But why does he walk away? It will be dark soon."

"That one," Rosa said, "can see like a cat. I think he is part *Chupacabra!*"

"He sees in the dark?" Marco asked.

"He does," I said.

Marco gazed at the sizzling bird. "Remarkable. Remarkable indeed."

Rosa leaned on her rifle but kept looking in the direction Monte had gone. "He has dreams. Bad ones. Sometimes I think he is a little *loco.*

"He could have gotten us all killed in Ojo Federico."

"Ah, yes," smiled Marco. "I heard the story. But the peasants love to embellish. They love to tell fairy tales."

"What did you hear?" I asked.

Marco continued to smile. "That *El Muerte* killed ten men with only his knife and pistol."

Rosa and I looked at each other, trying to read the other's thoughts.

After a moment, Rosa said, "It was only seven."

"Seven," repeated Marco, suddenly serious. "He killed seven Carrancistas?"

"They had," I said and then hesitated, searching for the right word, "kidnapped the mother of a small boy."

Marco stopped rotating the *pitoreal.* His face seemed to go blank for several seconds. "Fascinating!" he whispered. "Truly fascinating!"

"I say he is *loco,* " snipped Rosa. "Why else would a *gringo* go alone into Mexico and risk his life for Mexican women he does not even know?"

Shaking my head, I said, "It has something to do with Apaches. That's why we're here. Why he's here. He desperately wants to join up with them."

Marco looked up. He peered at me through the smoke for several seconds. "He looks to join the Apaches? I do not think *El Muerte* is the kind of man that would join with Apaches. More likely he seeks to kill them."

"Oh, don't think that, Marco," I countered. "Monte wants to scout with them, that's all. To catch . . ."

I caught myself but it was too late.

"To catch General Villa," interrupted Rosa. "But the Americans, even with *El Muerte,* will never find *El Jaguar!*"

Marco glanced at Rosa. "And you are a *soldadera.* Are you Villista or Carrancista?"

Rosa said proudly, "I am for *Villisimo.* And I am a captain in the army, not a *soldadera.*"

Rotating the bird slowly, Marco said, "Then you must need each other. That is why you travel together? You have a truce?"

I was quite impressed. Marco's deductions were as accurate as they were remarkable. "Yes. We have a truce."

"Good," Marco said. "A truce is rooted in honor. And this revolution has none."

The bird began to pop and sizzle. I detected a faint aroma of cooking meat and felt saliva oozing under the base of my tongue. "May I ask you a personal question, Marco?"

"Certainly."

"Clearly, you are an educated man. How

is it that you are wandering about in Mexico?"

Before Marco could answer, Rosa said snidely, "He is a Spaniard."

Musing why being Spanish was in any way relevant, I waited for an answer to my question.

"Yes," Marco admitted. "I am a Spaniard. And I was a priest. Neither is acceptable in this revolution."

I was taken back. "You were a priest?"

Marco nodded reluctantly. "For decades, I was a priest. However, recently my faith began to weaken. I prayed for a sign, something to restore my soul, but no sign came. So now I am only a beggar."

Being quite insensitive, I said bluntly, "I've never heard of someone leaving the priesthood. I didn't know you could quit something like that."

"Nor did I," sighed Marco. "Nor did I."

I glanced at Rosa. Clearly upset, she was staring at Marco. Her mouth was half open but she seemed unable to speak.

"Would you care to elaborate?" I asked.

Marco turned the bird, keeping it just above the flames.

"Confession is always good," said Marco, "even for one such as I. And sometimes it is easier to speak with strangers. My story is a difficult one to hear. Are you certain you want to listen?"

I was so intrigued, it didn't occur to me that Rosa might not wish to know Marco's story. Instead, I answered eagerly, "Absolutely."

Without taking his eyes off the *pitoreal,* Marco's brow furrowed as his eyes softened with sadness. "Not long ago, I was in San Pedro de la Cueva visiting with Father Flores. The revolution was being fought far from the village and we were not concerned. But one dreadful day it came upon us with no warning. It was that day I watched Father Flores, a devout priest, beg General Villa for the lives of seventy-seven men, every able-bodied man in the village.

"You see, the men had fired on Villa's soldiers mistaking them for marauders. All the villagers begged Villa for his forgiveness, especially Father Flores. But Father Flores begged too much.

"Villa became irritated and personally shot Father Flores in the head. Then he had all the men in the village shot as well.

"I left San Pedro de la Cueva and went to Santa Rosalía. I arrived there in time to help bury ninety women that General Villa had tied in bundles like cordwood and burned to death. I learned he had first doused them

181

with gasoline and then set them on fire.

"Later, I was called to a convent. There I tried in vain to comfort more than fifty nuns that the Carrancistas had kidnapped, raped, and impregnated.

"Seeing these atrocities, I realized that though the church had been in Mexico for three hundred years, all it had accomplished, all God had accomplished, was putting an end to human sacrifice."

Marco paused and brought the bird out of the fire. He inspected it and then again held it over the flames.

"I could see no reason to be a priest any longer."

Silently, Marco stretched out his hand and sprinkled more salt on the *pitoreal.*

Incredulously shaking my head, I said, "How can such brutality exist? It is madness."

Rosa was shaken. She had heard similar stories from me the night before and she had heard them from others. She had always attributed such accounts to lies spread by the Carrancistas. But Marco was a priest and an eyewitness to the atrocities.

"There was nobility in the beginning of the revolution," said Marco. "But no longer. Now there is only depravity.

"Both sides lust for power, for riches, for

182

women, and for blood. Nothing is sacred in Mexico. No one is safe. And justice, there is no justice in Mexico. None."

For the next quarter hour, no one spoke a word. Each of us was deep in thought when, without a sound, Monte stepped out of the darkness and took a seat by the fire.

"Billy," Monte said, breaking the glum silence. "I'm not Italian. My mother was Mexican. My father was white. They were murdered when I was just a small boy. Apaches are mixed up in it somehow. One of Pershing's scouts might be one of them. The best I can tell, that's the reason I'm here. To find out what happened and, if I have cause, to settle things one way or the other with the Indians. So, if this changes things, you should head back to Colonia Dublan."

Adding this news to what Marco had just divulged, I was in a state of total bewilderment. "I don't understand. You told me you were Italian and you couldn't remember your parents. And you said you wanted to join the scouts to help track down Villa."

"That's what I thought at the time," Monte admitted. "I can't explain why, not even to myself, but I'm beginning to remember things from when I was a little kid. For a month now, bits and pieces have been

183

coming back to me but I thought they were nightmares or hallucinations. They don't make much sense yet, but they're real memories. I'm sure of that, now."

Marco looked across the fire, squinting his eyes. "May I ask how old you are, Monte?"

"Thirty or thirty-one. Somewhere in there."

"And in your memories, how old are you?"

Monte thought hard. "I'd guess six or seven."

Bobbing the bird in and out of the flames, Marco said, "That would mean the events you are recalling occurred around eighteen eighty-five or eighty-six."

"Sounds about right," Monte agreed.

"I am almost seventy," Marco said. "I have been a priest in northern Mexico since I was twenty. Throughout all those years, all of them, the Apaches have killed Mexican men, women, and children.

"Eighteen eighty-five and six were especially bad. That was the time Geronimo and his band of renegades raided back and forth across the border. They murdered many Mexicans and whites on both sides. Very many. If one of those raids is the source of your memories, you may have lived in Arizona or New Mexico."

Instantly, a thought occurred to me. "When I was in Columbus, I heard that some of Pershing's scouts were used in the Geronimo campaign. Actually, several of them were."

Monte nodded. For the first time since leaving Columbus he thought of the folded page of newspaper in his back pocket. He took it out, unfolded it, and then handed it to me.

"The one on the left. He looked familiar to me the first time I saw that picture. That same night my nightmares got worse than ever before. And right after we met up with Rosa, crazy things started running through my head. I was seeing things, like a dream but in broad daylight. They were starting to worry me. But all that turned out to be memories. Pieces anyway.

"I didn't know what they were until that damned woodpecker showed up. Up to that point, I thought I was losing my mind."

I handed the photograph to Rosa. She studied it for several seconds, holding it close to the firelight. "The one on the left has a scar on his face. Do you see him in your dreams?"

"A scar?" questioned Monte.

"Yes. If you look close you can see it."

"There's a man's face in my dream, my

185

recollection, but it's mostly blacked out by shadows. I can't say what he looked like or if there's any scar, but I'm pretty sure it's an Apache."

"May I ask what that dream is about?" I asked.

Monte worked his neck side to side to loosen it. "Somebody's standing over me, holding my arms down, pushing me into a fire while I burn."

Rosa glanced at Monte and then held the photo up so Marco could see it. Marco took a brief look and then went back to cooking.

This time, with her eyes holding on Monte, Rosa handed the paper back to him and asked, "The woodpecker, it reminded you of something?"

"The sound of it did," said Monte, carefully folding the paper and sliding it back into his pocket.

"It was the sound that brought back a memory?" Marco asked.

Monte took a seat by the fire next to me. "Yeah. But it brought one back I hadn't had before, something I never saw in a dream. The sound that woodpecker made was just like a death rattle. The death rattle is what made me remember."

"I have seen this once before," Marco admitted somberly.

"How so?" I asked.

"A man came to confession one evening and said he no longer wanted to live. He had fought in the Mexican-American War two decades before and had not even received a wound. But then one day he caught sight of an old musket hanging upside down on the wall of a cantina.

"The moment he saw that musket, all the horrors he had experienced in the war descended upon him. He was never the same after that day. Other priests have told me similar stories."

"What happened to him?" I asked.

Marco sighed. "I tried to help him but I failed. His wife left him, finally. After that, he no longer came to confession. I do not know what became of him."

"Well," Monte said, "I sure as hell want to live. And I don't have a wife."

"Who would marry you?" demanded Rosa, but with a hint of flirtation in her tone.

Glancing at Rosa, Monte scratched behind his ear. "Knowing my luck, it'd be somebody just like you."

I had to laugh. Marco chuckled and even Rosa grinned. Sparks flew up from the dancing flames and swirled skyward. A pleasant breeze stirred the air.

Out of the blue, Marco asked Monte, "Which way would you say is north?"

Without hesitation, Monte pointed to his left and said casually, "That way."

Marco looked up, searching for the North Star. Finding it, he asked, "How did you know so quickly?"

Monte shrugged, half ignoring the question. "How does a wild goose know?"

At the time, I paid little attention to Marco's questions or the strange look on his face. I was too hungry, and seconds later he was lifting the roasted meat up and out of the flames.

Marco pinched off a strand of meat and tasted it. "Ah, it is ready."

Offering the meat to Rosa, he said, "Ladies first."

Rosa hesitated. It was the first time I detected any hint of uncertainty in her eyes. I assumed it was because she had never eaten a *pitoreal* but quickly realized it was because she had never been referred to as a lady. And I had a suspicion it was the first time she had been called on to act as one.

Sensing her predicament as well, Monte unsheathed his hunting knife, flipped it in his palm, and handed it to her grips first. "It's sharp."

I half expected a *"gracias"* but none came.

188

Instead, Rosa cut a thick slice off the breast of the bird and then handed the knife to me.

"Thank you," I said.

This time Rosa muttered an awkward, *"De nada."*

I cut a small piece for myself. Offering the knife to Monte, I smiled. "Change your mind?"

"Nope," returned Monte. "The rest is yours, Padre."

"Then I will need no knife. My teeth are yet strong."

Wiping the blade on his shirtsleeve, Monte sheathed his knife. Observing each of us as we ate, he asked, "Well? How is it?"

"Like a *gallo,*" said Rosa.

"Rooster, eh?" said Monte.

I looked curiously at Monte. He shrugged. "Some Spanish is coming back, too. My ma likely spoke some once in a while. And we must've had chickens around."

Marco bit off a mouthful. He chewed as he talked. "More will come back to you. Slowly at first. You should prepare yourself. These memories were not forgotten. They were too much for a child so they were buried."

Monte grimly stared at Marco for several seconds. "I think it would've been better if

189

they'd stayed buried. There's no stopping it now. It's got to be finished."

"And you're sure the Apaches are the key?" I asked.

"As sure as I can be."

"Then the sooner we find those Apaches," I said, "the better. I'm here to get a story and I'm not going back without one."

Rosa pretended to be busy eating but all the while she was wrestling with an array of growing doubts. That night was not the first time she had heard rumors of Villa's senseless brutality, and priest or no priest, Marco had no reason to lie.

Villa was revered by the peasants and Rosa was no different. She, like the others, had excused his early years of banditry and everyone was convinced his criminal days were behind him. Villa's war was a noble struggle and Rosa could not bring herself to abandon the myth of Villa or the desperate hope of *Villisimo*. Yet she also understood there was no way anyone could sanctify the murder of women and priests.

Finishing the last of her meat, Rosa wiped her hands on her skirt. "I had two *tios,* uncles, killed by Apaches. They were brothers herding goats. They died slow. I will help you find the Apaches. Unless we first meet Villa's army. Then I will go with them."

Marco was still gnawing on the *pitoreal* but his wrinkled eyes had not left Monte in several minutes. He paused thoughtfully. "I can speak the Apache language somewhat. Perhaps I could come along and be of some help."

"You couldn't keep up," Monte said.

Feeling a certain kinship for Marco, I ventured a question. "Can he ride behind me?"

Monte considered the idea for a moment. "It's up to you. The horse can handle the added weight for a day or two."

"Splendid!" said Marco, then surprising us all, added, "God is merciful."

CHAPTER 7

My riding skill was rapidly improving and though Marco was hanging on to me, I was able to brace my rifle on the saddle pommel with one hand and rein my horse with the other. Marco and I thus brought up the rear and, with Rosa leading, the four of us rode down off the mesa.

We stopped at midday by a spring and ate the last of our jerky and goat cheese. A half-hour later we were back in the saddle working our way down a narrow valley that was fringed with creosote and dotted with an occasional scrub oak.

As the valley began to open Rosa drew up suddenly. Both Monte and I reined in and waited. In seconds, we heard distant gunfire.

We closed the space between us, each searching the hills around us for any sign of danger.

"It comes from San Miguel," said Rosa. "The pueblo is not far from here."

Monte listened for a moment. The shots were spaced but erratic. "Can we go around?"

Rosa shook her head.

"The peasants are fighting against marauders," Marco said evenly. "They are hoping to protect their village."

I glanced back over my shoulder. "How do you know that?"

"Because," answered Rosa, "they would never fire on Villistas or Carrancistas. They try only to defend themselves from bandits."

Monte listened again. "Can't be too many of them or there'd be more shooting. If we get in close enough we can pick off some of the bandits. Even things up a bit."

Instantly, I was jolted by the thought of being shot. Fear gripped me as claws would a quivering rabbit. I felt dizzy and my palms started to sweat.

Monte turned his horse and faced me. "I'll be needing your rifle, Billy. This'll have to be done long range."

Trying to hide my prodigious relief, I offered a manly nod and, oh, so gladly, handed over my Mauser and belt of cartridges.

"Do we stay together," Rosa asked, "or go apart?"

Monte threw the cartridge belt over his

shoulder. "We stay together. I want to see how many times you miss."

Rosa tossed her head back. "You can shoot a pistol but we will see who can shoot the rifle."

Monte unholstered his pistol and handed it to me. "These are bandits, Billy. It won't do any good pretending to be a German. If you have to, shoot and don't ask questions. Then ride like hell."

"What's the plan?" I asked, hoping my trembling vocal chords went unnoticed.

"The four of us will ride up a little closer, then you and Marco will get out of sight and hold the horses. Rosa and I will move on foot to high ground. From there we'll pick our targets."

Monte briefly looked at each of us and then asked, "Agreed?"

We all nodded and then Rosa kicked her gelding into a trot leading the way up the valley. When the muffled gunshots became distinct cracks, she and Monte dismounted.

Handing their reins to me, Monte glanced around as Rosa took the binoculars from her saddle pocket.

Monte pointed. "That clump of creosote over there. Get in behind that and stay out of sight.

"Marco, you mount up on Rosa's horse.

If you have to make a run for it, it'll be fresher than mine."

"Vaya con Dios," said Marco, and then the two of us headed for the brush.

Watching us ride off, Monte asked, "You know this town?"

Rosa checked the bolt action of her rifle. "Yes. It is surrounded by hills except from the front."

"Good. Let's get as high as we can and back behind the bandits. A couple hundred yards would be good."

"This way," Rosa said and then trotted across a patch of dry grass that led up a steep brush-covered hillside.

Five minutes later and several hundred feet higher, Rosa took a knee to catch her breath. Below, clustered in a small meadow, the adobes of San Miguel were in plain view.

Monte squatted next to Rosa, breathing easily. "Only one road leads into town. They're boxed in."

Rosa glanced at Monte. Noticing he was not the least bit winded, she frowned.

Monte shrugged. "I'm used to high altitude. And living in the mountains."

Between gasps, Rosa muttered, *"Cabrón."*

Puffs of smoke followed by delayed booms came from some of the pueblo windows. Return fire was coming from a dozen scattered positions in the surrounding hills.

"They've got the town surrounded," Monte said. "Looks like ten or twelve bandits. About half are in the hills on our side and the other half over on the far side."

Rosa brought the binoculars up for a better look. "We take the ones on this side first?"

"Yeah. Once we get the ones closest to us, the rest will be a lot easier."

Breathing more easily after their brief rest, Rosa rose up to a crouch and crept along the side of the mountain, angling downward toward the nearest rifle fire. They had gone only a short distance when they spotted a shooter less than one hundred yards below them and slightly to their left. He was perched behind a squared-off boulder using a forked stick to steady his rifle.

A moment later Rosa caught sight of a second bandit fifty paces beyond the first but no higher.

"I will take the one behind the boulder," said Rosa.

"Alright. The other one's mine. I'll count to four. Slow even count. We fire on four."

Monte and Rosa sat down next to each other. Resting their elbows on bent knees they took careful aim.

Monte counted evenly, rhythmically,

"One, two, three, four."

Simultaneously, both rifles bucked. An instant later two bandits crumpled and then disappeared into the dense brush.

Both rifle bolts worked back and forth, ejecting and loading the next cartridge. Monte and Rosa looked and listened. The shooting around them and in the village continued as before.

Moving again toward the sound of the next shooters Rosa and Monte worked their way in behind three more bandits. Two were about the same distance as before but one twice as far and almost hidden by a stunted oak.

Again, Monte and Rosa sat. Just as they began to take aim the two nearest men rose suddenly and charged downhill toward the adobes. In seconds, they were out of sight.

Without hesitation, Rosa took aim at the far bandit and fired.

Rising straight up, the man then fell backwards.

"Good shot," admitted Monte.

Rosa ejected her empty and slammed in another round. "It would be for a *pistolero*."

Monte huffed as he studied the far hill that rose from the opposite side of the pueblo. He could make out a gray shirt and sombrero standing under a mesquite.

He pointed, holding his arm out at full length. "Look there."

Rosa leaned in, her face resting on Monte's bicep as she sighted down his arm and finger. "I see him."

Monte flipped the rear sight up, reading the numbers. He raised it to eight hundred. "You think this *pistolero* can make that shot?"

"You are *loco*," scoffed Rosa, viewing the target with her binoculars. "That is too far."

"Are you willing to help?"

Rosa dropped the binoculars in her lap. "Help what?"

Monte scooted back behind Rosa. "Don't move a muscle," he said, resting the rifle on Rosa's right shoulder.

"Wait," Rosa said and then stretched out her hand and snatched the empty casing she had ejected. Placing the small end of the brass in her right ear for a plug she said, "Now you can miss the bandit."

Monte took careful aim as Rosa plugged her right ear with a finger pressed against the shell casing. Inhaling gently, Monte then held his breath and squeezed the trigger.

Close to eight hundred yards away a man spun and then stumbled. He gained his footing and then hobbled downhill and out of sight.

"Windage must be off," muttered Monte.

Taking the casing from her ear, Rosa stared across at the distant hillside.

The shooting stopped. Minutes later, a dozen horses appeared on the road below. Only half had riders.

The men and horses gathered into a group and then took off at a run heading away from San Miguel.

"Guess we spooked them," Monte said, bolting his rifle. "Now maybe we can get something decent to eat."

"How is it you shot like that?" demanded Rosa.

Monte stood up, a faint smile on his lips. "Idaho National Guard training helped some, but mostly hunting elk for the last twenty years."

Sitting on our horses deep in the brush thicket, Marco and I listened to the reports of the Mauser rifles. We could only guess what was happening, my heart racing faster and faster with each shot fired.

"Rosa is a remarkable woman, is she not?" Marco said softly.

Hiding as I was, my face flushed with shame. Attempting to disguise a wave of guilt, I answered weakly, "Yes, she certainly is."

Glancing at the expression on my face and reading it as easily as he would a road sign, Marco remarked, "This is not your fight, Billy. It is enough that you are here with them."

"But she's a woman," I said. "It seems shameful for me to be here in the trees and her out there."

"No Billy, you must not think that way. Life has hardened Rosa in ways you do not understand. She, like so many Mexicans, has seen too much death. Her life has been a primitive one, one in which fang and claw prevail. You, on the other hand, are clearly an American gentleman, one unaccustomed to the harsh reality of predator and prey."

I hung my head. "I wish I could be more like Monte."

"Monte Segundo," said Marco, "is like no other you will ever meet. He is proof that God works in obscurity, for if you lived a thousand years you would not meet another like him."

"What do you mean?"

"Do you not sense it yourself? Is there not something about him that tells you he is not like us?"

I thought of my immediate reaction to seeing Monte on the train platform and then how I had, on impulse, followed him into

Mexico. "Yes, I would say he is . . . well . . . charismatic?"

"He has tremendous physical strength, does he not?"

"Without question."

"He sees in the darkness and instinctively knows the direction of north. Though he had blocked out his childhood memories, he recalled the location of an obscure Bible verse. That is proof he possesses an astounding memory.

"And does he not go into battle with absolute confidence, with unbounded courage?"

"I would say so. Certainly, from what I've seen."

Marco beamed with satisfaction. "I believe he is the sign for which I prayed, desperately yearned for, and did not receive. I had given up hope and with it my faith. But now I am certain Monte Segundo is that sign. He is a sign that God has not forsaken me."

"What do you mean, Monte is a sign? What kind of sign?"

"The veins of Monte Segundo," Marco said, "course with the blood of the Mighty Men, great warriors spoken of in the Bible and elsewhere. The 'giants' mentioned throughout history. Those with phenomenal strength and abilities that once were common but, with the passage of centuries, have become exceedingly rare. Monte is a remnant of that noble race. To meet a descendant of the Nephilim is a miracle. It is my sign."

"Nephilim?" I asked.

Marco smiled, patiently. "You are not Christian?"

"No."

"Then you would dismiss the ancient writings of Genesis that declare 'the sons of God married the daughters of men.' And you would likely discount the Greek's account of Hercules as a baseless myth. But surely you have heard of Leonardo da Vinci."

"Certainly."

"Did you know he could, amongst his other extraordinary talents, bend horseshoes with his bare hands? Bend horseshoes!"

"So . . . you're saying he was a Nephilim?"

"Merely a distant relative, like Monte. Da Vinci was the last of such men recorded in history. But now I have met my own 'giant.' Monte Segundo is a sign, an assurance sent from God."

I was taken aback that such an educated man as Marco, even if he were a priest, could believe such nonsense. However, I respected him far too much to express my opinion, especially under the circumstances.

Instead I gave Marco a scholarly nod and said, "I see."

We both stopped speaking and listened. The shooting had stopped. Moments passed and then we heard galloping horses.

Peering through the mesquite we saw a group of bandits riding south. We remained in the thicket until we caught a glimpse of Monte and Rosa walking up the road.

Riding out into the open, I called out, "You alright?"

"For now," answered Monte, and he waved us down to the road.

When we reached them, Marco started to slide off of Rosa's horse but Monte held up his hand. "Stay put, Marco."

Monte glanced down the road and then back at us. "Rosa, you take my horse. You all go on into San Miguel. I'll be along in a while."

Rosa and I looked at each other. A scowl reflected her disapproval.

"I will go with you," Rosa said.

"Not unless you were raised by Indians," returned Monte.

Totally befuddled, I asked, "Where are you going?"

"Those bandits," Monte said, "won't go far before they stop. They'll want to figure out what happened. And I'm thinking they'll come back tonight if not sooner. I doubt they'll give up so easy."

Handing me the Mauser in exchange for his pistol, Monte added, "And besides we could use some extra horses."

Thinking of what Monte had done in Ojo Federico, I shuddered. Then I remembered his unusual ability to see in the dark. "Will you wait until nightfall?"

Monte considered my question for a moment. "If it works out that way," he said, starting down the road. "But that's a damn good idea."

Rosa mounted Monte's gelding and the three of us sat our horses watching Monte. He walked several paces, paused to study the tracks, and then continued on. As I watched him, the thought of Leonardo da Vinci bending horseshoes popped into my head. Entwined with that thought was a whisper of uncertainty, a fleeting consideration that Monte Segundo might be precisely what Marco believed.

With an inward chuckle, I shook my head and the fanciful speculation vanished. And for a long while, I thought no more about it.

I glanced at the hills to the west. The sun was already behind them. "We'd better get to San Miguel," I said. "They'll need enough daylight to see that we're not bandits. I don't want to be shot by mistake."

"That may be difficult," Marco said. "They will shoot at us long before we can get close to town. They will think we are the bandits returning."

We started down the road holding the horses to a slow walk, giving us time to think. Just as we veered onto the road that led to the village Marco said, "I know of a way."

He offered no more until we were in sight of San Miguel. When we passed a fallen tree, he reined in and then dismounted.

Going to the tree he selected a long, relatively straight but limbless branch and snapped it off. He then searched around and found a shorter piece no longer than his arm.

Rosa peered at the distant pueblo. "They see us, Marco. What is your plan?"

Taking the fishing line from his pocket, he began wrapping the twine around the shorter branch and tying it near the top of the longer one. "I will walk in front of you one hundred paces," he said, jerking a final knot in the fishing line.

Hoisting the makeshift cross high over his head, Marco spoke proudly, "I will go into

San Miguel on foot. I go not as Marco the wanderer but as Padre Marco Ortiz. It is time. I have been away far too long."

"But you said yourself," I protested, "that priests are not safe in Mexico. Won't they shoot anyway?"

Rosa shook her head. "No matter how difficult their lives, villagers never lose their faith."

Facing San Miguel and holding the cross in one hand, Marco knelt on one knee and bowed his head. A moment later he stood. Slowly, he turned back toward us. With a knowing smile on his face and a queer gleam in his eyes he said, "Truly, God has chosen the simple to confound the wise. Destiny awaits."

As Marco started for San Miguel Rosa spoke softly, "Only the rich and powerful become heretics. It is they that seek to harm the church."

Rosa's comments carried a tone of reverence. It gave me pause. "So, are you a villager, Rosa?"

Looping her rifle over her shoulder, Rosa replied flatly, "Yes. I am a villager."

Marco slowed his pace, and then began taking rhythmic, almost majestic strides. When he was out far enough in front we fell in behind but made certain to keep the same pace and distance.

In minutes our procession was recognizable to the people of San Miguel and over one hundred excited men, women, and children rushed out to meet us.

After a few words of explanation from Marco, the people erupted with cheers and then greeted us as heroes. In moments, the cheers were mixed with chants.

Of course, looking down from my lofty saddle, I understood not a word of the adoration and praise, none except the often-repeated name of *"El Muerte."*

A spontaneous, albeit humble, celebration was hastily organized. Blazing fires were started, which lit up a small dusty plaza in the center of the pueblo. Dogs barked and howled as a primitive three-piece band assembled and started to play. Dozens of villagers began to sing and dance. Women that were not dancing busied themselves baking something referred to as *pan dulce,* a delicious variety of sweet bread.

As for me, I was quickly swept up in the festivities and soon had my second taste of tequila. Shortly after that I was dancing like a fool and singing words I didn't understand in what I considered to be perfect pitch.

Rosa, too, was dancing but I noticed she left the very intoxicating *aguardiente* alone and was never far from her rifle. But that is about all I remember of that night.

I would like to say that I simply awoke the next morning. However, it is more accurate to state that I regained consciousness shortly before sunrise and crawled out of a pile of putrid smelling hay to vomit on all fours like a dog.

Feeling worse than I ever dreamed possible, I heard a rasping sound mixing with the ringing in my ears. I managed to raise my head a few inches and focus my bloodshot eyes.

Monte was sitting on a nearby adobe wall sharpening his hunting knife. Rosa was standing next to him leaning on her rifle and staring down at me. Behind them I could make out the bulk of three saddled horses."

"I see you had quite a time last night," Monte said, dragging his knife blade over a sharpening stone.

My stomach rolled. I half drooled and then spit. "When did you get back?"

"Late. After the fiesta."

"What happened?" I asked, still on my hands and knees.

Monte stopped sharpening his knife and sheathed it. "Got us some fresh horses. I'm leaving ours here to rest up."

Even in the state I was in, I had a good idea of how Monte acquired the horses but I was too sick to ask many questions. I rolled over and sat up. It was light but the sun was not up. The village was quiet. Here and there, in every conceivable position and combination, men and women lay asleep on the ground.

"Is this a hangover?" I asked.

"You're damned right it is," answered Monte. "And we're packed and ready to go."

"He is welcome to stay here with me," said a voice to my left. It was Marco.

I rubbed the grit from my eyes. "You're staying in San Miguel?"

"Yes. It was my destiny to be a priest. I hid from that calling for a while but no more. I will finish what has been set before me, no matter what the cost."

Struggling to my feet, I looked around the plaza. "But you're leaving so early. Wouldn't the villagers want to meet you, Monte, to get a look at *El Muerte*?"

Monte shrugged. "They won't miss much," he said as he and Rosa stepped onto their saddles. He grabbed the reins of a third horse and pointed to a fourth tied to a post. "Your rifle and writing pouch are hanging on the horn. Catch up to us if you want."

I staggered to the fourth horse. Thankful he was a bit shorter than the one I had been riding, I pulled the reins free. "Right behind you," I mumbled.

Fighting down the urge to vomit a second time, I hoisted myself up, collapsed over the horn and drug my leg over the cantle.

Monte and Rosa stepped out at a fast, jostling walk. Not to be left behind, my horse naturally took off after them.

It was a morning from hell. When we stopped at midday, all I wanted to do was lie down and close my eyes. It was nearing sundown before the mere thought of goat cheese or *pan dulce* didn't make my stomach churn.

The road south had been pulverized by truck-trains and each hoof fall sent a cloud of dust into the blistering heat. Late in the afternoon we veered west off the main road onto another. An hour later, when we rounded a small butte, Rosa finally put up her hand, ready to call it a day.

Rosa shaded her eyes with her fingers and gazed at some object dancing in the undulating heat waves. "That is the San Miguelito hacienda. It is a ranch. The rancher will let us sleep there. His water is cold and sweet."

"Looks like a small fort from here," Monte said, taking in the high adobe walls and series of heavy wooden doors.

"The rooms are inside the walls," Rosa said. "Haciendas are built for protection. For hundreds of years there have been bandits and Indians."

I rode up next to them. "Are those at the hacienda friendly?"

"To me they are. It is better for us if I first ride in alone."

Without waiting for us to respond, Rosa kicked her horse into a gallop.

Tugging my cap down to ease the glare, I studied the hacienda for a moment. "It's like the Middle Ages."

"The what?"

Fatigued and thirsty, I waved my hand at the horizon. "Mexico. It's like living in the Middle Ages. With castles and warlords. And peasants living in squalid little villages. It's like they're five hundred years behind the times."

Monte kept his eyes on Rosa and the dust rising behind her. "I wouldn't know about that."

Craving a simple glass of cold water, I rubbed my burning eyes. "We have no idea, or at least I had no idea, of how good we have it back home."

The hacienda was almost a mile away but we could see figures coming through the gates as Rosa approached. Then her dust blocked our view for several minutes.

"Think she'll be alright?" I asked.

Monte licked his chapped lips. "I don't hear any shooting."

"No shooting," I huffed and then added sarcastically, "Good day, sir. Thank you so much for not shooting us today. What a country!"

"Here she comes," Monte said, pointing toward the hacienda.

Rosa's gallop toward us seemed slow to me but at the time I deemed that observation of no significance. A quarter mile out, however, she drew up and waved for us to follow.

Monte and I galloped to meet Rosa, but before we came up beside her she wheeled her mount and, at a full run, headed back toward the hacienda's main entrance.

We continued at an easy gallop and saw Rosa slide to a stop in front of a massive oak door. She dismounted in a cloud of dust and then stood waiting beside her horse.

Nearing the entrance, we slowed to a walk. I was about to ask Rosa a question when she shouldered her rifle and aimed it squarely at Monte.

"Manos arriba!" she demanded.

Monte and I came to a sudden halt. I

froze. I could see Monte glancing around and slowly raising his hands.

"Raise your hands, Billy," Monte said as calmly as if he were asking that I pass the potatoes.

Speechless, I followed his directions.

In seconds, the wooden door flew open and two dozen Mexicans flooded through it, each with a rifle and two bandoliers of bullets across their chests. Atop their shaggy heads, they wore the usual sombrero but with one notable exception. A bright band of gold cloth had been sewn onto the edge of every hat brim.

"These are Dorados," barked Rosa. "They are the general's best men. Move and they will kill you."

"So, you're back with your army," said Monte.

I must have been suffering from shock for instead of remaining quiet I blurted, "But you and Monte had an agreement."

"And what agreement was that?" asked a man just then emerging from inside the hacienda walls.

Wearing what in Mexico would pass for an officer's jacket, the speaker walked through the Dorados and stood beside Rosa. "Speak up, *gringo*," he said smiling, "and maybe I don't shoot you until tomorrow."

My lips seemed to go numb. Trying not to babble, I said, "They had an agreement. One would help the other."

"Do what, *gringo*?"

"Monte would help Rosa get by the Carrancistas and Rosa would guide Monte until they split up."

The officer laughed. "And you believed her?"

I hesitated. "Of course."

Shaking his head, the officer ordered, "Bring them inside."

Rosa repeated the order in Spanish and the Villistas goaded us with their gun barrels until we dismounted and our guns were taken.

As we were prodded past Rosa, I was impressed by the fact that Monte did not even look at her. Whether he didn't want to give her the opportunity to gloat or he just didn't care, I couldn't say. But I did see the look in Rosa's eyes when he ignored her. There was a glimmer of surprise in them. And then a hint of admiration.

At gunpoint, we were marched through the front door of the hacienda, across a plaza, and then into an expansive room with yellow and green walls. In the center of a red tile floor rested a heavily constructed wooden dining table. Across from it was a hulking fireplace constructed of melon-sized river rocks.

Rosa, along with a dozen of the Dorados, filed in behind us. We were escorted to the foot of the table where we stood while the Mexican we assumed was an officer took a seat at the opposite end.

"I am Julio Cárdenas. I command the Dorados for General Villa."

Monte only stared at Cárdenas so I spoke up. "I'm Billy Cabott of the *Chicago Tribune*. And this is Monte Segundo."

"You are *gringos*. *Gringos* in Mexico. For that it is *ley fuga*. You will be shot."

I looked to Rosa for help but her eyes were locked on Cárdenas.

Thinking as fast as I could, I said, "Monte saved Rosa from the Carrancistas in Las Palomas. We're not here to fight against General Villa. Not at all."

Cárdenas took out a cigar and lit it. He puffed and then exhaled a stream of smoke. With his serpentine eyes and sunbaked skin, he looked like the devil himself.

"All you *gringos* have a sad story to tell before you die. Why can't you just die like men?"

Finally, Rosa spoke up. "The big one is

215

here to find the Apache scouts," she said
and then surprisingly added, "He seeks to
kill some of them."

At the mention of Apaches every head
snapped to attention. Even Cárdenas sat
up.

"What Apaches?"

"Then you have not heard?" Rosa asked.

Rosa switched to Spanish. Cárdenas spoke
rapidly, his voice laced with near panic.
Every Villista in the room was instantly uneasy.

The very mention of Apaches had sent a
shock wave through the room. Their fear
was palpable.

"You know these Apaches?" asked Cárdenas in English, his question directed at
Monte.

"At least two, maybe five or six were
involved with Geronimo. Some of them
killed my family when I was a boy."

The name of Geronimo, only pronounced
with an *h* instead of a *g,* echoed off of every
man's lips. That fact was not lost on Monte
and he quickly took advantage of it. "That's
right. Heronimo. There are twenty-four of
his kind with the Americans and there'll be
more if they're not stopped."

"And they are after the general?" asked
Cárdenas.

"Sure. But you know how they are. They'll kill any Mexican they can along the way. You can't hide from them and they like to kill slow. The old ones are teaching the young ones."

Cárdenas thought for a full count of ten, then waved his hand and barked out an order. All but Rosa left the room.

"Agua," yelled Cárdenas and in seconds a rotund Mexican woman laid several clay mugs and an olla of water on the table in front of us.

"Sit," ordered Cárdenas. "Drink."

I sat immediately. Monte turned, glared at Rosa, and then took a seat. I filled my mug and started gulping. My mouth had never been so dry.

Rosa took a seat midway between us and the officer. She stretched for the olla and a mug but they were just out of reach. Monte could have reached it and shoved it to Rosa but he didn't move a muscle.

Without taking the mug from my mouth I reached in front of Monte and shoved the water jug toward Rosa and then a mug.

I expected her to at least mouth a venomous *cabrón,* but she said nothing. Instead she filled her mug and then, very surprisingly, shoved it back toward Monte.

That tiny gesture sent a message to both

Monte and myself. Regardless of our circumstances, we knew Rosa had not betrayed us. At least not completely.

"General Villa is not well," sighed Cárdenas, returning to English. "His leg wound is healing poorly. He is in much pain and has much difficulty traveling.

"He is hiding with only a few men to protect him. Not even I know where he is. The army is scattered all over and waiting for his recovery.

"But there are many defectors. And we have to threaten men with the death of their families to get them to join us, now."

Rosa seemed genuinely taken aback. "Is General Villa in danger of being caught?"

Cárdenas thoughtfully inhaled from his cigar. "Not by the *gringos*. But the Apaches. They could find him."

We all knew enough to let Cárdenas consider his predicament in silence. As he did, Monte filled his mug with water. He glanced briefly at Rosa and then looked away.

"The general's orders are to kill all Americans," said Cárdenas. "How do I know, Señor Segundo, that you speak the truth about the Apaches?"

Monte took a long drink of water and then refilled his mug. "I was a small boy when the Apaches came. They raped my mother and then crushed her skull with the butt of a rifle. My pa came riding in from the field and they jumped him. They stripped him and tied him to a fence. Then they made me watch while they cut him open. They pulled out his insides and stretched them out on the ground so he could see his own guts. Then they threw me into a fire."

Cárdenas's eyes narrowed. "Yes. I have heard such stories. But if yours is true, you would have scars. I see none."

Monte seemed stumped for the moment but I didn't hesitate to jump in.

"Monte, show him your back."

Monte shot me a knowing glance and then shoved his chair back and came to his feet. Unbuttoning his shirt, he took it off and then turned. Rosa's eyes widened as did those of Cárdenas.

As Monte turned back around, put on his shirt, and started re-buttoning, Cárdenas said solemnly, "It was not fire. They threw you into cactus. This I have seen before."

Monte stopped buttoning. His eyes went blank but not his mind. For the first time in his life he clearly envisioned a thick mat of spiny cholla that grew next to his house. He saw two Apaches holding him by his arms and legs. They swung him high and let him go. He heard the crunch of cactus needles as they tore into his skin. The pain was unimaginable.

A gruesome sigh escaped from Monte's lungs. "Yeah. You're right. Come to think of it, it was cactus. Not fire."

Cárdenas barked out another order and a pair of Villistas entered and returned our weapons. "You will leave immediately. Go, before I change my mind."

Monte finished buttoning his shirt. As he holstered his pistol I stood and said, "Thank you, Señor Cárdenas. Thank you."

We hadn't taken our first step before Rosa lunged to her feet. "I will go with them. They are of no use without a guide. And if they fail, I will be there to carry out the general's orders and kill the *gringos.*"

Without a second thought, Cárdenas agreed, "Excellent. Yes, excellent. That was my plan also."

Trying not to appear too eager, the three of us made our way back out to the plaza and casually mounted our horses. Allowing Rosa to lead, we passed through the Dorados and out the gate at an easy walk.

We never looked back and kept the same pace for miles. Near dark we reached the main road and picked up the pace. After an hour, Rosa wanted to stop for the night but

Monte would have none of it. When he pointed out that Cárdenas could easily have changed his mind and be following us, we decided to ride most of the night.

An hour before daybreak we found a good place to camp. Only then did we feel safe enough to speak freely to one another.

I built a fire while Monte tended the horses and Rosa got what food we had ready to eat. In silence, we busied ourselves as if our menial tasks were of utmost importance. All the while, each of us was anxiously waiting for the other to bring up what had happened at the hacienda, what had almost gotten Monte and I killed.

It was nearing first light when Monte joined Rosa and I at the fire. He squatted, warmed his hands, and gazed into the flames. "That was quick thinking back at the hacienda, Billy. About my shirt. I'd never have thought of it."

Somewhat ashamed of myself, I said, "I was desperate, Monte. The idea just popped into my head. I was hoping your small pox scars would pass for burns marks. We were unbelievably lucky Cárdenas thought they were from cactus thorns."

Monte sighed. "It wasn't luck. It was cactus thorns, not fire. As soon as Cárdenas said it, it came back to me. Part of it anyway. I saw it happen as plain as if I was watching a moving picture show."

I jerked my head around and stared at Monte. "My God, Monte," I whispered. "Cactus!"

"In my dreams, it was always fire. In the dream the sky above me is blood red. Maybe that's why I thought I was on fire."

Rosa handed me a piece of jerky and then held one out to Monte. His eyes met hers and then he grimly accepted the offering.

Monte paused and then asked sternly, "Why did you wave us in to the hacienda, right into the hands of Cárdenas?"

Rosa had been waiting for that question. She looked squarely at Monte, and answered forcefully, "I was at the gate of the hacienda before I learned there were Dorados inside. They saw us ride in and were already circling behind you.

"I did not know Julio Cárdenas was at the hacienda or that there were any Dorados there. When I discovered it, it was too late. And I knew your only chance to live was for me to tell Julio about you and about the Apaches. To prevent you from fighting like you always do, I turned my rifle on you. I did it to save you."

Monte thought hard for several long seconds. Seemingly satisfied with Rosa's answer, he eyed her closely and took a bite of jerky.

"My soul," Monte said, with a slight smirk, "was saved one summer when the priests came to convert the Kootenais. But I do believe you're the very first person who ever cared enough about me to save my natural born life."

At first Rosa drew a blank and then she stiffened. "I did not do it for you, *gringo,*" she scowled. "I did it for Villa!"

Sinking his teeth into the jerky again, Monte tore off another piece and chewed lazily. With his eyes still on Rosa he said with an edge to his voice, "Well, I should've known better. But then, I forgot how much you admire your big strong general who kills women."

Rosa's eyes flashed. I swear she laid her ears back like a cat and was about to pounce.

"Personally," I interjected loudly, "I thought we were going to die. I'm thankful to be alive."

My proclamation had the desired effect of diffusing the smoldering feud. Rosa was first to break the stare-down by glancing at me.

"The two of you were very close to being shot," she said, her voice simmering with stifled rage. "Like Father Marco said, no one is safe in Mexico."

Monte sat back and crossed his legs, Indian style. He took a deep breath and let it out slowly. He flicked a finger toward Rosa. "You lost your sombrero."

Rosa palmed the top of her head. "I left it in the hacienda. We left so quickly."

"So, what do we do now?" I asked.

Rosa slowly leaned to one side resting on her elbow. "Julio said the general is going south as fast as he can, away from the *gringo* army. But even he, Julio Cárdenas, head of all the Dorados, does not know where he is hiding.

"The general's men are scattering. For now, his army is finished. He hides in a secret place and has only the protection of a few men, men that are his cousins.

"The Apaches will learn of this and find him. Since we cannot hope to find General Villa, we must find the Apaches before they find him."

"To locate the scouts," I reasoned, "we'll need to talk to someone in the army again, like we did at Colonia Dublan."

"We passed Namiquipa hours ago," Rosa said. "Julio told me there were soldiers camped there. We could go back."

"No," said Monte. "My gut tells me we should keep going south."

Rosa thought for a moment. "Then, I say we go to La Quemada. It is a small pueblo out in the desert. I think some soldiers will go there looking for Villa. It is not far from here."

"Good. If we meet any Americans, I'll approach them as before, as a reporter, and see what I can find out."

Monte studied his jerky. "The scouts got here a week ago. They'll likely be down this far already. If the stories are true about them going out at night and killing Mexicans, maybe we can ask around and see if that's happened. That'll tell us where they are."

"I can do that," offered Rosa. "The villagers at La Quemada will know of such things."

With that settled, we did nothing but eat for several minutes. We hadn't slept in twenty-four hours and were finally beginning to unwind. Gazing into the hypnotic flames of our small fire, our bloodshot eyes soon grew heavy with fatigue.

Breaking the silence Rosa began to speak. Her tone was subdued. "The general once said he could whip the Americans if he had to. He could go all the way to Washington. He told us the Americans were cowards."

Monte started to say something but I saw

him catch himself. His eyes narrowed with curiosity and he let Rosa continue.

"Julio said," continued Rosa, "the general cried, cried like a baby because of his wound. He even swallowed poison trying to kill himself. But he vomited it up."

Monte and I glanced at one another, unsure if we were hearing Rosa correctly. She seemed almost in a trance. Her normally defiant eyes now reflected disappointment and doubt.

I didn't know how to respond but my heart went out to her. Monte and I had never discussed what might have happened to Rosa at the hands of the Carrancistas. But there was no question she had fought and endured unspeakable suffering for the sake of the charismatic Pancho Villa and for the dream of *Villisimo*.

Not knowing what to say, all I could think to do was ask a question. "How was he wounded?"

Rosa's expression did not change. "He was shot in his leg," she said dejectedly. "It is said, by one of his own men. An accident."

What happened next astounded me and revealed a part of Monte Segundo I thought was nonexistent.

"Rosa," Monte said, "it seems to me you

226

and your people have been fighting and dying so Mexicans can have a better life, not for the sake of one man."

At that moment, Monte was very much aware that he was trying to comfort Rosa but wasn't sure why. He didn't understand what he was feeling because it was completely foreign to him. For the first time in his life he was experiencing not the usual extremes of rage or indifference, but a hint of genuine compassion.

Rosa sighed. She seemed not to have noticed the subtle change in Monte Segundo. "Who can say?" she said wistfully. "Without a leader, there are no soldiers. And then, we again become nothing but sheep."

CHAPTER 8

We slept for an hour and then decided to take a shortcut to La Quemada using a trail that stretched across twenty miles of barren sand. At the trailhead, I was pleasantly surprised when Monte silently took his campaign hat from his pommel and handed it to Rosa.

Without a word, she accepted the hat and tried it on. It was far too big for her dainty head and I expected her to hand it back. Instead, she cleverly wound her braided hair on top of her head and then twisted the hat into place.

Rosa looked up at Monte. Monte nodded approvingly. That was all there was to it and yet that simple exchange was a marvel to behold. Not a word had been spoken and yet a profound agreement had been reached and accepted. The war between them was over.

Rosa led off and Monte and I followed in

single file but this time the distance between the three of us was only a few feet. We were halfway to the village, quite in the middle of nowhere, when we heard a muffled, metallic rattling.

Drawing up close together, we looked all around but, though we could see for miles in every direction, we saw nothing but rippling heat waves. Then the sound disappeared.

"What do you think that was?" I asked, taking a drink of warm water from my canteen.

"Sounded like a machine gun," said Rosa. "Very far away."

Monte scoured the horizon. "I don't see any dust."

"I couldn't tell which direction it came —" I said but hearing the sound again, I stopped in mid-sentence.

Now the rattling was more distinct but also more erratic. Again, we searched the desert but saw nothing.

Monte glanced up into the cloudless sky. "What the hell?"

Rosa and I followed his eyes and caught sight of a black speck coming out of the south.

"It has to be one of Pershing's airplanes," I said, watching the dot grow larger. "It's coming our way."

Again, there was silence but the airplane continued toward us. The engine fired again, then sputtered, only to die again.

Shading my eyes, I said, "I think he sees us. He's coming down."

In a matter of seconds what resembled an enormous box kite hissed through the air just above our heads. Our horses flinched and mine started to spin. By the time I got him under control, the Jenny was rolling and bouncing to a stop one hundred yards ahead of us.

As we rode forward, the pilot got out to greet us. He waved, *"Buenas tardes."*

The pilot began walking toward us holding his hands out to his sides. He was average height with a slight build. The only thing that caught my eye, other than his tight-fitting leather cap, was his two-toned face. The lower half was browned by the sun but the skin around his eyes was white. He reminded me of a raccoon.

"Amigos. Do you speak English?"

When we were within ten feet of the pilot we came to a stop.

"Habla English?" repeated the pilot.

Monte tilted his sombrero back. "As good as you."

Glaring at Monte and his serape and then

230

glancing at Rosa and me, the pilot asked, "Are you Americans?"

"Never mind, that," Monte said, "The question is, who are you?"

"Ben Foulois. Captain Ben Foulois. First Aero Squadron, United States Army."

"What are doing out here?" Monte asked.

"Looking for General Pershing. I have dispatches to deliver. Damn desert winds. I ran out of gas."

Monte glanced around. "You sure picked one hell of a spot."

"The general goes wherever he feels like. I never know where he'll be, just general direction is all. Word is, he may be near Satevó."

Foulois eyed our fourth horse. "I could use a ride."

"We're headed to La Quemada," Monte said. Turning to Rosa he asked, "Think they'll have any gas there?"

Suddenly uneasy, Rosa demanded, "What are dispatches?"

Turning his attention to Rosa, Foulois hesitated and then answered, "Messages for General Pershing."

"About General Villa?" snapped Rosa.

Rosa's hostile demeanor was not lost on Foulois.

"No," Foulois answered casually. "Nothing at all about Villa. Villa's nowhere to be found. But there's been trouble with the Carrancistas down in Parral. They attacked us yesterday. The general needs to know about it right away. In fact, there's trouble with the federal troops all over Mexico. If you ask me, this expedition's going to hell in a handbasket."

Monte turned in his saddle facing Rosa and me. "What do you say?"

"We can't leave him here," I said, and then looked at Rosa.

Rosa was torn. Earlier that morning she had all but lost faith in Pancho Villa and yet she wasn't ready to let go of the *Villisimo* dream. She was struggling with her doubts but still a loyal soldier clinging to the hope that the revolution was not dead.

Rosa sat on her horse, considering the situation. The pilot, she knew, was a messenger for the American general pursuing Villa. The pilot was also carrying information concerning Villa's enemies, the Carrancistas. But she was also convinced that if the Americans and the Carrancistas went to war, Villa would have time to mend and rebuild his army. And that was enough for Rosa.

"We take him," muttered Rosa. "He will die out here."

232

"You have a hat for the sun?" Monte asked.

The pilot shook his head, "Only goggles."

"Better get them. They may come in handy in this desert."

Watching the pilot return to his airplane, Monte said, "Let's see what all he knows. He might know where the Apaches are. And the less he knows about me the better."

"He'll be wondering what we're doing out here," I said.

"Alright," agreed Monte. "Me and Rosa will make like we're married and live down here. You're just who you are, Billy Cabott, a reporter that got lost. Me and Rosa are guiding you until you can hook back up with the American army."

I half expected Rosa to make a snide comment about the hasty marriage arrangement but she appeared comfortable with the ruse. And that brought a smile to my cracked lips.

"Good thinking," I said. "I think we can fool him easily enough."

"Hot down on this sand," said Foulois, returning with his goggles perched on the top of his head. "It's not so bad up high."

Monte pointed to our fourth horse. "You'll have to straddle our grub sacks."

Foulois hoisted himself into the saddle. He shoved the sacks aside and took the reins. "I haven't ridden much."

Rosa started off but not before she said, "Any fool can sit a walking horse."

Monte glanced at the pilot and grinned. "She's always like that. Don't take it personal."

As the three of us started off together, Foulois squinted at Monte. "She your wife?"

Monte shook his head. "Don't remind me."

I laughed and so did Foulois.

"I guess we're both lost," I said. "I work for the *Chicago Tribune.* I was with the press corps but got separated. This fine couple offered to take me to La Quemada."

Offering my hand, I introduced myself. "Billy Cabott."

"For a price, Mr. Cabott," said Monte, adding to the charade. "Don't forget that part. Me and my woman don't work for free."

"Certainly, Mr. Smith," I responded. "I have not forgotten."

Monte threw a look at Foulois. "You got any money?"

Foulois flinched. "Just a few dollars. But I need that for fuel."

"Well now," grunted Monte. "Mrs. Smith won't like that. She favors Villa, you see. But she does hate those Carrancistas. Me

234

personally, I don't give a damn about either side."

Taking the last comment as my cue, I asked, "What happened down in Parral, anyway? You said we were attacked by Carrancistas?"

"Well," began Foulois, "it seemed like a setup from the start. The Thirteenth Cavalry under Major Tompkins was headed toward Parral when they went through a small village. A captain there named Mesa told the major that he'd telephone ahead to Parral and make sure they had food and forage waiting when the company got there."

Rosa, who had been listening, turned in her saddle. "Telephone!" she scoffed. "The lines in Parral have been cut for years."

Foulois shrugged. "Anyway, when the Thirteenth got to the outskirts of Parral, no one came out to meet them like Mesa said they would.

"So, Tompkins took a small squad and went into town. He got ahold of the *jefe de armas,* a fella named Lozano."

"What's a *jefe de armas*?" I asked.

"Oh, that's the officer that heads the army garrison, the man in charge. Him and the mayor run the town.

"General Lozano tells Tompkins to get out of town but the major says he won't go until he gets the food and forage Mesa promised.

"Lozano says he'll get it but Tompkins still has to leave town right now. While they're talking a mob forms and starts screaming 'Viva Villa, Viva Mexico' and the like.

"And Tompkins sees a German in the crowd stirring them up, too. So, everybody's all wound up when Tompkins leaves town. But as the troops are riding out, the women dump their slop jars and spittoons on them from some second-story windows.

"Before the troops are out of town, somebody in the mob shoots at the men. Tompkins takes all the insults without doing anything and joins back up with his cavalry. Then he sees Carrancista soldiers gathering on a hill nearby. Pretty soon the Carrancistas open fire.

"Tompkins retreats for sixteen miles in a running battle with the Carrancistas. They made it to another village and took cover. But then they were completely surrounded.

"A couple of hours went by and Tompkins was thinking he was sitting in the second Alamo when he heard a bugle call. That came from Colonel Brown and the black Tenth Cavalry. When the companies joined up that put an end to the fight. But a good many men died on both sides."

"And General Pershing doesn't know

anything about this?" I asked.

"Not yet. That's one of our biggest problems down here. Communication. A lot of the time he's completely out of contact with the whole army, not to mention Washington.

"We've got radios, but they don't go but twenty-five miles and that's if no mountains are in the way. And our buzz-wire keeps getting cut."

"What's a buzz-wire?" I asked.

"Like a telegraph only laid out on the ground. Maybe you've seen it along the main road going south?"

I shrugged. "No, haven't seen that."

"Well, we just started laying it out from Columbus to Colonia Dublan. It's not this far south yet, I suppose."

"Guess not."

Foulois wiped sweat from his face with his shirtsleeve. "Anyway, Carranza already sent a note to our Secretary of State blaming Tompkins for everything. There's lots of talk about a full-scale war breaking out now but not with Villa. With the damned Carrancistas and that means the whole country of Mexico.

"But, except for the one division that's protecting Washington, D.C., our entire army is already down here. All we have left is state militias, and, according to the general, they don't amount to anything at all. He says about all they can do is wear a uniform."

"I'll bet the Germans like what's happening," I said.

"That's not the half of it," agreed Foulois. "There are Germans all over south Texas stirring up the Mexicans and German immigrants, trying to get them to revolt against the United States. And there're lots of rumors that Carranza himself is behind the border raids. It's as if he wants to start a war with us.

"Like I said, it's nuts all over."

"It sounds to me," Monte said, refocusing the conversation, "that if the American army can't find Villa, it's time for them to go home. Years ago, the Apaches used to hide from us down here but Villa's no Apache. If the army had any good trackers they'd have had the general weeks ago."

Clearly unaccustomed to the desert heat, Foulois shifted the muslin bags that hung near his legs. "As a matter of fact, we have some Apache scouts working for us. But they just got here."

Acting surprised, I said, "Hey, that would make quite a story for the folks back home. Do you have any idea where they might be?"

"I heard they were going to be assigned to

Major Howze," Foulois said. "But I think for now the scouts are waiting in San Antonio. They're commanded by a Lieutenant Shannon, I believe."

Monte sneered. "Hell, bringing Apaches into Mexico is like taking anthrax into cattle country. The Mexicans won't like that one bit. They've been at each other for three hundred years."

"Rosa," I said, only slightly raising my voice, "how far to San Antonio?"

Looking up at the sun, Rosa replied, "One day's ride."

Foulois glanced at Rosa and then curiously looked up in the sky. "Sure hot down here on the sand."

A thought came to me and I opened my satchel and tore out several sheets of paper. I folded them in half and handed them to Foulois. "Tuck this under the edge of your goggles."

"What?"

I pointed to the small bill on my Carrancista cap that was drawn down close to my eyes. "Like this. Make a shade."

"Gotcha," said Foulois and then stuck the edge of the papers under his goggles. He made a few adjustments and then smiled. "Hey, that's swell. How do I look?"

"Preposterous," I said, laughing.

Monte glanced at Foulois and then gave me a nod. "You're learning fast, Billy."

Foulois was a happy-go-lucky sort and seemed to enjoy our company. As we rode, he and I continued our conversation.

"You mentioned the Germans, Captain. What's new on the European front?"

"Those Huns are a crafty bunch but President Wilson knows what they're up to. General Pershing, now, he wants to bust out and take over all of Chihuahua but Wilson doesn't want to get us tied up down here in Mexico. The president, you see, is thinking there's a good chance we're going to end up fighting the Germans in Europe.

"The Germans are thinking the same thing. But they know good and well we've got most of our army out looking for Villa. So, if the Germans can keep us occupied with Mexico, which is exactly what they're trying to do, they know we'll never join the fight in Europe.

"If we end up declaring war with Mexico our hands will be tied. Then the Germans will use their submarines to sink every ship of ours that's headed for England and there'd be nothing we could do about it. That would mean no more of our military supplies or food would make it to England. That little island would fall in weeks and the war would end before you know it."

As I listened to the pilot, it became clear to me that a disaster was in the making. The Apache scouts were now of vital importance to the army. If they quickly located Villa our forces would soon go back home. When that occurred, the United States would be free to enter the war in Europe if it became necessary. And yet Monte Segundo was on a mission to kill one if not more of the Apaches. Monte's success would only benefit Villa, thereby prolonging Pershing's expedition, which in turn could lead to war with Mexico.

In the blistering heat, a tortuous thought sent a chill down my spine. Despite the massive armies clashing on the other side of the Atlantic Ocean, despite the vicious advances in war machinery and the intricate plotting of government powers, the future of the world could possibly hinge on the actions taken by one man, one man virtually alone in the middle of a desert wasteland.

"This Parral mess," continued Foulois, "could be just the thing that triggers that war, like it or not. I know it's what General Pershing and his officers want. They've already got their strategy figured out, have had for some time."

Rosa turned. Even shaded by the brim of

the campaign hat, the hardness in her eyes was unmistakable. "Your army has done enough. The general is wounded and in hiding. His Dorados have deserted him as has much of his army. No one wants you here, not the Carrancistas and not the Villistas. You are invaders. You should go back where you came from."

Foulois glanced at Monte as if asking permission to respond but Monte was expressionless. "As a matter of fact, I agree with you, ma'am," Foulois said. "But we were invaded first and we have the same dislike for invaders as you do. It's a matter of national pride now. And, too, if we leave Mexico without having done something other than chasing the wind, we'll look weak to the Germans. And that would be bad."

"Damn the Germans," snarled Rosa. "Damn the *gringos.* And damn the Spaniards. This is our revolution!"

"Yes, ma'am," agreed Foulois, wiping sweat from his face using the bend of his elbow. "My sentiments exactly."

"I know the *jefe politico* in La Quemada," Rosa said. "He has a motor car. He will have gas for it." Rosa kicked her mount into a trot. "Then you can go. And take your army with you!"

We watched Rosa ride a short distance,

far enough to be out of hearing range, and then slow to a walk.

Foulois was uneasy. "Well, like you said, she's for Villa."

"She was," answered Monte. "But lately she's having doubts. That's why she's boiling over. She's flustered."

"And what about you?" questioned Foulois. "Are you having any doubts?"

Monte ran his tongue over his teeth to moisten them. "None of it's any of my business."

With that answer Foulois and I avoided politics all together. We spent the remainder of the day talking of restaurants, sports, and moving picture stars.

The sun was setting when we rode into the plaza of La Quemada, a cookie-cutter Mexican village replete with barking dogs, darting children, and the penetrating stares of distrustful adults.

Rosa entered ahead of us and had already dismounted when we rode in. An elderly man with deep creases at the corners of his eyes emerged from an adobe at the edge of the plaza. He was dressed in a surprisingly well-fitting suit and possessed an air of importance. As he approached us the inhabitants of the pueblo gathered behind him in a tight cluster.

He spoke in Spanish to us and Rosa answered. She then pointed to Foulois and spoke again. When she finished speaking, the man in the suit and most of the villagers frowned.

"I have four gallons," the old man said, switching to English. "I am the *jefe politico* here. I will sell the gas but the pilot must go immediately."

"The pilot," said Monte, "needs a ride back to his airplane, tonight if possible. The three of us will keep heading south after we get some water, if that's the way you want it."

The *jefe politico*'s eyes turned to Monte, running over him head to toe. The mayor then looked appraisingly at Rosa. Next, he looked me over and then his eyes flared with recognition. *"Madre de Dios,"* he said softly, making the sign of the cross.

"The armies have taken all our horses. And there is barely enough gas to use my automobile. Four gallons is all I can spare."

Monte grunted and thought for a moment. "Captain, do you think you can find your way back to your airplane? There should be enough moonlight to see our tracks."

"Sure."

"Alright. You'll take the horse you're on.

Let him loose when you get back to your airplane. He'll find his way back here."

Foulois nodded. "I could use some water. Lots of water. And something to eat."

"We will fill a goatskin," said the *jefe,* "and give you some tortillas. But you must go quickly. You endanger our village."

Stiffly, Foulois dismounted. "Then I'll go. I gotta stretch my legs first, though."

The *jefe* barked out some orders in Spanish. Two women and a small boy broke from the crowd. The women disappeared into the darkened doorway of an adobe but the boy trotted to a tattered, sun-bleached canvas that covered a large bulky object. He pulled the canvas to one side, exposing a rear axle, two rubber wheels, and a dented rectangular gas can sitting in the sand.

Grabbing the can and flipping down the canvas, the boy returned with the gas can and set it down at Foulois's feet.

Rosa went to Foulois's horse. Ignoring him completely, she lifted the muslin food sacks off the saddle and draped them across her own saddle horn.

Foulois worked his legs up and down attempting to get the blood to circulate. His eyes darted over the Mexicans but wisely, he said nothing. In seconds the two women returned and one handed him a large goatskin bulging with water and dripping wet. The other gave him a bundle the size of a baseball, wrapped tightly in a white cotton cloth.

Without hesitating, Foulois looped the strap of the goatskin over his saddle horn and stuffed the cotton bundle inside his shirt. He then handed a handful of paper dollars to the *jefe*.

Rosa picked up the gas can. "Mount up," she ordered.

Foulois stepped into the saddle and took the reins in one hand and the gas can in the other. He glanced at me. He cracked a faint smile and then offered a casual salute to Rosa.

"Good evening ma'am," he said and then rode out of the plaza at an easy walk.

The *jefe* seemed to relax but only slightly. His movements were stiff, almost formal, as he turned his attention from Foulois to us. "I am Rafael Hernandez, *jefe politico* of La Quemada. You are welcome to eat with us and stay the night."

"Our horses need to be fed and watered," said Rosa, still with her rifle over her shoulder. "Is this possible?"

"We have good water and *maiz.* The *caballos* will be well cared for."

Following Rosa's example, I kept my rifle

on my shoulder as I too stepped down. Monte, however, was edgy. He sensed that we were getting close to the Apaches and knew word had a way of spreading quickly in Mexico. He figured it was even possible the Indians already knew he was coming and why. If they did, they would not wait to be attacked. They would strike out on their own, regardless of any orders given to them by the army.

Monte glanced up. The sun had just set behind the jagged bulk of the Sierra Madres, leaving a faded blue sky and dingy orange glow just above the mountain peaks. "I'll have a look around the desert first," he said, and then wheeled his horse and abruptly trotted out of the pueblo.

The villagers began to disperse but did not go far, choosing instead to gather in smaller groups here and there along the walls of the adobes.

"Venga," the *jefe* said, waving his hand. "Come. We will go into my home. My wife, Maria, will care for you."

"What about our horses?" I asked.

Rafael Hernandez waved again but this time with several jerky flicks of his wrist. "Come, come. They will be well cared for."

With Rosa ahead of me, I followed her into a large room, surprisingly cool, with an ornate, well-polished oak table and chairs in its center. Several paintings of patron saints adorned the otherwise bare walls, but the walls were painted bright green with orange trim. The floor, like the hacienda in Santa Rosalita, was checkered with large slabs of red tile.

A short, plump woman with braided gray hair and a factory-made dress was lighting two kerosene lanterns and setting them on the table.

Indicating the table with a nod of her head, the woman said, "*Siéntate, por favor.* Sit, please."

Sitting was the last thing I wanted to do but not knowing any of the customs, I wasn't about to protest. And besides, I suddenly smelled something delicious, the aroma coming from a dome-shaped clay stove just beyond the far end of the table.

I slid my rifle off my shoulder but must have been staring at the stove for Rafael Hernadez said, "Tamales. Maria makes tamales. Please lean your rifles against the wall if you wish or lay them near you. Is no matter."

Rosa leaned her rifle on the wall behind her, tossed her hat next to it, and then took a seat. I did the same with my rifle but removed my hat and placed it in my lap as I took a seat beside Rosa.

Maria went to the stove. Rafael followed close behind her and then said something to her we couldn't hear. Her back was to us but I saw Maria stiffen. He spoke again and she went back to work at the stove, using her bare hand to turn over what looked like small tawny-colored bricks.

Rafael came back to the table with his hands full. Placing two mugs in front of us, he filled them with cool water from a large jug. "You have come far, *amigos*. You surely have much thirst."

I waited for Rosa to pick up her mug and then take the first drink. After she emptied the mug without taking it from her lips I eagerly followed suit.

Without hesitation, Rafael began refilling our mugs. "Did you perhaps pass by San Miguel on your way here?" he asked lazily. "I have cousins there."

"Tal vez," answered Rosa, and then took another long drink of water, but as she drank her eyes peered over the mug, studying Rafael. Taking the mug down, Rosa wiped her lips with the back of her hand. "Why do you ask?"

Only half listening, I drank again, enjoying the cool, crystal clear water as it washed down my parched throat and trickled into my belly.

"We hear strange stories from that pueblo and some from north of there," Raphael was saying. "Stories sometimes hard to believe."

I had no idea if Rafael and Maria Hernandez were Carrancistas or Villistas but it sounded as if what had happened in San Miguel had already reached La Quemada. Since we had been invited into his home to eat, I surmised the mayor harbored no sympathy for the dead bandits.

Regardless, I was far too tired, too sore, and too hungry to be suspicious of Rafael's questions. I didn't care much about anything save my own comfort. At that moment, I was satisfied just to know that I was out of the burning sun, had plenty of water, and was anxiously waiting to discover if a tamale tasted even half as good as it smelled.

"There are always stories," Rosa said, flatly.

"Not like these," returned Rafael. Setting the pitcher down, Rafael took a seat across from us. "Some bandits were caught and hanged there at San Miguel."

"Hanged?" questioned Rosa, genuinely surprised.

"Yes. Four were hanged only a few miles from the village."

I stopped thinking of tamales for a moment and recalled the horses Monte returned with that evening at San Miguel. That night I dared not ask him how he came by the bandits' horses. I knew better. Or, more honestly, I didn't want to know. Rosa didn't want to know either or just didn't care to ask. Both of us left well enough alone.

"It is not unusual to hang bandits," Rosa said, regaining her apathetic composure. "That is nothing unusual."

Maria came to the table with a steaming platter of palm-sized, rectangular packets wrapped in some sort of leaf. She set them in the middle of the table and then sat down next to Rafael. Immediately, she bowed her head as did Rafael and then Rosa.

I dropped my head a bit but kept my eyes half-open. Rafael said a few quick words and then all three traced the sign of the cross over their chests.

Reaching for a tamale, Maria Hernandez said, "It is how they were hanged, *amigos,* that has caused all the talk. It was an evil way to hang them."

I watched Rosa take a tamale and then begin to unwrap it by stripping off the folded brown leaves, corn husks as it turned out.

"Hanging is hanging," Rosa said and she

251

then took a bite of tamale.

I took a tamale and began unwrapping it, trying not to burn my fingers or to think of the hanging.

"Not so," returned Maria. "These bandits were hanged like no others have ever been hanged. Like fish on a string, like clothes on a line. Not like men at all. It was evil to hang men that way."

Rosa stopped chewing and I stopped unwrapping. Rosa glared at Maria and then at Rafael. "Four men on one rope? How could one man do such a thing as that?"

Rafael shook his head. *"¿Quien sabe?* But they were stretched high off the ground between two trees. Like so many fish. And on one shirt, in charcoal from the campfire nearby, is written, *'Pasó por aquí'!"*

Rosa began to chew again but slowly, thoughtfully. "That is not evil. But it is a fearful thing to hang men so."

I finally took my first bite of tamale, hot and moist and wonderful. I savored its taste for several seconds, seconds in which the idea of four men hanging on a rope was shoved aside to make room for a moment of self-indulgence.

Savoring my good fortune, I half-heartedly asked, "What is *'pasó por aquí?'* "

Rosa looked at me with a glint in her eyes.

"It means, 'I passed through here.' "

I nodded and continued eating, oblivious at the time that I had completely suppressed the barbarity of what had happened at San Miguel.

Rafael grew more serious. "Some say such a hanging was made by a devil. Others say by an angel. An angel of death."

"It was but a man that did this thing," scoffed Rosa and then paused to consider some hidden thought. "But I think maybe he is not like other men."

"Then it is true?" asked Maria. "*El Muerte* is real?"

Rosa finished her tamale and reached for another. "You have seen him with your own eyes. He is more real than not."

"Tengo miedo!" Maria said. "He is a demon!"

Unwrapping her tamale, Rosa shrugged. "You have nothing to fear from Monte Segundo. Nor does any peasant. He has no interest in any of you. Only bad men, very bad men. But especially Apaches."

Rafael took a bite of tamale. He considered what Rosa had said as he chewed. "We have heard this, too, about the Apaches. What kind of man, unless he is crazy or a demon, hunts Apaches?"

"No lo sé," admitted Rosa. "I cannot say."

"Well, I can assure you he is not crazy," I offered, enjoying every morsel of tamale.

Rosa shook her head. "Monte Segundo has no fear. Maybe for this reason some say he is *loco*."

Rosa's observation sobered me somewhat. My mind drifted to what Monte must have seen as a small boy, how he had watched his parents being mutilated and murdered. I thought of how, while enduring incredible pain, he had seen them die, certain that at any moment he would be next. Little Monte would have been horrified beyond anything one could imagine. But very likely, in order to maintain his sanity, he had buried that memory deep and perhaps, just perhaps, buried parts of himself as well. Then I found myself wondering if Monte Segundo had somehow buried fear itself.

I glanced at Rosa, wondering if she had not done something similar, buried what could not be endured. How long had she been fighting for the revolution, and very likely killing? And how long had she been a prisoner of the depraved Carrancistas before Monte rescued her?

I found myself questioning how anyone could bring themselves to kill another human being and yet I was in a country where death was an everyday occurrence, accepted as casually as the midday heat.

Rafael peered at Rosa, his eyes uncertain. "They say *El Muerte* can see in the dark, that his eyes glow like a cat. They say he kills with a gun, a knife, a rope, and even his bare hands. He breaks necks like twigs and has the temper of a mad dog. All of the villages are hearing these things and more."

Rosa's reply was nonchalant. "Much you say is true. Much is not. But as I said, it is only bad men that need to worry."

"Then he is a devil come to take his own," said Maria.

Considering the comment for a moment, Rosa's eyes narrowed but only briefly. "Maybe yes. Maybe no. We will see very soon.

"No quiero el diablo en mi casa," demanded Maria. *"No quiero!"*

We ate the rest of the meal in silence, each of us sporadically glancing at the open front door, watching uneasily as the meager light within slowly faded into darkness. When we finished eating, Rafael brought out a bottle of wine and a handful of long-stemmed glasses.

He carefully set the glasses down but his hand trembled as he filled them. "We do not get many guests since the revolution. Tonight is a night for wine."

A cool breeze funneled in through the door. I felt the tension drain from my aching body. "I don't think he will come," I said. And then with more confidence I added, "No. He would have been here by now."

Rafael filled a glass for himself and then went to the doorway but did not go out. He listened as he sipped from his glass, turning his head from side to side as the wind ruffled his loose-fitting cotton shirt.

Shaking his head, he turned and slowly strolled back to the table and took a seat. "The village is quiet. There should be much activity since it is cool now. They are afraid, I think, to go outside. Very afraid."

Going to a cupboard, Rafael took down two candles with holders, lit them, and brought them to the table.

"We will be gone in the morning," said Rosa.

"The two of you are welcome to sleep in my house," offered Rafael. "We have beds."

At that moment, the warming glow of the wine was starting to take effect. I slouched in my chair to ease the hours-old ache in my lower back. The thought of a soft bed brought a smile to my face. But before I could accept the offer Rosa's voice shattered my thoughts.

"*Gracias,* but we will sleep with the horses."

My smile melted away. I took a long swallow of wine. I wanted to let down for a bit, to forget about everything Mexican, to just enjoy myself for a while. Oh, bloody hell, how I wanted to sleep in that bed.

Taking my last swallow of wine, I rolled my eyes toward Rosa. She was sitting up straight, her eyes bright and clear in the candlelight. If she had the slightest pain in her body, she covered it well. All things considered, she was simply magnificent.

As inconspicuously as possible, I eased myself upright and leveled my not-so-broad shoulders. I set my glass down and found myself thanking the God whom I had never particularly believed in that Rafael filled it once again.

"Thank you, sir," I said, wrapping my grateful fingers around the glass stem. *"Gracias!"*

"De nada," Rafael said with a nod. Some of the stress lines in his face relaxed. He picked up his glass and held it out. Glancing at me and then at Rosa he said, *"Salud. Vaya con Dios."*

CHAPTER 9

When Rosa and I went back to the horses we expected to find Monte somewhere near the corral. He was nowhere in sight so we went to a small shed that covered a pile of sweet-smelling hay and lit a candle. I laid out my blanket on the hay only half aware that Rosa was doing the same hardly more than an arm's length away.

I sat down, took off my shoes, and dropped back on my blanket, instantly feeling the knotted muscles between my shoulder blades begin to unwind. It was then that I noticed Rosa laying out a second blanket, Monte's blanket. Keeping my head steady, I slid my eyes toward Rosa, watching her in the flickering shadows.

Monte's bed was no closer to Rosa's than mine but it was the mere fact that she was preparing it that stirred me. It was the same sensation I'd felt when, the day before, Monte had offered Rosa his campaign hat.

Trivial acts by most standards but for Monte and Rosa, guarded gestures not only of a truce but perhaps even a developing friendship.

As if I'd seen nothing, I rolled away from Rosa onto my side. Feeling the warmth of the wine pulsing through my body, I closed my eyes and smiled.

In what seemed like seconds, something poked the bottom of my foot. I cracked open my eyes and it was dawn. In fact, the rising sun was in my eyes.

Wiping the crust from my eyelids, I propped myself up on my elbows and was relieved to see that Rosa was also just getting up. Monte, however, was standing by his saddled horse looking down at both of us.

I expected him to say something about sleeping so long but he waited for us in silence. I was yawning and cinching up my saddle when I glanced down where Monte stood. I blinked and looked again.

"What happened to your boots?" I asked.

Rosa was buckling on her headstall but she stopped and looked. "Moccasins?"

Monte nodded. The sun painted his face with a red-orange hue. His eyes were hard, not angry, not irritated. Just hard. "I found a cobbler. I traded my boots. He stayed up all night making these. From now on I've got no use for boots."

The moccasins were light brown with turned-up toes and were tied with a leather thong from the ankles to the bottom of Monte's knees. "These are styled after the Apache moccasin. They'll leave a similar track in soft dirt. It's the toe that does that."

Rosa finished buckling her headstall and I went back to my cinch, gave it a heavy tug, and tied it off. I pulled some straw from the collar of my shirt and then some from my hair. Dragging a hand over my face I yawned again and asked, "Where to today?"

"The cobbler said there's rumors of Apache killings near a village called Agua Caliente. The army around those parts deny it. They say it's just stories, lies made up by the Villistas or Carrancistas to turn the Mexicans against the army. But the cobbler says they're true.

"No matter what though, nobody's denying the Apaches are somewhere near Agua Caliente."

Looping her rifle over her shoulder, Rosa said, "Agua is on the main road from Colonia Dublan to San Antonio."

Rosa bent to adjust her sandal. When she straightened, her rifle strap slipped, causing her loose-fitting blouse to fall off her left shoulder, leaving it bare almost to the elbow. She was fully engulfed in the rising sun, its amber rays penetrating the thin cotton blouse draped over her breasts. With her black eyes sparkling, her lips full and red, the beauty and sensuality of the moment was impossible to ignore.

My stomach turned somersaults. I swallowed hard, forced myself to avert my eyes, and then glanced at Monte. I could see that he, however, was taking in every inch of what was on display.

Looking steadily at Monte, Rosa deliberately hesitated for a moment before teasing the edge of her blouse back over her shoulder and then slowly tucking it under her rifle sling.

Monte's eyes met Rosa's and held. Each remained poker-faced, unwilling to betray the slightest emotion. It was a contest of wills, a battle of sorts that neither wished to lose.

"I suppose Agua Caliente is a day's ride," I said, verbally inserting myself between them. "Seems like everywhere in Mexico is a day's ride from one place to the next."

Rosa looked away first but not before turning up one corner of her lips in a knowing smirk. She raised an eyebrow and turned toward me. "Of course, it is one day.

261

Does it not make sense? A day's ride and then one needs water, food, and sleep. Another day's ride and the same is needed."

Stepping into my saddle I said, "Never thought of it that way. It does make sense."

Rosa's campaign hat was hanging on a peg on the wall above where she had slept. Monte indicated its location with a nod of his head. "Don't forget your hat," he said, knowing good and well Rosa needed no reminder.

Rosa reached for her hat and pressed it onto her head. Stepping onto her saddle, she looked down at Monte. Her eyes narrowed tauntingly. "Did you sleep well?"

Monte chuckled softly and then led his horse out into the full sun. He mounted, the saddle leather creaking as he adjusted his weight. "The cobbler said we should get on the main road headed south, the one that runs from Colonia Dublan to San Antonio."

"Then we go south first," Rosa said. "Then east to Rubio before we head south once more. Then we hit the main road."

"Why the main road?" I asked.

"Because," Monte said, "that's where they're laying that buzz-wire. And the Mexicans have been cutting it. Rumor has it that some of those same Mexicans have been found dead, killed Apache style."

I nudged my horse ahead of Rosa's, hoping to get one more glimpse of her silhouetted by the rising sun, but she wheeled her horse to the south before I got into position. I felt a twinge of guilt at what I had tried to do. But that guilt was nothing compared to the excitement of the attempt and the realization that for those few moments every ache and pain in my body had completely disappeared.

We rode south for several hours with the sun low and to our left. Well before noon we passed through the dusty, dog-infested village of Rubio and then headed southwest until we came in sight of the main road. By then it was midafternoon and we decided to dismount and rest in the shade of an overhanging creosote.

I drank hot water from my canteen but the heat had taken away my appetite. Seemingly unfazed by the temperature, Monte and Rosa dined on our usual fare of goat cheese and jerked meat, meat whose origin, especially after riding through the dog-town of Rubio, I was beginning to question.

The ache in my knees and backside had hardly started to subside before we heard the jingling of trace chains coming from the main road.

Monte stopped chewing. He had been

leaning back on his elbows but now sat up and listened. "Wagons. Sounds like a lot of them."

Ten minutes passed and the first southbound wagon appeared. It was pulled by four mules and was stacked high with bales of hay. Behind it was another wagon also pulled by mules and loaded with hay. By the time the train passed we counted eighteen wagonloads of hay.

Shaking her head, Rosa scoffed, "Your army has no chance to catch the general. They can barely keep their horses fed. The general has no wagons of hay. He moves wherever he wants."

Taking a bite of cheese, Monte nodded, "That was a bunch of feed, alright. They must've trucked it a couple of hundred miles by now. But a handful of Mexicans could take that train just about anywhere along the way. Pershing's supply line is long and paper thin. Without those supplies, he'd be in mighty big trouble."

At that point, even I could see the danger our army was in and how easily disaster could strike. Captain Foulois had said that virtually the entire U.S. army was now in Mexico and that it was scattered all over the state of Chihuahua.

I was suddenly agitated. "Surely General

Pershing knows his supply lines are vulnerable. If they're broken, our whole army could be cut off and surrounded. Then what would happen? If Mexico decided to invade us we'd have no way to defend ourselves. And that pilot said the Carrancistas had attacked us down in Parral. Not the Villistas but the government troops!"

"You should leave at once," said Rosa. "There are already two plans to invade Texas. The general has one and so does Carranza. And the Germans will help either one that attacks. The Japanese, too. Your army should go back before it is too late."

Monte tore off a piece of jerky and chewed thoughtfully. "Well, no matter what happens the Mexicans sure as hell won't reach Idaho. Not even with the Germans' help. In fact, if the Mexicans invaded our country, those boys in the Southern states would pour into Texas so fast it'd make your head spin. They're still not over losing the Civil War and they've been carrying a chip on their shoulder ever since. And everybody knows Southerners are always itching for a fight.

"No, it'd be messy at first, but Mexico would lose. And then we'd take another big chunk of their country for our trouble. It's best the Mexicans not listen to those Germans. The last thing you want to do is rile up a hoard of Anglo-Saxons."

"Still," I said, "I think we should get out of Mexico."

"Yeah," agreed Monte coming to his feet. "But they attacked us. Some scores have to be settled. There's no getting around it. Blood debts have to be paid in blood."

Riding out of the shade we soon discovered that horses' hooves, steel-rimmed wagon wheels, and solid rubber truck tires had pulverized the main road into a fine powder six inches deep. Resembling a dry riverbed, the road stretched out in front of us, winding south around a ragged range of hills that rose sharply to the west.

We held up for a moment and listened. In the silence my eyes drifted to the side of the road and I caught sight of something unusual.

Lying off to the west and tucked haphazardly under the low branches of creosote was a short strip of what appeared to be a black rope. On a hunch, I stepped down for a closer look.

"What is it, Billy?" Monte asked.

Walking and pointing, I said, "I think it might be the buzz-wire, the one Pershing uses."

I stooped down and took hold of an

insulated wire not more than a half-inch thick. Thinking it was only a fragment I pulled upward but all I did was uncover a continuous cable that had been buried by all the dust.

"This has to be it," I said. "This is the buzz-wire."

Monte turned half-around and adjusted his sombrero. "Seems kind of flimsy. I hope they're not counting on it for anything important."

Shaking her head, Rosa snorted. "Do they think we are so stupid? A child with two rocks can break that in two."

What Rosa said made perfect sense, which further shook my confidence in Pershing's judgment. Recalling what Foulois had told us, the general's whereabouts were often unknown and now I could see his best means of communication was a flimsy wire lying on the ground in plain sight. And on top of that, Pershing was bent on leading the entire U.S. army deeper and deeper into hostile territory, all the while relying on a fragile supply line that stretched over hundreds of desolate miles.

"No doubt you are correct about the wire," I said and mounted my horse. "I only hope General Pershing knows what he's doing."

Once again, we headed south but had ridden less than an hour when we rounded a bend and saw where the buzz-wire had been pulled out of the sand and seemingly drug off into the brush. Monte dismounted, followed the wire, and in a few feet picked up a loose end. Examining it closely, he rolled it between his fingers.

"It's been cut alright." Glancing at the road ahead, he added, "Looks like the ones that did the cutting took a good piece of it with them. And not that long ago."

Monte came back to the road but instead of remounting, led his horse forward while scanning the side of the road. Occasionally, he squatted and then for several seconds peered off into the hills before continuing on.

Finally, I ventured a question. "What are you looking for?"

Monte answered but continued his search as he spoke. "For whoever took the wire. They'll leave tracks. Those tracks'll be on top of the ones left by the wagon train with the hay or they'll be underneath them. That'll tell me something about when they cut the wire. The army'll be sending somebody out to find the break . . . and maybe somebody to find the cutter. That'd likely be a tracker, a good one. Maybe even an

Apache. Whoever they're sending will already be on their way."

My pulse jumped and my heart began to race. Before Columbus, I'd scarcely even heard of an Apache, much less seen one. I knew nothing about them. But south of the border, the mere mention of Apaches invariably triggered a wave of fear and sometimes outright terror.

Watching Monte search for a sign, I told myself that the Mexicans' fear of the Apache was surely based on a liberal mixture of folktales, ignorance, and superstition. I also attempted to convince myself that the Apache scouts were nothing like the renegades of the last century. Now they were uniformed soldiers of a modern army.

I found my line of reasoning reassuring until I saw Rosa take the rifle from her shoulder, jerk the bolt back, and slam a cartridge into the chamber.

I glanced from Rosa back to Monte. He had stopped and gone to one knee. He stared at the dirt in front of him and then lay flat on his belly. With his eyes almost at ground level he glared into a narrow gully, a notch carved out of brush that carpeted the side of the road and hills beyond. I could not see well from where I sat but Monte was looking at the sandy bottom of that narrow ravine, reading what had happened as easily as I would read a book.

"How many?" Rosa asked.

How many what, I wondered but kept my ignorance concealed.

Swinging into his saddle, Monte adjusted his pistol, bringing it within easy reach. "The first two had their feet wrapped in cloth. After them, four horses came up the road from the south. One rider, in moccasins, got down to study the tracks of the two that went up the ravine. Those four horses went up the draw after the hay wagons passed by.

"The shoes on the horses are fairly new, so those riding the horses would be Americans. And they were looking for whoever cut the wire. The other tracks, the ones made by the cutters, are almost invisible. You have to get down low to see them, especially this time of day. And it would take a mighty good tracker to have found that kind of track."

Like a fool, I blurted, "Like an Apache?"

"I'd say at least two," replied Monte. "I doubt one would go out by himself. And there's no tracks coming back down. Unless they came out a different way they're still up there somewhere, all six of them."

Rosa rode up next to Monte and I closed

in behind her. Without thinking too much about why I was doing it, I unslung my rifle. I had enough wits about me to keep the muzzle pointed in a safe direction, but it didn't occur to me to put a round into the chamber.

"I'll take the lead," Monte said softly. "Keep ten horse lengths between us. If I stop, you two stop." Monte nudged his mount forward. "Don't bunch up."

Monte rode out slowly, then after several seconds, Rosa followed. Waiting by the side of the road, I got a good look into the ravine for the first time. I could have touched both sides of it had I stretched out my arms. It was deeper than I'd imagined and full of shadowy twists and turns. Had I waited as long as I should have I would have lost sight of Rosa all together. With only five horse lengths separating us I nudged my horse forward.

Monte could not see the tracks of the wire cutters from the back of his horse but he knew it didn't matter. Four horses left a trail a blind man could follow and if an Apache was on one of those horses, he knew the wire cutters would have no place to hide.

The trail began to ascend, its sandy bottom giving way to loose gravel. In minutes the ravine widened and then forked, with the horse tracks veering to the right into a dry riverbed that drained a small canyon. Creosote peppered the sloping walls of the canyon with an occasional juniper twisting its way through piles of speckled gray boulders.

Entering the canyon, Monte spotted a small hut in an opening less than a quarter mile ahead. It appeared to be made of stone with a brush roof. Four horses stood in front of the hut and on the shaded side he could make out the gray silhouette of a man standing.

Monte turned as Rosa emerged from the ravine and waved her forward. Rosa in turn waved to me and we rode up side by side.

Pointing in the distance indicating the hut, Monte said, "Whoever's standing by that hut up there'll see us if he hasn't already. My guess is that he's not a scout, just regular army. I wouldn't expect him to be any trouble. I say we ride right in and see what he's up to."

Glad to be out of the dark ravine and back into the open, I felt a sense of relief. "Seems like a good idea. Once he knows we're Americans there shouldn't be any problem."

Rosa rolled her eyes and shook her head. My face flushed with heat. "I mean, Monte and I, of course."

Taking off her campaign hat, Rosa held it out to Monte. "We should trade. You look too much like a damned greaser. And that is not a hut. It is called a *jacal.*"

Monte removed the sombrero and handed it to Rosa. "Now that I know I'm half Mexican, I wonder if that makes me only half American."

My face flushed even hotter. I had no idea what to say. My eyes drifted to Rosa and I could see she was as stumped by the comment as I, perhaps even more so.

Putting on the hat, Monte's eyes narrowed. "Doesn't matter much. Not to me, anyway."

"Well," I said emphatically, "not to me either."

Monte looked at Rosa, a genuine question in his eyes. "What about you? Does it matter to you so much?"

Rosa looped the big sombrero over her saddle horn. Looking straight ahead, she answered sternly, "Maybe yes." But then, taking a strand of hair that had worked loose from one of her braids, she tucked it behind her ear and said thoughtfully, "Maybe no."

Monte grunted and turned his attention back to the hut. "That being the case, Rosa, remember this is my fight and not yours. No matter what happens, I can't have you killing American soldiers. You being a Villista and them up there after your general, I imagine the temptation to shoot them will cross your mind if it hasn't already."

Rosa stiffened. "You cannot tell me what to do in my own country!"

Monte sighed and then said evenly, "I'm not telling you to do anything. I'm telling you what I'll do. Lord knows I wouldn't want to, but I will."

Hesitating for a moment, Monte turned his head in Rosa's direction but his eyes never left the ground. "I'm asking you . . . to stay out of it."

Rosa fumed in silence for several seconds. "And I am telling you," she said rolling her shoulders and defiantly lifting her chin, "I will not fight for you. I'm telling you this, not asking for your permission to do anything."

Showing a wisdom I had not expected, Monte replied simply, "I understand."

"How should we ride in?" I asked.

"We'll stay close to each other now but I'll lead. I want whoever that is to see me and my uniform first."

Without being asked, Rosa slung her rifle over her shoulder and then I did the same. Monte glanced at us, nodded, and then started toward the hut at an easy walk.

When we were fifty paces from the *jacal* the man in its shadow stepped into the sunlight. We could see that he was white and a lieutenant. When we were a few feet from him Monte reined in and saluted.

The lieutenant returned the salute. "What is it, Private?"

"I'm looking for the Apache scouts," Monte said.

"That makes two of us, private," said the lieutenant, noticing Monte's moccasins. "What business is it of yours?"

Monte dismounted. I could see the lieutenant was tall, at least two inches taller than Monte, with an athletic build. His face was sunburned. He had an aquiline nose, thin mustache, and wide-set blue eyes.

"First of all," said Monte, "who are you, Lieutenant?"

"I'm Lieutenant Shannon. I command the scouts. And you?"

"I'm Private Segundo," Monte said, noticing that all four horses had scabbards with rifles still in them. "Idaho Militia."

"Militia? National Guard?"

"That's right," said Monte, his eyes searching the sand around the hut and then the horses tied out front.

"I wasn't aware we had called up the Guard."

"Where are the three scouts?" Monte asked as he took one knee and rubbed his hand over a sandal print in the sand.

Shannon studied Monte for a moment. "They were gone when I got here. We spotted tracks down on the road. The scouts took off up a gully so quickly that we got separated.

"I've been waiting here for over an hour. There's a roll of our buzz-wire inside this hut and wire cutters. Whoever lives here cut our wire. It's been happening all along the road. We were sent out to put a stop to it."

"I'll go look for your scouts," offered Monte. Coming to his feet, he gathered the reins of his horse. "You might want to stay here in case they come back, Lieutenant."

Shannon looked at Rosa and then at me. "Who are they?"

"The woman's a local guide. The other man is assigned to me."

"Billy Cabott," I said. Then thinking quickly, added, "I work for the *Chicago Tribune*. I'm assigned to Private Segundo. I'm to go where he goes."

Frowning at me with obvious disapproval, Shannon said, "Alright, Private. I'll wait here. Report back in one hour if possible. The scouts are led by a private named Norroso. You'll recognize him by the scar on his face. Make it clear to him he is to return immediately."

Recalling Norroso was one of the scouts in the news photo in his hip pocket, Monte saluted. "Yes, sir," he replied in proper military fashion and then swung back into his saddle.

Without any hint of uncertainty and yet with no sign of a trail, Monte headed off to the southeast. With us close behind we rode upward around dozens of jutting boulders and stands of gnarled juniper until reaching the crest of hill high above the hut. We then angled down a gentle slope that led into what Rosa called a box canyon, slowly being engulfed in late afternoon shadow.

Halfway to the bottom of the canyon, Monte drew up beside a lone juniper, dismounted, and tied his horse. As we did the same, he spoke softly. "From here, we go on foot."

"Why did we come this way?" I asked.

"Tracks. The Mexicans were in a hurry. Theirs were easy to see. The Apache tracks were harder to pick up but they were following the Mexicans at a dogtrot. Those Mexicans are probably dead by now. If they're lucky."

Monte palmed his Colt. "Rosa, what I said earlier don't apply to Apaches. Them you can kill if you want."

Every trace of belligerence was clearly missing from Rosa's usual demeanor and the change in her unsettled me. When she slipped the Mauser off her shoulder she glanced at me. I was completely unnerved when I saw that her eyes were rimmed with fear.

She nodded her head, indicating my rifle. "Put a bullet into the chamber," she whispered. "Do it quietly and keep your finger on the safety."

"You two stay back aways and stay together," Monte said. "Try to keep me in sight but watch your back trail. Keep your eyes and ears open. Be as still as you can. Don't look for men. Look for movement. Any kind, any size."

Bending low, Monte crept along the side of the hill, while shoulder-to-shoulder, Rosa and I rested on one knee and watched. I could hear my breathing. I could hear Rosa's breathing. But Monte moved over the rocks and through the brush like a ghost. Not even a pebble rolled.

When he was a stone's throw ahead of us, Rosa looked left and right. Understanding I was to follow Rosa, my eyes swept the hillside behind us.

"Ready?" she asked, her voice hushed and

seemingly calm.

"Ready," I answered feeling a pounding deep in my chest.

Monte studied the winding canyon in front of him. The fading light was making it difficult to see the tracks but he knew that people and animals would naturally select the easiest path through any terrain and that the fleeing Mexicans would be no different.

He had seen no track in several minutes but was following the most likely escape route when he caught sight of a heel print made by a Mexican sandal. Lifting the branches of a creosote he saw another but both were facing the direction he had come.

Monte looked closer. The heel prints were too deep. They had been made by walking backwards, by men trying to confuse those tracking them.

Knowingly, Monte shook his head. The wire cutters knew they were being pursued but such a simple trick would never fool a good tracker, much less an Apache. The Mexicans had wasted valuable time attempting a ruse.

A gentle gust of wind, stirred by the setting sun, drifted down the canyon and brushed Monte's cheek. He sniffed and then sniffed again, detecting the faint smell of smoke.

The vision he had seen so often, of him being thrown into a fire by a faceless Apache flashed in his mind. For the first time, he realized that on that day there had also been the smell of smoke. If he had been in cactus instead of flames the fire had to have been coming from something else.

Shaking off the distorted memory, Monte moved forward, every sense alert. He dropped into a shallow ravine that marked a turn in the canyon. Under a bush, he eased his head over the crusted rim of the arroyo. One hundred yards in front of him, the canyon flared into an acre of smooth sand. In its center was a cluster of basket-sized granite boulders and a single juniper, a large tree that had clung to the dry riverbed. A wisp of smoke curled above the top of the branches.

Monte strained his eyes. The ground was turned over at the far end of the acre of sand. And there were drag marks.

Swearing bitterly, Monte scoured the steep walls of the canyon. If the Apaches were up there he knew there was little chance of seeing them but he looked anyway, taking the time to think.

The scouts had left their rifles with their horses and he had never heard of an Indian being a good shot with a pistol. And he was in uniform. That would confuse them. And the scouts had intentionally left Shannon behind assuming he could never follow them. Whatever they had done to the Mexicans they had done thinking the army would never find out. But since shooting a soldier would be difficult to cover up, the Apaches would most likely run, circle, and get back to their horses undetected. Then they would deny any involvement in killing the Mexicans.

There was a chance the three scouts were still nearby but if they were they would have scattered. The only chance remaining was to go directly to the juniper, pick a set of tracks, and follow them.

Making his decision, Monte climbed out of the ravine and stood upright. With no attempt to conceal himself, he walked down a slope and onto the flattened bed of sand. Checking his back trail, he was pleased that he saw no sign of anyone.

Monte gazed up at the hillsides surrounding him on three sides. He saw nothing but knew the Apaches were near. He could feel it, feel it the same as he could feel a spider crawling up his leg or the wind in his hair. Some called such an ability a sixth sense. Monte Segundo, however, never gave it a name or a second thought. He merely trusted his instincts.

Striding across the riverbed toward the smoke, Monte tried to brace himself for what he would see. The vivid image of his tortured father darted in and out of his thoughts. He began to take deep anxiety-filled breaths, the same breaths he took each time he tried in vain to gut a deer or elk.

Sweat broke out on his forehead and upper lip as he approached the juniper. The smell of smoke mixed with that of burning hair.

Rounding a small boulder that lay at the trunk of the juniper, Monte slowed and then stopped. He saw two sandal-clad feet stretched out over the sand. They were tied at the ankles with strips of leather and had been staked wide apart.

Monte gritted his teeth and took two quick steps, forcing himself not to take his eyes off the Mexican.

The head of the Mexican was down. His arms had been tied backwards around the trunk of the juniper. Coals still glowed in the fire that had been built in his crotch, now a black mass of smoldering, oozing flesh.

Shifting his eyes to his right, Monte saw another rope encircling a larger boulder that stood higher than his head. Hardly feeling his legs, hardly aware that he was walking, Monte approached the boulder knowing full well the second Mexican had been lashed to the other side. Again, he braced himself, trying desperately to keep his wits about him.

When he saw the Mexican, he froze. The man's arms were tied wide apart, tight enough to suspend him several inches off the bloodstained sand. His legs had been tied together. From a distance, he looked as if he had been crucified on the face of the rock. But where his stomach had been there was a gaping hole.

The instant Monte saw the disemboweled Mexican he also saw his own father's gruesome death and the face of the Apache who had thrown him into the cactus. Only this time, the face of the Apache lingered in his mind and was crystal clear. So was the fresh, purple scar that ran from the corner of the Indian's mouth to the bottom of his ear. There was no more doubt. The Apache who had murdered his father and mother was Norroso.

At the sight of the Mexican's intestines splayed out on the sand, Monte leaned forward and vomited, and then vomited again. When he raised himself up, tears began to roll down his cheeks. Wide-eyed at the thought of weeping, he wiped the tears away, blinking hard to clear his vision.

"Pa!" he moaned softly. "Oh, Pa."

He had not remembered ever having shed a single tear over anything or anyone. But now he knew that was not the case. The day of the raid he had screamed and cried when they attacked his mother and tortured his father. He was still crying when Norroso threw him into the cactus. It was coming back to him, in torn, ragged fragments, his buried memories once again being forced to the surface.

Hearing heavy footsteps in the sand, Monte swiped his eyes with the back of his sleeve. Turning he saw Rosa and I skirting the edge of the juniper. We jerked to a halt and stared at the first Mexican.

The fear that I had bottled up inside me now churned with nausea as shock set in. Rosa, on the other hand, seemed immune to it all. Recovering from her initial surprise, she went to the man, cupped his chin, and raised his head. He had been gagged with a dirty strip of cloth torn from his shirt. His eyes were half open but seeing nothing. Somehow, he was still breathing.

Rosa looked at Monte. She saw the look on his face but from where we stood neither of us could see the second Mexican. "The other is there?" she asked.

Monte nodded, pointing with the barrel of his pistol. "What's left of him."

Taking long strides, Rosa went around the large boulder and directly to the second Mexican. This time, however, she hesitated long enough to gulp down a few breaths of air before lifting the man's dangling head.

The man had also been gagged but, mercifully, he was dead.

Glancing at Monte, Rosa took out her pistol. I had not moved. I saw her coming toward me but my mind was not registering. Nothing seemed real. Things were happening in slow motion, in a haze.

I saw Rosa walk up to the burned Mexican, saw her put the pistol to the back of his head, and heard the shot. But in all that, nothing was real. No time passed. No breath was taken. No sensation was felt. And it was serenely quiet, even the blast of the pistol was muffled, no more than the sound of a popping cork.

Monte and Rosa met in front of me. At first nothing they said was more to me than a dull hum. Slowly, I began to hear them speaking but the words sounded distant and made no sense. But even in that thick, swirling, nauseous moment I knew that my life had changed; I would never be the same person I was only seconds before. Death has a way of doing that. Until we see it, experience it, we are but fools on a picnic.

Taking a few steps away from Rosa, Monte started walking in a zigzag pattern. With his eyes fastened on the sand he worked back and forth taking several dozen paces one direction, then turning, taking a few paces, and then coming back in the opposite direction. He was searching for sign and in what seemed like seconds, though I'm certain it was longer, he started off angling up the far side of the canyon, opposite the one we had come down.

Noticing the rope encircling the back side of the large boulder, I started toward it, stumbling with my first steps. I heard my shoes churning the sand beneath them, I was aware of the sickening stench of burned flesh and hair, yet my mind was blank.

I saw a hand first, clinched tight into a fist, the rope cutting into the wrist. I dropped my eyes and kept walking until I was directly in front of the dead man. I could see where Monte had stood. I saw his moccasin prints or at least I thought they were his. There were tracks everywhere, not cut sharply into the river bottom like those of a boot but dull and rounded. They would have landed softly, quietly.

Stopping, I slowly raised my eyes. My stomach seemed to catch fire. I felt dizzy. It was hard to breathe, no not to breathe but to get enough air into my lungs, at least enough to do me any good. Gasping, I turned away.

Suddenly very aware of the rifle in my hand, the steel trigger guard, the smooth wood forestock, and thick front sight, I staggered back to Rosa.

"How," I asked, struggling to get the words out, "how could anyone do that?"

Rosa ignored me. She was watching Monte work his way up the east side of the canyon through the rocks and clumps of brush. And with her rifle at the ready, she was watching everything around him as well.

"We are losing the light," Rosa said. "If you cannot see your front sight, aim and shoot anyway. You will be close."

Realizing Monte was in danger, my head began to clear. I followed Rosa's eyes and caught sight of Monte as he passed in front of a light-colored slab of granite. He seemed little more than a speck from where we stood.

Minutes passed and I knew I was all but useless. I could never hit a target that small and I could barely see Monte, his green uniform blending with the drab creosote and juniper. For some inexplicable reason, I looked behind us and gazed at the fading outline of the western side of the canyon.

At first I thought it was nothing but then it moved. It moved slowly but it did move. Perhaps one hundred and fifty yards out, the object, a mere patch of darkness, darted behind a bush.

Without thinking, I fingered off the safety and raised the rifle. The front and rear sights were fuzzy. I focused on the bush the best I could. I squeezed the trigger. The muzzle blast flashed and the recoil knocked me backwards. I completely lost sight of the bush.

Rosa spun. "You saw something?" she demanded.

"I did. Moving back the way we came."

Turning back, Rosa tried to find Monte again but it was growing too dark. She lowered her rifle. "Soon it will be no use. Not even *El Muerte* can see moccasin tracks at night."

"I hope we find them," I said. "I hope we find whoever did this. They're animals. Worse than animals."

Rosa nodded slowly. "They are Apaches."

It was dark when we heard Monte's voice.

"It's me. I'm coming in."

We saw him approaching across the open stretch of sand, now painted silver-blue in the starlight. A steady warm breeze came from the north but the heat of the day was gone. Rosa and I were waiting upwind to avoid the sickening stench of the bodies.

"We best get back to the horses and hope they're still there," Monte said, still walking toward us. "Who shot?"

"I did. Something was moving on the other side of the canyon. I think it was one of them."

"It was," Monte said, stopping an arm's length in front of Rosa and me. "I saw him from where I was. He went on over the ridge and back toward the *jacal.*

"At least he wasn't heading for our horses. But I didn't see the other two. They must've left in a hurry."

"You think they'll come back?" I asked.

"No. They'll want to get back to their lieutenant and hope what they did here isn't found out."

I was confused. "Aren't we going to report this?"

"Thought about it. But what would we say? We found two dead men but never saw who killed them. We know who did it but the Apaches would say they weren't anywhere near here or they came here and the men were already dead. These are Pershing's Pets, remember? Who do you think the army would believe, us or them?"

"This wasn't war," I said. "This was murder. No, it was worse than murder. It was torture."

"Yep. Apache style."

"Why would they do such a thing?" I asked.

"They enjoy it," Rosa said. "To kill is one thing, even to enjoy killing, but to torture is an evil thing. It is of the devil. They find pleasure in it."

"We better get back to the horses," Monte said. "We'll need a place to camp for the night."

"We should bury them," Rosa said. "They died hard. It is the least we can do for them."

Monte sighed. He thought of his father, wondering if anyone had buried him. And then he wondered the same about his mother. "Alright. I'll get the horses. I saw a well back at the *jacal* so I'll take them back there and water them. And I want to make sure the Apaches and Shannon aren't still there.

"You can go ahead and make a fire if you want. If there's anything to eat at the hut

I'll bring it back. I shouldn't be gone more than an hour or so."

"If they're there," Rosa said grimly, "kill them all."

We built a fire with waist-high flames, which gave us enough light to dig in the sandy river bottom. We used sticks and our hands but had barely gone down two feet when we hit cobblestones. On our knees, we finished the second grave and stopped digging. Our eyes met. One side of our sweaty faces glistened in the dancing firelight, the other half was blackened by the night.

"Which one first?" I asked, wishing I could dig a little longer.

"The one I gave the mercy shot," answered Rosa. She brushed her palms on her thighs, knocking off some of the grit. "He will be easier."

I nodded faintly. "And the other. How do we . . ."

"Do not think, Billy. Do not even think. We do it. That is how such a thing is done. Without thinking. We know what to do."

Rosa stood first and then I got to my feet and slapped the sand off the legs of my trousers. The knots that bound the men's arms were too tight to untie so Monte had cut them loose before leaving. Thankfully, he had intentionally left a foot of rope dangling from each wrist and ankle.

I grabbed the rope tied to the Mexican's left wrist and Rosa the right. We dragged him on his back. I looked ahead, concentrating on the grave, grateful for the darkness of it. I thought of nothing but the hole, the black hole.

We slid him in. His feet dropped with a thud. Resting his arms beside him, we began shoving the sand in with our feet. When the body was lightly covered and unrecognizable, we dropped to our knees and shoved with the palms of our hands as quickly as we could. In less than a minute the deed was done.

Rosa looked at me. "Stay here until I call you," she said as she picked up a forked stick and stood up.

I glanced at the stick. I tried not to think what it was for but my mind was too quick. I dropped my head and turned away from the fire, but I was well aware that Rosa was going to use the stick to scrape up as much of the second man as she could and then put it back inside him. As soon as Rosa stepped away I crawled into the night and vomited.

I wiped the acid from my lips. Looking up at the stars, I shut out all thought. A few moments later Rosa called. "Come now."

I avoided looking directly at the corpse but in my peripheral vision I saw that Rosa had tossed sand over the entrails she had piled back into the man's body. In the firelight, it could have been a layer of dirt, nothing more, nothing as gruesome as it could have been.

The second grave was covered as quickly as the first. They were close together, side by side. It only seemed right.

"Rocks," said Rosa. "We must cover the graves with rocks now."

"Because they were Catholics?" I asked.

"No. Because of the coyotes."

Another horrible thought tore through my flimsy mental blockade. Not even the dead were safe. "What kind of a place is this?" I muttered.

"Rocks," repeated Rosa. "As big as your head or bigger. Lots of rocks."

Monte found the horses undisturbed and led them back through the brush and over the hills to where he'd last seen Shannon. He stopped on a rise and stood motionless. A quarter moon lit the bare dirt that surrounded the hut and he could easily see the four horses were gone. There was no fire outside the hut and no smoke coming from the crooked metal pipe that jutted from its roof.

Knowing the lieutenant and his scouts were long gone, Monte mounted and rode down to a stone-lined well that was at the mouth of a nearby ravine. A metal bucket was there with a rope tied to it.

Taking one last look around, Monte dismounted. He lowered the bucket and then hoisted it up, thankful the well was shallow. Holding the bucket under his horse's nose he let him drink his fill and then lowered the bucket and did the same for the other two horses.

After tying them to a nearby post, Monte went to the front door of the hut, which was wide open. He struck a match and stepped inside. Two ragged blankets lay on a dirt floor that was littered with corn husks. A pair of rusty wire cutters leaned in one corner next to a gallon-sized cooking pot. Other than that, the hut was empty.

Dropping the match, Monte crushed it under his foot and then stepped back outside into the moonlight. He stood for a moment, listening to the night sounds. He was about to take a step when he caught a flicker of movement from the corner of his eye, a movement at the edge of the brush fifty feet to his right. Moving only his eyes, he focused on a gray-blue lump the size of a man's head. It moved again, but this time it hopped a few inches and then stopped.

Monte slid his pistol out of its scabbard. He was tired of cheese and jerky and he was hungry. He cocked the hammer back and eased the pistol up. The front sight gleamed in the moonlight and he settled it on the dark lump. Holding the sight dead-center, he touched the trigger, flooding the blackness with thunder and flame. And then it was quiet, the night instantly absorbing the sound and light as if nothing had happened.

Waiting for his eyes to recover from the muzzle flash, Monte listened. A distant coyote barked and then yipped warily. After that there was complete silence.

The forty-five slug would do a lot of damage to a rabbit. If the entrails weren't cleaned out quickly the meat would spoil. But Monte knew that when he took aim. He knew it in the back of his mind. And still he had pulled the trigger. No, it was not a deer, an animal the size of a man, but animals and men were all the same on the inside.

Monte holstered his pistol and then pulled out his knife, holding it low by his side. He told himself the night would help. Blocking everything from his mind, he thought of nothing but the rabbit. He started forward, rolling the knife in his hand so that the blade was up.

Kneeling next to the rabbit, Monte grabbed a hind leg and spun the animal around on its back with the head pointing away. He felt the knife in his palm, vaguely aware he was not clinching the grip and that he was raising the blade and moving it closer to the white underbelly.

Not thinking, not feeling, Monte placed the tip of the blade in the crotch of the rabbit. He sunk the tip ever so slightly into the skin and flicked the blade upward. A tuft of hair and skin came up as he lifted the blade.

For a split second he paused, expecting the usual wave of panic to overwhelm him. But then he quickly lowered the blade, this time slipping the razor-sharp edge just under the skin of the rabbit and sliding it all the way up the rib cage.

Monte watched the glossy mass of organs ooze out of the body as if they were being shoved out by an unseen hand. Even though he had taken hundreds of animals from the forest, it was a sight he had never seen.

Still holding the rabbit's hind leg with his left hand, Monte sheathed his knife and clenched his teeth.

Reaching into the slime, he jerked the

entrails free and flung them to the side.

He held his right hand up. Even in the moonlight he could see the blood covering it and could smell the acidic stench.

Holding the rabbit, Monte came to his feet. He started for the well. Only then did he take a deep breath, held it, and then slowly exhaled. He felt his heart beating heavily but realized his stomach was not nauseous. And his hands were steady.

"Damn," he whispered. He smiled faintly. "All this time. I'll be a son of bitch."

Our fire illuminated the lower branches of the juniper tree and reflected off the surrounding boulders and rocks. We worked hard covering the graves, desiring to protect them from scavengers but also to keep our minds occupied. We had barely finished stacking the stones when we heard the crunch of horse's hooves gouging their way across the packed sand.

Rosa tossed a few sticks on the fire. She grabbed her rifle and backed into the shadows of the juniper. I merely stood between the two graves staring blankly into the darkness.

"That you, Monte?" I asked raising my voice but not calling out.

"It's me."

Monte spoke no louder than he always did but in the box canyon sound traveled well and it was a full minute before his ghostly outline drifted into the light.

"If you let that bonfire cool off some," Monte said, coming into sharper view, "we can cook some rabbit. I got a nice cottontail over by the hut. Found a pot, too, and filled our canteens."

Monte rode closer and stopped. Handing the reins of the led horses to Rosa, he glanced at the graves behind us.

"The Apaches were not there?" Rosa asked.

"Nobody was," said Monte, dismounting. "Just the rabbit and the pot."

Rosa led our two horses to the juniper and tied them. From mine, she began untying the pot Monte had lashed to the saddle horn.

Monte stepped over to the far side of Rosa. "The rabbit's in the pot," he said and then tied his horse.

Rosa stopped working the knot and glared at Monte. "I am not your *soldadera.*"

"Soldadera?" repeated Monte with just a hint of sarcasm in his tone. "Now, I don't remember. Didn't you say that was the same as a soldier?"

"No," Rosa said indignantly, "a *soldadera*

is anything but a soldier. She is a wife or girlfriend, sometimes just a woman that takes care of her man, her 'Juan.' They carry the blankets and food, even the stone mortar and pestle to grind the corn for the tortillas. They make the fires, cook and keep the beds warm at night. I have no 'Juan.' I am a captain!"

"Well in that case, Captain," Monte responded, offering a mock salute, "I'll cook the damned varmint myself."

Rosa jerked the knot free and grasped the pot. "You would burn it. That is why I will cook your puny rabbit."

I saw Monte smile. "Want to use my puny knife?"

Rosa huffed, "No one needs a knife to skin a rabbit."

Still smiling, Monte replied, "Not if you have a sharp enough tongue."

This time Rosa was confused and she glanced at me for clarification.

I shrugged. "It's just a saying."

Rosa reached inside the pot, pulled the rabbit out by its ears, and held it in the firelight. The fur was damp and there was no blood on it anywhere.

"At least I won't have to clean it," Rosa said.

"No," said Monte, suddenly serious. "No,

299

you sure as hell won't."

Rosa took a few steps and then sat on a small boulder near the fire. She began to strip the skin off the rabbit using only her fingers.

I watched her for a moment, amazed at how quickly she worked. I then turned to Monte. "What do we do now? Tomorrow, I mean."

"First, I'll try and pick up the Apache's trail. Likely, they met back up with their lieutenant and rode back to the road. And it's just as likely their base camp is nearby. That buzz-wire couldn't have been down too long before the Apaches found the cut. My guess is they're camped no more than a day's ride from here.

"If they are, we do what we did in Colonia Dublan. Sooner or later they'll be sent out again. That's when I'll get my chance to even things up, now that I know for sure it was Norroso that killed my Ma and Pa."

"How do you know?" I asked.

"Because," said Monte, "when I came across that gutted Mexican it came back to me. The face of the Apache that threw me into the cactus had a fresh scar on his face. Just like the one Rosa noticed in my newspaper picture. It was Norroso alright. I saw him clear as day."

"San Antonio de las Arenales," Rosa said, still peeling the rabbit as one would a banana. "If your army is camped near here, that is where they will be. Many roads go into and leave San Antonio. If Pershing has to withdraw because of what happened in Parral, he will make a base near San Antonio."

The flames of the fire danced wickedly in the black of Monte's eyes. "Then tomorrow we go to San Antonio de las Arenales."

CHAPTER 10

Four miles southwest of San Antonio the desert began to buckle and then gradually roll its way up to the base of another mountain range. At the base of the mountains we camped in a natural bowl with high ground encircling our campfire. Using the binoculars, we could easily see San Antonio below us, and by taking a few steps to the north we could watch the roads that led east to Guerrero, west to Chihuahua, and south to Cusi. In fact, we could observe a military column leaving San Antonio in any direction.

Rosa and Monte had agreed that if Villa was in the area he would hide in the mountains and there were none east of San Antonio. If the army sent a column after Villa or his men, they would most likely deploy it to the west or southwest.

The first two days in our camp we were puzzled to see clouds of dust rising from all points of the compass but all drifting toward San Antonio. Eventually we deduced that the entire United States Army was concentrating forces there but we had no idea why. The third morning Rosa left her rifle with us and rode down to San Antonio to discover what was happening and, if she was lucky, what the army's plans might be.

That night Monte and I sat around our campfire staring into the flames. It was the first time Rosa had not been with us in nearly two weeks and her absence made both of us uneasy. But we were uneasy for completely different reasons.

I stirred the fire with a crooked juniper branch. "Do you think the Apaches would recognize Rosa if they saw her?"

"I think they were too far away to get a good look at her. They know there was a woman with us but that's about it."

"She's a brave woman," I said, thinking how she had gathered the remains of the Mexican with a stick not unlike the one I held in my hand. "I've never known a woman like her."

Monte sighed heavily. "You got that right."

I glanced at Monte from the corners of my eyes. "I think she likes you."

"Me?" Monte snorted. "She'd sooner claw my eyes out than look at me."

"I don't think so. I think she likes you."

Monte was quiet for several moments. "What would a man do with a woman like that?"

I flicked a glowing coal back into the fire. "Maybe she's asking herself the same question about you."

Shaking his head, Monte laughed. "We'd make quite a pair, wouldn't we? Probably kill each other in a week."

I brought my stick out of the flames and studied the smoke that whirled upward from its tip but hadn't yet caught fire. "You'd have to learn to talk to each other, that's for certain. But I've seen her look at you when she doesn't know I'm watching. She admires you. I'd bet on it."

Monte shrugged. "She's a pretty one. Anybody can see that. And she's tough. A good woman's gotta be tough. Sooner or later everybody runs into hard times."

I smiled at Monte's comments but only faintly. "She's been through a lot. If it were me, I'd start out slowly. Give her time to adjust."

"I'm not about to start anything with her." Monte paused and for a moment looked up at the stars. "Oh, hell, Billy, she's *loco* and so are you."

A voice sounded from the darkness behind

us. "Who's *loco*?"

It was Rosa and she was leading her horse into the light. She stopped a few feet from us both. There was dust on her blouse and face. "So, you think I'm *loco*?"

"No, Rosa," I said. "We were talking about someone else. About a woman that liked Monte."

Rosa huffed and wiped her face with the back of her hand. "Poor woman. She would have to be *loco*."

Monte glanced at me, rolled his eyes, and then frowned at Rosa. "What'd you find out?"

"That we must leave tonight," Rosa said flatly. "A gray-haired major called Howze is packing in a hurry. He has a machine-gun troop and at least two hundred fifty soldiers of the Eleventh Cavalry. He is loading a pack train with three days' rations. He and the Apaches are going to Rancho Ojos Azules to attack the Villistas that are there, about two hundred of them. If they can find a guide tonight, they will attack in the morning."

"How do you know all this?" I asked.

"Howze was looking for guides to take him to the *rancho*. He asked many Mexicans in San Antonio but none would go. But the Mexicans that would not guide for him told me of his plans. That is how I know."

Monte stood slowly. "Do you know where that ranch is?"

"Yes. We follow a road south to the village of Cusi and then head southwest. Howze must stop at Cusi and will try to get the Carrancistas there to guide him to the ranch. They will refuse, but there are some Americans living there and they may agree to show him the way. All of this will take time and it will give us a chance to get to the *rancho* ahead of him."

"Can you find the ranch in the dark?" asked Monte, as he lifted his saddle blanket and saddle.

"Yes. But we must hurry. Howze may have left already."

I scrambled to my feet, feeling my heart jump inside my chest. This would be different than anything we'd done before. We were headed for a battle between two armies, hundreds of men trying to kill each other and likely us, too, since we were sticking our noses right in the middle of it. Once again, I suppressed my fear and, doing my best to appear eager, jumped to my feet. I couldn't handle both my saddle and blanket at the same time so I snatched my blanket, took a few steps, and tossed it on my horse.

"How far is it to the ranch?" I asked

returning for my saddle.

"Maybe forty miles. It will take all night."

Inside I winced. It would be another long, painful ride but, looking on the bright side, I had just enjoyed two days' rest. And besides that, my posterior seemed to be getting tougher by the day.

"What does the ranch look like?" Monte asked, sliding a steel bit into his horse's mouth. "How's it laid out for a fight?"

Rosa picked up her rifle and slung it over her shoulder. "It has three big adobes that are built like forts. The roofs are flat and can hold many soldiers. Behind the ranch are hills that run up into the mountains."

Monte swung into his saddle as I finished cinching mine and tying it off. He thought for a moment and then said, "If they do things by the book, the army will try and surround the place and cut off any retreat. And that retreat would be the hills behind the ranch. They'll want a surprise attack and sending a bunch of horses into those hills would make too much of a racket. I'm thinking that's where Howze will send his Indians. They'll sneak in first and on foot. Then the rest of the company will come in three groups, one straight on and the other two flanking from the sides."

I saddled up and happened to glance at

Rosa, who still stood by the fire holding the reins of her horse. She was staring down but I could see she was deep in thought. With the toe of her sandals she began shoving sand over the flames. Before she buried the last ray of light, I saw her look up at Monte. What I saw in her eyes worried me.

As Rosa started off, cutting across the hills to the southeast, I wondered what I had seen, what filled her eyes with such perplexity. The pace she set across the rugged terrain was almost more than I could handle and I had no time to ponder. It wasn't until we reached the road to Cusi that I was able to think of anything but sticking to the seat of my saddle.

We could see from the lack of tracks on the road that we had managed to get ahead of Howze and his troops so we settled into an easy gallop. My mind began to clear and when it finally did I knew immediately why Rosa had looked so perplexed.

The Villistas at the Ojos Azules ranch were Rosa's people, her comrades. They were about to suffer a surprise attack, likely an all-out assault from four different directions. She would naturally want to warn them, warn them any way she could.

I thought of Monte. He had figured out the army's strategy in a matter of seconds.

Would he also predict what Rosa would try and do? If she warned the Mexicans in time, the surprise attack would fail and the Americans would ride into a waiting barrage of bullets. Knowing that, would Monte try and stop Rosa from warning the Villistas or, I wondered, did he even care what happened to the troops? Was he, after all, only interested in avenging his parents, in killing Norroso no matter the cost?

And what if Monte did try and stop Rosa, what then? Would he shoot her? Would she shoot him? Would she then shoot me?

Throughout the long ride, I thought about the inevitable dilemma awaiting us. I thought about Villa attacking Columbus, of the United States invading Mexico, of the brutal Mexican revolution, the war in Europe, and, above all, the unimaginable cruelty of the Apaches. To me, the entire world was going insane.

And yet, barely a month had passed since I arrived in New Mexico. Up to that point, the world to me was nothing more than my personal playground, a bowl full of cherries picked and handed to me on a silver platter.

Ahead of me now was a battlefield of death and destruction. Minute by minute, that reality began to consume me, to compress my entire being into a single moment in which there was no past and no future. The present was all that existed, and in that razor-thin moment of time; life itself hung in the balance and the black threat of death reigned supreme.

Even so, like a slave to my own destiny, I rode on. God only knows why. And suddenly I found myself believing in God and for the first time in my life I was praying. I prayed not to die. And if I was to die, I prayed not to suffer.

The horses were lathered in a soapy sweat when we slowed to a fast walk and rode through the sleeping village of Cusi. Not a single lantern or even a candle was seen burning in the entire pueblo. A dog barked bravely from the security of the shadows. It was answered by another and then another. We were a half-mile out of the village before the barking ceased but no curiosity was aroused and no light was ever lit.

A few minutes beyond Cusi we reached a fork in the road and took the western branch, which was little more than a cart path sliced through the sand and cactus. The road soon began to rise and fall as it rolled steadily higher, climbing toward the dingy expanse of a mountain range. I glanced over my right shoulder, finding the

North Star and the Big Dipper. Calculating the time and our speed, I figured we had to be more than halfway to the ranch and that we would be there, or nearly there, in two hours. We would be ahead of the U.S. Cavalry but likely only by minutes. When they arrived, I knew there would be little time to think.

Rosa was still in the lead and several horse lengths in front of Monte. I kicked my horse but, not allowing him to break into a trot, came up beside Monte. He guessed I wanted to talk and we both slowed slightly allowing Rosa to gain some distance.

"What is it?" Monte asked, keeping his voice low.

"I'm worried about Rosa."

"About what?"

I hesitated. "Well, she said Howze was planning a surprise attack. That puts the Villistas at a disadvantage." Biting the inside of my lip, I hesitated again. "And Rosa is a Villista."

We rode for a few seconds before Monte responded. "I thought of that, too. I figure she'll make a break for it when we get close. She'll go in and warn her people. She'd naturally want to do that."

I nodded vigorously, thankful that Monte was not angered by my concern. "And that will put our troops in danger. More than they would have been in, anyway."

"Yeah. It will do that."

I waited for Monte to say more but all I heard was the dull thud of horses' hooves and the creak of saddle leather. Finally, I spoke up.

"But that's not right. We've got to do something."

"Yep. We do. All three of us," Monte said flatly. "You know it, I know it, and Rosa knows it."

Shaking my head, I said, "I don't get it."

"Think about it, Billy. Rosa found out there was to be a surprise attack on her people and she came and told us about it. She could've ridden straight to warn them and left us out of it all together. You got to ask yourself why she did that."

It was a question I hadn't even considered. "What do you make of it?"

Monte glanced up at the stars, no doubt checking the time. "There's a couple of ways to look at it but I figure it's this way. She's gonna run off and join up with the Villistas because she's one of them. And she wants me to be there to go after the Apaches."

"But what about me?" I asked. "What does she think I'm going to do? I can't just sit by and watch our men ride into waiting gunfire."

I was glaring at Monte as I spoke. I saw him look at me and even in the starlight I saw him smile. "She knows that, Billy."

It took several seconds for Monte's words to make sense to me. Slowly, my head cleared. "Then I'm to warn our troops? Tell them that the Mexicans are waiting for them?"

"That's your decision."

We rode through a dozen more hoofbeats before a thought occurred to me. "You said there were a couple of ways to think about this. What's the other way?"

Monte shrugged. "She's planning on killing us both within the next hour or so."

A jolt of something resembling electricity shot through my body and down the length of my arms and legs. My heart jumped as it had a habit of doing and I knew immediately what Monte had said was a surefire possibility.

"Do you think she would do that?"

"I guess we'll find out soon enough. You'd best be ready for anything."

At that moment, I was silently asking, "Oh, God, what version of hell have I gotten myself into?" and yet, what dribbled out of my mouth was an unconvincing lie. "Oh, no. I'm not worried about Rosa. She wouldn't do such a thing. Not to us."

"You never know with a woman," Monte said.

"What about you? What about the Apaches?"

"Nothing changes."

"But there'll be no surprise attack after I warn them," I protested. "Major Howze will call it off."

"No. Even if you get to the major and he believes what you have to tell him, they'll keep coming. They're not about to turn back."

"Why wouldn't I get to Major Howze?" I asked. "Won't he be coming up the same road we'll be on?"

Monte looked over at me, his face too shadowed for me to read. "The Apaches will be out in front of the main column. Most of them will be fanned out on both sides of the road. But a few will be on the road and they'll have seen our tracks for miles. It's likely they'll put two and two together and figure those tracks belong to us, to the same three riders that found the dead Mexicans.

"Those Apaches may not want you to talk to the major. Could be, they'll figure you're gonna tell Howze what you saw in that dry gulch."

314

Thinking of the tortured men I shuddered. "I never thought of that."

"Two things I'd do if I was you. I'd tie a white rag on the end of your rifle barrel and ride with it up in plain sight. And as soon as they get close enough, I'd order them, order them real loud, to take you to Lieutenant Shannon or Major Howze. Don't show any fear. Act like you own that road and everything on it."

"You think that'll work?"

"Maybe. And just maybe, if you're lucky, Shannon will be right there with them."

Realizing the next hour might be my last, time seemed to evaporate. In what seemed like seconds the three of us were gathering in the middle of the main road that led to Ojos Azules.

The horses were lathered and blowing hard, their chests heaving as they sucked in the night air. Rosa was first to speak.

"A mile ahead there is another fork in the road. The hacienda, the ranch, is to the left."

Neither Monte nor I replied, each of us waiting for Rosa to make her move.

Rosa hesitated. "I will go to the ranch," Rosa said, her voice softening with uncertainty.

"I don't want you to do that," said Monte.

"I am a Villista," said Rosa, her tone more forceful now.

"I know that, Rosa," Monte said. "I know you are."

I felt it was time to say my piece so I said, "And I'm an American. I have to warn those behind us that the Villistas know they're coming."

"Then you will let me go?" asked Rosa. "You will not try and stop me?"

"No, I won't," Monte answered. "But I will ask you not to go."

"Ask me not to go?" questioned Rosa, clearly confused. "Why?"

Monte looked to the side and then rubbed the stubble on his jaw with his knuckles. "Because, damn it, I don't want to see you get hurt. That's why."

I don't know who was more stunned, Rosa or me, but amidst my fear and anxiety, I somehow smiled. I came to realize that emotions of all sorts can sometimes mix together. At that moment, for all three of us they were churning like butter.

"You talk of me being hurt, Monte Segundo," snipped Rosa, "and yet you are going off to be killed by the Apaches?"

Monte dropped his hand and rested it on his saddle horn. "Where can I find you after this is over?"

Rosa thought for a moment. "I will go to my village, Sabinal." She paused. "I will wait there. For a short time."

Monte nodded. "Then I'll look there. For a short time."

Reaching back into her saddle pocket, Rosa brought out her binoculars. She handed them to Monte. "You will need these."

Monte accepted the binoculars but said nothing.

Rosa looked at Monte and I could see him looking at her. It was too dark for her to see the expression on his face but she knew he could see hers. But even I saw her offer a faint smile. *"Vaya con dios,"* she said as she spun her horse and then bolted into a dead run.

Monte reached out to me. We shook hands. "She said to us both, 'Go with God,' Billy. I second that. You have a white rag to tie on your rifle?"

"Almost forgot," I said, untucking my shirt and pulling it up to my teeth. Biting down hard, I ripped a long piece off my shirttail. "This part's still clean enough."

"It'll do. Can you tie a square knot?"

I fumbled for words as I unshouldered my rifle and lowered the barrel.

"Let me tie it on for you," Monte said,

taking the piece of shirt from me and tearing one end partway, making two strips.

"Starting from right here," advised Monte as he tied the cloth tightly over the front sight, "you keep this barrel up high. Keep it in plain sight and keep it moving back and forth. As quick as you can, you tell anybody you see that Major Howze is riding into a trap. That'll get their attention."

"Got it," I said. Then as valiantly as I could I added, "It has been a pleasure, Monte. Good luck."

I tried to spin my horse but it only made a mediocre turn. I heard Monte say, "See you in Columbus."

I waved as my horse broke into a trot. Holding the forestock of the rifle in my left hand, I rested the butt on my thigh. I glanced up then and was shocked to my see my bright, white flag of truce was little more than a drab strip of cream-colored cloth. Riding on, I waved it left and right, fluttering the rag as best I could.

I was retracing the same stretch of road we had just ridden and yet I felt suddenly lost. Every shadowy outline that I had ignored only moments before now loomed up from the desert floor offering a perfect hiding place for an Apache. My hands began to sweat. The rifle began to slip in my hand. The reins felt oily and slick.

The hoofbeats of my horse sounded like thunder. I slowed to a walk but feeling too vulnerable, soon resumed the trot. My thoughts began to run wild. I waved the rifle barrel, wondering if the Apache scouts even knew what a white flag meant. Could they see in the dark like Monte? Would they recognize me? Would they know that I had taken a shot at one of them? Would they think I had come to tell Howze about the tortured Mexicans? God, why had I ever come to Mexico? If they tortured me, would I scream? Would anyone hear me? Why was it so dark? Where was the damn sunrise?

I looked up at my flag, hoping it would be brighter. I strained my eyes as if that would help. When I leveled my eyes, there was a black bulk in the middle of the road in front of me. Before I could rein in, two forms bolted from the darkness to my left and right.

Somehow, I got the words out. "I have a message for Major Howze!" I yelled, though it was later reported that I screamed, "I want to see Shannon!"

A hand shot out of the darkness and ripped the Mauser from my hand. Another jerked the reins from my fist. For some reason I bellowed, "I am with the *Chicago*

Tribune, damn it!"

"Hold it!" demanded a voice somewhere farther down the road.

I heard a galloping horse. It slid to stop in front of me. I could make out an army hat on the rider's head. "Who the hell are you?" demanded the rider.

"Billy Cabott. I have an urgent message for Major Howze. The Mexicans know you're coming."

The rider leaned close to me, taking a better look. "You're the one that was with that deserter. You and the woman. You're under arrest. For treason."

I was so glad to hear a white man's voice I didn't care about the charge of treason. "Did you hear what I said? The Villistas are waiting for you no more than two miles up the road."

More horses were galloping forward. It sounded like a dozen or more. "Who warned them?" asked the soldier. "You or that friend of yours?"

The band of horses surrounded me. One man spoke. "What is it, Lieutenant?"

"This man is the one I told you about, Major. The one that took a shot at one of the scouts. Now he claims the Villistas at Ojos Azules know we're coming."

"You've got tell Major Howze," I insisted.

"They know you are coming."

"I am Major Howze, damn it. How do you know this?"

I hesitated but only a few seconds. "The woman who was traveling with us, our guide, bolted and got away. It turns out she was one of them, a *soldadera*."

"Captain," ordered Howze, "take this man to the rear and put a guard on him. If he tries to escape have him shot."

A soldier broke from the group and took the reins of my horse from the Apache who was holding them. I was led away but not before I heard Howze say, "It makes no difference if he's lying. We proceed as planned."

I took a deep breath and let it out slowly. I had done what I could. And I had survived. Monte was right. The warning had made no difference. But still, I had done what I had to do. It felt good. Damn good.

Rosa's bravery received a similar reception at the hands of the Villistas. When she was just coming in sight of the hacienda, a half-dozen Yaquis guards had lunged out of the darkness blocking the road. She slid to stop in front of them, immediately smelling the pungent fumes of marijuana.

She told them she had an urgent message for the *jefe* but the men were more interested in the fact that she was a woman. One grabbed the horse's headstall. Another taunted her, asking why she was alone and why she was in such a hurry. Several offered to be her Juan.

Rosa swore viciously and tried to kick her horse in the flanks but hands shot out and grabbed her ankles. It wasn't until those groping hands slid up her dress and discovered she was wearing pants that the men began to listen to her.

The Yaquis finally let her go and she rode directly to the main building of the hacienda, a two-story flat-roofed adobe. She went inside but the men were scattered about on the floor still asleep. A half-awake cook appeared and then took her into a kitchen. There, he told her to wait.

Minutes passed and then a captain of the Villistas entered. He yawned. Glaring at Rosa with one eye closed, he demanded to know what she wanted. Before she could answer, the Yaquis guards burst in, frantically reporting their position was being surrounded by American soldiers.

Monte had watched me ride back down the road. He listened for several minutes and then thoughtfully nudged his mount into an easy walk.

First light was no more than a half-hour away. He reasoned that the attack would begin shortly after that, as soon as there was enough visibility to see the front and rear sights of a Springfield rifle.

In minutes, the vague shadow of the hacienda came into view as did the black outline of the hills behind it. As he suspected, for purposes of water, the buildings of the ranch had been built only a few hundred yards from the base of the hills.

From his militia training, Monte was aware that the army would most likely make a frontal attack while flanking both sides of the buildings. But Monte also knew the Apaches, unlike the plains Indians, preferred ambush-style fighting, always choosing caution over foolhardiness. The scouts would never agree to fight in the open but would gladly take to the hills behind the hacienda where there was cover. There they would wait until the time was right and then hunt down those that tried to escape into the draws and canyons.

Monte glanced down at Rosa's tracks. She had put the tired horse into a full run. She was likely at the hacienda already and would no doubt fight alongside the Villistas. She would try to kill Americans just as he would try to kill Apaches. He had no thought of his own death but the vision of a bullet crashing into Rosa's forehead flashed through his mind. He shoved it aside, reminding himself this was no time to think of her, no time to be a fool.

Rosa's tracks shortened suddenly and then stopped where track upon track had been stomped into the ground. Monte dismounted and read the sign. She had been stopped by several men before she again broke into a run.

First light was rapidly approaching and a quarter mile to the south Monte could now make out the distinct profiles of three large buildings, one of them two stories high. He could see movement on its roof.

Quickly remounting, Monte galloped off the road heading east across a flat of scattered juniper and dried grass. After darting between a thicket of stunted trees, the ground began to rise rapidly, the juniper growing taller, and the grass giving way to a thin layer of loose sand and gravel.

He started a steep climb. As he did, he veered back to the south working his way up and to the rear of the hacienda's adobes. When he was a good five hundred feet above the ranch he dismounted on the uphill side of a tree that had been toppled by lightning.

Monte glanced at the glow in the eastern sky as he tied his horse behind the tangled mass of dead branches. Reaching inside his saddle pocket, he took the binoculars and immediately glassed the road below him. But, to his relief, he saw no troops.

A cool breeze stirred the branches of the junipers next to him. Sunrise was only minutes away. Monte swung the binoculars back to the hacienda. He could make out dozens of men on the roof of the two-story adobe but none anywhere else. There was no doubt Rosa had told them Howze was coming with a machine-gun troop but clearly the Villistas had decided to make a stand, hoping to use the thick-walled adobes for protection.

Monte lowered the binoculars. The Idaho Militia had no machine guns, but he knew what they could do. "God, help her," he whispered. "God help her."

He rubbed a hand over his eyes and down over the wiry stubble on his jaws. Straining to push thoughts of Rosa aside, he caught a flicker of movement on the road below.

A gray column of mounted soldiers was snaking its way down the winding road toward the ranch. A moment later the entire column, close to three hundred men, came to a halt.

Raising the binoculars again, Monte watched a handful of riders gallop to the head of the column. From his training, he understood those were the officers and they were receiving their final orders. Carelessly scattered around the tight-knit group of officers, a dozen riders sat their horses.

"There you are, you Apache sons-a-bitches. Finally!"

A half a minute later the Apaches wheeled their horses and galloped directly toward Monte's position. Then, as he expected, the column divided into three smaller divisions, one circling to the west of the buildings, one to the east, and the largest of the three positioning itself for a frontal attack.

Monte quickly lost sight of the Apaches as they disappeared in the brush and rough terrain. Occasionally he caught a glimpse of one or two but was confident all were coming his way and in minutes would take a position a few hundred yards below him.

Monte knelt behind a stunted juniper. He refocused the binoculars as he listened to the sound of steel horseshoes clattering over loose rocks. Still out of sight, Monte knew the Apaches were slowly working their way into position. Far below, however, the pincer movement of the cavalry had not even begun when muzzle blasts, like a string of fireworks, lit up the edge of the two-story adobe roof. The Mexicans, either too eager or too afraid to hold their fire, had started shooting at the cavalry, targets that were more than one thousand yards away.

All three columns appeared to be disorganized and so far, none had advanced or bothered to return fire.

The sun crested the mountain peaks to Monte's right just as the Apaches, still on horseback, rode into the open no more than four hundred yards below. In the sunlight, though, he could see their glistening black hair hanging down from their olive-colored campaign hats.

"Keep coming," Monte whispered. "That's right. A little closer."

Watching the Apaches slow their horses, Monte counted eleven scouts and one white officer.

"So, Lieutenant Shannon," sneered Monte. "Let's see what you're made of."

Shannon and the Apaches dismounted in the clearing and tied their horses. The lieutenant then pointed several times downhill toward the hacienda as the columns below began to maneuver into position. When the frontal column mounted their charge and opened fire, Shannon immediately darted downhill, waving for his men to follow. Instead, the Apaches turned east, cutting across the mountainside and then scattering into the brush.

Even at that distance, Monte heard Shannon screaming out orders, all of which were being ignored.

"Thought so," Monte whispered and then turned his attention to the Apaches.

At one point the scouts stopped and fired a few ineffective shots at the hacienda, still nine hundred yards away.

Seconds later, Shannon reappeared to the rear of the Apaches. This time he was waving both arms like a madman but again with no effect.

The hacienda was now under full attack from three sides. Rifle blasts and the unmistakable rattle of machine-gun fire roared up the mountainside and bodies could be seen falling from the roof. Only then did the Apaches break cover and follow Shannon downhill. But the scouts advanced no more than fifty yards when they again took cover and began firing, no doubt drowning out the furious orders of their commanding officer.

Monte watched at least a dozen more Mexicans plummet to the ground. At that point, some of the Villistas began scrambling off the roof. In seconds, they were fleeing out the back of the adobe. Curiously, Monte noticed that none seemed to be carrying rifles. However, all were undoubtedly running away from the battle, heading for an arroyo that gouged its way deep into the hidden folds of the mountain.

Seeing the retreating Mexicans and ignoring Shannon completely, the Apaches sprang to their feet, running down the mountainside but angling sharply for the mouth of the arroyo, less than a quarter mile away.

Monte came to his feet. Tossing the binoculars aside he started after the Indians. In a dogtrot, he kept a steady pace down through the junipers until, near the base of the mountain, he skirted thorny patches of mesquite trees and cat's-claw. He didn't stop running until he caught a glimpse of sand that fanned out onto a gentle slope. Crouching, he slowed his pace to a walk. But the steps he now took were no longer those of a white man.

Cautiously approaching the mouth of the arroyo in his moccasins, Monte eased each foot into place, feeling every pebble before it rolled and every twig before it snapped. He rolled the soles of his feet over the jagged terrain like the belly of a snake, gliding across it in deathly silence.

He stopped at the edge of the arroyo to scan the sand below. It was one hundred feet to the opposite bank. The tracks of the running Mexicans went right up the middle of the arroyo. The Apaches, all eleven, had chased after them. From the length of their strides, Monte could see the Apaches were still running full-speed.

The battle was still raging at the hacienda but Monte heard a single shot that came from the mountain to his left. It was followed by a piercing scream and then several more shots.

Monte drew his pistol and slid down to the sand. Keeping to the eastern side of the drainage, Monte moved quickly up the arroyo. Along the way, he saw several bandoliers, still full of cartridges, that had been tossed into the brush.

Paying close attention to the tracks, he also noticed that even though most of the Villistas wore sandals, many were barefooted. It was then Monte realized that without a rifle and bandolier these Villistas would look like any other peon. Had it not been for the Apaches, it would have been a good trick. But now they were defenseless against the Apaches.

Monte hurried on, hearing more shots and more screams. The arroyo began to narrow, its banks growing steeper and its course more erratic. Rounding a sharp turn, he saw the first dead Mexican.

Dressed in ragged, dirty muslin he lay facedown. The sand around his head was soaked with dark red blood. One hand clutched a tattered straw sombrero.

Monte paused and studied the tracks. Most of the peons were still in the bottom of the ravine but one had gone up the crusted bank and out into the brush. The Apaches had not followed that one, at least not yet.

Moving quickly up the ravine, Monte passed more dead Mexicans, all shot in the back. Passing three more that were sprawled in a grotesque pile, Monte came to a point where the ravine fractured into a labyrinth of smaller arroyos. Here the Mexicans had scattered and so had the pursuing Apaches.

Shots were now coming in front of him and to his left and right. He glanced down at the tracks, taking a closer look. He noticed one particular set. It had been left by someone very small and wearing sandals, someone the size of Rosa.

Swearing softly, he turned to his right and followed the single set of sandal tracks. They led up and away from the main drainage and deeper into the mountain. Mixed with the small tracks was a second set, a set made by someone wearing moccasins.

The ravine narrowed as it twisted, now no more than ten feet across but still sandy at the bottom. The sporadic firing all but ceased as he continued up the draw.

He had taken only a few steps when he heard a twig snap ahead of him. He froze. Someone was ahead just beyond a sharp turn.

He heard a grunt. There was a thud. And then the hot, dry air of the arroyo was filled with vicious, defiant swearing.

Monte cocked the hammer of his Colt. Knowing the Apache had his hands full, Monte moved quickly. Rounding the bend, he saw a uniformed Apache jerk Rosa up off her knees and then spin her around to hold her in front of him as a shield. The Indian's left arm was locked around Rosa's waist. His right hand held a knife to her throat. The three of them were no more than five paces apart.

Half of the Apache's face was visible behind Rosa's head. But half was enough. Monte recognized the scar along the exposed cheek and he recognized what he saw of the face. It had not changed in nearly thirty years. This was the Apache who had killed his mother and mutilated his father.

This was the face he had seen in his nightmares. This was the dark figure that had, for so many years, thrown him into the flaming fire.

"Go!" demanded the Apache in guttural English. "Go! I kill! You go. I kill!"

The Apache's pistol was in its holster. All he had was the knife. Monte raised the pistol.

"Let her go."

The Apache was unfazed. "You go! Your woman, I kill! You go!"

"So, it was you that killed those two Mexicans. Does Shannon know about that?"

Pressing the knife blade against Rosa's throat, the Apache repeated, "Go!"

"She's not my woman," Monte said and then the Colt bucked in his palm.

The bullet tore through a thatch of black hair and ripped off the Apache's earlobe.

Instantly, the knife was withdrawn from Rosa's throat. Wide-eyed, she let out a hoarse agonizing gasp as the Indian sprang to his right and out of sight.

Rosa staggered a step forward and then dropped to her knees, trying with both hands to clutch her back.

Monte bounded forward, passing by Rosa, only catching a glimpse of the Apache scrambling up and over the rim of the ravine.

Glancing back at Rosa, Monte saw blood pouring from a stab wound to the kidney. She could not reach it.

Monte looked back at the rim of the ravine. The hated Apache could not get away, not now.

But Rosa was bleeding and would die in minutes without help.

Swearing bitterly, Monte spun and went to Rosa. Holding his Colt at the ready he kneeled beside her and said gruffly, "Lie down. Lie on your stomach."

Rosa was gasping painfully. She eased herself flat onto the sand.

Scanning the rim of the arroyo, Monte pressed his empty palm hard against the stab wound. Rosa winced. "Will I live?"

"I don't know. But if he wanted you dead quick he'd have stabbed you higher."

"What do you care?" muttered Rosa.

Monte shook his head. "Keep quiet or you'll get us both killed."

"All you want is revenge! Leave me, you half-*gringo*. You . . ."

"Shut up, Rosa," demanded Monte, his voice suddenly changing to a commanding whisper.

Rosa was instantly quiet. Both of them

listened to the raspy thuds of horses' hooves. Riders were working their way up the sandy arroyo.

"Horses," Rosa whispered.

"Maybe they'll pass us by," returned Monte.

But the horses grew nearer, then stopped. They were close enough that Rosa and Monte heard the creak of saddle leather as several riders stepped down.

"He goes here," one of them said.

"I want him alive," said another.

Monte swore softly. "That's Shannon. The other's got to be an Apache."

Easing the hammer down on his Colt, Monte shifted his weight to face the advancing Americans. He held the pistol across his knee and continued pressing on Rosa's wound with his left palm.

In a half-crouch a soldier slowly appeared around a jagged, vertical wedge of crusted sand. Catching sight of Monte and Rosa he froze.

Monte did not move but glared at the soldier. He wore moccasins but had short hair and was no more than twenty-five years old. He gripped an Army issue forty-five automatic pistol.

"If I wanted to shoot you," Monte said evenly, "you'd be dead already."

The Apache slowly stood erect and then took another step, exposing himself completely. "Here, Lieutenant," said the soldier in perfect English.

Shannon came up behind the scout. After a hard look at Monte he glanced at Rosa and then stepped around the Apache, aiming his pistol at Monte. "Drop your weapon and put your hands in the air."

Monte hesitated. His attention shifted to the Apache, paying close attention to the young buck's eyes. Instead of seeing the sinister stare of a cold-blooded killer, Monte saw inexperience and uncertainty. And he guessed Shannon was a by-the-book officer.

Easing his Colt down onto the bloody sand, Monte raised his right hand. "I can't raise both hands or this woman will bleed to death."

Shannon started to protest but instead craned his neck for a better look at Monte's bloody left hand. "Alright then. You're under arrest for treason. Any wrong move and I'll shoot you down, no questions asked."

Three more soldiers stepped past the Apache, all of them white, all of them privates.

Monte wasn't sure what treason meant but he knew that if he was to get another chance to kill the scar-faced Apache he would need to say as little as possible and keep what he knew to himself.

Even to someone as inept as Shannon it would be obvious the Apaches had chased unarmed Villistas into the mountains and shot them, many in the back. Those same Apaches were under his command, but they had ignored his orders repeatedly.

Monte also doubted that Shannon knew anything about the two Mexicans that had been tortured to death. But Monte was also certain the scar-faced Apache was part of that murder. And no matter what treason might be, Monte figured it wasn't half as bad as what the lieutenant and his Apaches had done.

"She needs a doctor," Monte said, indicating Rosa with a nod. "She was stabbed."

Shannon flinched. "Who is she? Is she a Villista like you?"

"I'm no damn Villista," Monte sneered, "and she looks more like a cook or a whore than a revolutionary. You expect her to stay in the hacienda while you were blowing it to hell?"

Glancing at the young Apache, Monte asked, "Did you see any guns up here? Any weapons at all?"

The scout didn't answer. There was no

reason. They all knew what had happened in the arroyo.

Monte thought it curious that Shannon didn't ask about the origin of Rosa's stab wound, a wound inflicted upon an unarmed woman. Instead, the lieutenant leaned forward and picked up Monte's Colt. He turned to the three white privates. "You men go back and get a stretcher up here. Double quick."

The privates scrambled out of the drainage. When they were heard galloping away Shannon shoved Monte's Colt behind his belt. The lieutenant fidgeted, nervously rolling his head as if he had on a tight necktie.

Pointing at Rosa with the stubby barrel of his automatic, Shannon asked, "Does she speak English?"

"Why ask the damned *gringo*?" snapped Rosa. "How would he know? Ask me if I speak English."

Shannon sneered, his eyes shifting from Rosa to rest knowingly on Monte. "Sure. Sure. I get what the two of you are up to. But you can't fool me. Well, get this. The less you say today and at the court-martial the better it will go for your woman. Do you understand what I'm saying?"

Monte smiled, looking hard at Shannon.

338

"Oh, I understand plenty, Lieutenant. You can bank on that."

CHAPTER 11

I was held at the head of Major Howze's pack train, guarded by a surly corporal who had orders, which I thought entirely inappropriate, to shoot me if I tried to escape. I was in no position to protest so I quietly sat my horse and tried to gather my thoughts. But there was little time for that.

The pack train rode only a short distance and then halted as the cavalry rode on. We were a safe distance from Ojos Azules but close enough that I saw the flashes from Mexican rifles erupt and light up the flat roofline of the largest hacienda. The American troops, however, offered no return fire and seemed to be having trouble forming their lines.

We heard hundreds of muffled rifle blasts coming from the Mexicans but all we could make out of our mounted cavalry was clouds of dust. Finally, the bone chilling, crisp notes of bugles pierced the air and from the dust three magnificent lines of cavalry thundered straight into the flying bullets of the Villistas. Behind the troops, cover fire from Benét-Mercié machine guns opened up and instantly bodies began falling from the hacienda roof.

In seconds the cavalry, while riding full speed and bounding over rocks and leaping fences, blasted away with their Colt automatic pistols. It was like a Fourth of July fireworks display, beautiful, thrilling, and horrifying at the same instant.

It was hard for me to grasp that men were dying. They were tiny figures, totally unknown to me and indistinct in the distance. But I did know Rosa and the thought of her being caught in the melee promptly extinguished my exhilaration.

Entangled with thoughts of Rosa were the recollections of the jolting recoil I'd felt when firing my Mauser and what such a powerful bullet would do to a man. The disemboweled Mexicans crossed my mind as did the Apaches and the relentless desert heat. And too, I thought of the plight of the Mexican people, of the unimaginable poverty of the peons.

What, I wondered, was the point of it all? Why were Americans charging into gunfire only to die hundreds of miles away from the ones they loved? And why on earth were we in Mexico in the first place? Mexico had nothing we needed, nothing we didn't already have. In fact, what it did have was an overabundance of deeply rooted problems that we didn't want any part of.

Thinking of Rosa, I began to feel sick. She could be killed or maimed. And for what? Such a beautiful woman, a needless sacrifice for a country that was hopelessly corrupt.

I looked more closely at the battle. Horses were darting left and right, dust was swirling, guns were blasting rapid-fire in every direction.

Monte, I thought suddenly. Where in all that chaos was Monte Segundo?

I shook my head. No, I told myself, Monte doesn't fight like that. No need to worry about him. Not Monte. There was something about Monte Segundo, something intangible that made him seem invincible. I assured myself that Monte was like a cat. No matter what happened out there he would land on his feet.

The sun had crested the ridgeline just as the shooting began to wane and a few minutes later the rifle fire stopped all together. Shockingly, it had only been twenty minutes since the first bugle blast and yet the two hundred Villistas defending the hacienda had been totally routed. But more astonishing was the casualty report that came in a half-hour after the battle ended. When I overheard the body count I, as well as those around me, thought surely there had been a mistake. But minutes later the bizarre report was confirmed.

Cheers erupted, backs were slapped, and hands shaken, but for the sake of pride, no one dared mention what had to be on the minds of many. Barring the direct intervention of God Almighty, the only plausible explanation for such a one-sided victory was that the Mexicans must have been intoxicated with either *aguardiente* or their coveted marijuana smokes.

How else could one explain how sixty Villistas had been killed and seventy captured while, despite the close nature of the fighting, not one single American was killed, not even one trooper so much as wounded?

By the time the supply train was brought up to the hacienda, the Villista prisoners had been herded into a large pole corral just east of the bullet-riddled fortress. I, along with my guard, sat our horses watching several soldiers dragging bloody corpses to an open area. There, like sacks of potatoes, they began tossing them into piles. Other men were breaking down fences and tossing the wooden rails onto the mounds of twisted bodies. Sickened by what I saw I turned away.

"Too much for you, paper boy?" jeered my guard. "Wait 'til we set them on fire. That's what we did with all them dead greasers back in Columbus. Stunk up the whole town for days."

"I know. I was there."

I swallowed hard, forcing down the acid that squirted up from my stomach. I carefully looked over the prisoners in the corral and when I didn't see Rosa my heart immediately sank. Sitting there in the rising sun, I felt life itself draining from me. I couldn't bring myself to search the dead.

The casualty report, however, had also included an estimate that forty Mexicans had escaped into the mountains. Desperately, I held onto the hope that one of them was Rosa.

Lifting my eyes, I gazed past the corrals to the mountains.

And where was Monte, I wondered? And what of the Apache scouts? They were nowhere to be seen. Had they gone after the escaping Villistas? And if they had, what chance did the Mexicans have? What chance did Rosa have?

"Look smart, paper boy!" ordered the

corporal. "Here comes Major Howze."

I glanced to my left and saw a rider coming toward me. He was in his fifties, lean and distinguished-looking with a trimmed mustache and handsome age lines around his eyes and cheeks.

The major's gray eyes, shaded by his campaign hat, were steady and unblinking. "Who are you, sir, and what are you doing here?" he asked in a surprisingly polite tone.

"I am Billy Cabott. I'm a reporter for the *Chicago Tribune.*"

The major studied me for a moment. "And the second part of my question?"

The major's easy manner was disarming. Amidst all the carnage and brutality, he was being a gentleman. Perhaps it was because of that I felt I owed him the truth. Or a decent version of it, anyway.

"I followed a story that started in Columbus. It led me across the border and then, by unfortunate circumstance, deeper and deeper into Mexico. I had no way to return."

Howze mulled over what I had said for several seconds. "You may consider yourself still under arrest, Mr. Cabott. You will be interrogated by General Pershing when we return to base. In the meantime, do I have your word that you'll not try to escape?"

"Yes, sir."

Glancing at the guard, Howze said, "You are relieved, Corporal."

"Yes, sir," replied the trooper and immediately galloped away toward the piles of dead Villistas.

"Mr. Cabott, you may circulate. Take notes if you wish." Howze paused. "You are aware that we have Apache scouts in our ranks?"

"Yes, sir."

"Then you are aware that escape is impossible?"

"Yes, sir. Quite aware."

"Good," said Howze. "You may go about your business of reporting. Good day, sir."

Somewhat bewildered, I watched the gray-haired major ride away. He was hundreds of miles from the border, had ridden all night and just fought a small war, and yet looked as fresh as if he were riding across a parade ground back in the states.

Dead men lay everywhere. Minutes before the air had been filled with flying lead, yet here was a man conducting himself as though such unspeakable carnage was no more than a daily routine.

It was too much for me. Knowing it was impossible to make sense of what was happening, I hung my head, trying to bury my emotions and my conscience as deeply as I could. And I must say there was a palpable comfort in giving up. Or was it giving in, callously accepting the horrors I had witnessed as simply the immutable realities of war?

Clenching my teeth, I inhaled deeply, detecting the lingering smell of gunpowder now mixing with the pungent odor of kerosene and burning wood. I nudged my horse and quickly rode upwind and over to the prisoners, who were now being escorted out of the corral in small groups to be interrogated.

Dismounting for the first time in hours, my legs buckled under me. I caught myself and worked my knees until the blood began to circulate. When my strength returned, I took a few unsteady steps. I tied my reins to a corral pole and studied the prisoners more closely. Most wore large dirty sombreros, ragged muslin, and worn-out sandals. A few were well dressed, likely the officers.

I made eye contact with one of the peons. Taking a chance, I said, "Rosa? Have you seen Rosa?"

The Villista I was speaking to responded with a blank stare but others near him looked in my direction. "Rosa?" I repeated. I pointed to my chest. "Friend. Friend."

One of the men nodded and then pointed

to the mountains. *"Alla."*

"The mountains?" I asked.

"Sí. Tal vez."

I didn't know *"tal vez"* but I did know *"sí"* and I started walking toward the back of the hacienda hoping to get a better look at the path Rosa might have taken. On my way, I recalled what Major Howze had said, that he had Apache scouts. Did he know what they had done to the wire cutters? Could a man of apparent refinement condone such cruelty? If he did, could such a man grow so insensitive that he would accept torture as just another weapon of warfare?

Monte told me to trust my instincts and at that moment my instincts told me that Major Howze knew nothing of the Apache atrocities. And that was something to remember.

The ground immediately to the rear of the hacienda was packed too solid for me to see any tracks but I continued south for several more paces and the hardpack gave way to smooth drifted sand. There even I could see tracks, lots of them, heading for the mountains.

I glanced over my shoulder and realized I was as far from the soldiers as I dared get. I stood there hoping upon hope that somehow Rosa might see me, or that Monte would.

Standing there alone, I began to worry. Not for Monte or Rosa but for myself. As long as I was with them I felt confident, sometimes even brave. But really, what was I without the two of them? What if I never saw them again? What if I were now completely on my own? Was I even a news reporter? Would I ever make a report or had I been fired weeks ago?

I felt my resolve fading as if it were draining out through the soles of my feet and into the Mexican sand. I fought down a wave of panic but couldn't ignore the question that suddenly dominated my thoughts. Had I been bold and ambitious, perhaps even courageous to join up with Monte and venture into Mexico, or had I been nothing more than a tagalong fool who was now thousands of miles from home and facing a charge of treason?

Wiping my forehead and squinting my eyes, I tried to keep my head from spinning. I thought of the saddle sores I had endured, the sweltering deserts I had crossed, and the anxious nights I had slept on the hard ground. I saw the faces of the dead Mexicans and entrails strung out over the sand. And then I recalled how I had gone so far as to take a shot at an Apache, a scout for the United States Army.

I rubbed my sweaty palms on the seat of my pants, vaguely aware the painful saddle sores were now healed over. Fighting down the urge to turn and run, I glared at my hands. Then, for a long while, my eyes focused on the calluses. I raised my hands for a closer look.

For the first time, I recognized strength in those hands, a strength and toughness that had never been there before. It was a strength that, of all people, belonged to William Cabott Weston III.

Oddly, I suddenly felt a sense of pride in those calluses. A fledgling I might be, but I had indeed earned every one of them. Had I not ridden hundreds of miles across Mexico with Monte Segundo, learned to build a fire, shoot a rifle, and sleep on the ground? Had I not gone with Rosa trailing armed Apache killers and just this morning risked my life to deliver a vital message to the United States Cavalry?

I wasn't much compared to Monte and Rosa but I had ridden with them. No one else could make that claim. And that counted for something, something mystifying and profound that I could not put into words.

At that moment, I realized that I was not the same person who, only weeks before, had walked out of Columbus, New Mexico. I had changed and changed for the better. With that realization, my confidence returned and with it, my resolve.

From a wide funnel of sand at the base of the mountain, a nondescript figure appeared rippling through the heat waves. Soon, I could make out three soldiers on foot, all walking in a tight cluster.

When the three soldiers were well out of the mouth of the drainage a whole platoon of cavalry galloped into the open. Passing those walking, they rode directly toward me. In seconds they were on me, some coming within inches of where I stood as they barreled toward the hacienda. The leader was Lieutenant Shannon. Most of the others were Apaches.

I watched them for a few seconds but then turned my attention back to the walking soldiers. As they trudged closer I could see that two of the men were carrying a stretcher with someone on it. The third soldier had a rifle slung over his shoulder and paralleled the other two.

After seeing the Indians ride by, my first thought was that it must be Monte on the stretcher, that he had been outnumbered and wounded by the Apaches. Without hesitation, I started forward, but it didn't take long before I recognized that it was Monte holding onto the head of the stretcher. I was within ten paces of them before I realized it was Rosa being carried. She was unconscious and very pale.

Before I could react, the soldier with the rifle, a corporal sporting a heavy growth of stubble on his face, put his hand on his Colt pistol but did not remove it from its holster. "Who are you?" he demanded.

"I'm a reporter with the *Chicago Tribune*," I answered but kept walking closer. "Major Howze is aware of my presence."

The corporal relaxed. "Not much here. Just a wounded *soldadera* and a traitor. Nobody will want to read about these two."

"What happened to her?" I asked.

I glanced at Monte but his eyes were locked on the hacienda. He seemed deep in thought so I turned and started walking alongside the corporal. "Did she get shot?"

"I don't know," grumbled the corporal, wiping sweat from his neck with the palm of his hand. "Didn't ask. Just following orders."

"She was stabbed," said Monte.

I blinked incredulously, "With a bayonet?"

"A knife."

That short answer was all I needed to piece together the basics of what had happened. The Apaches had Rosa, they stabbed her, and Monte stayed with her trying to save her life. As a result, he was captured.

"She's been bandaged up," offered the corporal, casting a pair of lecherous eyes on Rosa. "Be a damned shame if one as purty as this one dies. Not many greasers look that good."

I expected Monte to react to the insult but he said nothing. Part of me wanted to ask him how badly Rosa was injured and part of me wanted to know if he had found the scar-faced Apache. However, Monte was holding his tongue and I decided it was wise to follow suit.

Nothing more was said until we reached the rear of the hacienda and its bullet-riddled double door. The corporal stepped forward and pounded on the heavy oak planks with the meat of his fist. "Wounded prisoner," he called out and the door opened.

"You stay here," ordered the corporal and then followed the stretcher inside.

The heavy doors closed. I heard a metallic clang as some sort of locking bolt was snapped shut. I heard moaning inside, no doubt from the wounded. It was only later that I learned the Villistas were being attended to by two competent doctors.

I waited by the doors for over an hour but Monte didn't come out. I didn't see him again until late that afternoon when the army column was mounting up for its return to San Antonio. I was at the rear of the column but Monte was kept in the front. And it was several days before I saw Monte again but at least I did learn that Rosa would fully recover.

CHAPTER 12

Ojos Azules was forty miles south of Pershing's base camp at San Antonio and it was there we headed after the battle. After riding northeast for three hours, we stopped in the village of Cusihuiriachic. Cusi, as the soldiers called it, was a substantial town with two resident doctors so we left Rosa there along with the Villista wounded.

I had no grasp of the trouble I was in until we reached San Antonio a few hours later. As soon as I dismounted I was handed over to a military escort composed of four guards. They prodded me through a maze of parked trucks, tents, and bustling soldiers until we came to a spacious quadrangle. In its center, two dusty black touring cars and one old Model T were parked in front of a large army tent that resembled those used in a traveling circus.

Avoiding the large tent, I was taken across the open space to a line of smaller tents on

355

the west edge of the open square and ordered inside a ten-by-ten-foot wall-tent. A single guard was then posted outside.

The only amenities inside the tent were a cot and one wool army issue blanket. It was midafternoon and with the tent flaps down, the heat under the canvas was stifling. I immediately went to the front of the tent and jerked one of the flaps aside. A private, with a rifle over his shoulder and a Colt pistol on his belt, turned and glared at me.

The soldier was a few inches taller than me but looked to be close to my age and about my weight so I ignored him and started tying the tent flap back.

"It's like an oven in there," I said flatly and then gathered up the second flap. "What's the idea, anyway, putting me in here? What's going on?"

The private shrugged. "You're under arrest."

I jerked the knot tight that held the second flap. "What for?"

The private hesitated, looking me over carefully. "I heard you were with that deserter fella. They say you're both going to be shot for treason."

"That's preposterous," I said boldly though I felt a jolt hit the pit of my stomach. "I'm a reporter for the *Chicago Tribune*. And

I can vouch for Monte Segundo. He's neither deserter nor traitor."

I eyed the soldier, doing my best to intimidate him. "And what is your name, soldier?"

The private took a half-step back, his eyes narrowed with uncertainty. "Darby."

"Well, Private Darby, I'd like to speak to someone in charge."

"I'm just the guard. You're to stay in the tent or go to the latrine. That's all. Those are my orders. And they'll stay that way unless General Pershing says different."

"General Pershing?" I blurted. "You mean Major Howze?"

Darby shook his head, a rank smile turning his lips. "Nope. They say you and your friend are headed for the general. And down here General Pershing can do whatever he damn well pleases with traitors. They say it's like marshal law while were in Mexico."

"We're not traitors," I repeated adamantly, but inside I began to quiver. If Monte and I were being brought before General Pershing our predicament was far worse than I had imagined.

And why was I being charged with treason? Was it because the Apaches told Major Howze I took a shot at one of them? If they had, would the circumstances at the time be enough to justify shooting at an American soldier during a time of war? Would anyone believe my explanation of those circumstances? I had no proof, no witnesses other than Monte and Rosa.

And then there were the horses. Monte and I had ridden out of Las Palomas on stolen horses, horses that belonged to Carrancista soldiers. No one forced me to ride with Monte. I just went. Without regard for the consequences, I had stolen horses from a friendly government, an ally in the war against Pancho Villa.

I backed up to the cot and sat down. The wooden frame creaked. I thought of a gallows, a rope, of how it might creak as I swung back and forth, back and forth. And then I envisioned a firing squad taking aim and wondered if the bullet would hurt.

Fighting down those morbid thoughts, I swiped my face with my shirtsleeve, wiping away the nonsense. I was, after all, a Weston. All I had to do was make that fact known and wheels would start turning. Powerful wheels. Father had influence and that influence extended to Washington, D.C., and even into the White House.

No. I was safe. A stern reprimand was all that awaited me. I took a deep breath and exhaled a sigh of relief. I had expelled only half of that selfish breath when I thought of Monte. For a split second I stopped breathing. Monte was in real trouble.

I sprang to my feet and went to Darby. "What do you know of my friend, of Monte Segundo?"

"That his name, is it?" asked Darby, half interested. "Sounds like a greaser name to me."

"Do you know anything about him?"

"Only that he's being held somewhere just like you. But with two guards instead of one."

"What about the Apache scouts? They're not the guards, are they?"

"No. Major Howze put them in charge of the Villista prisoners. But I ain't seen none of them Indians anywhere around here."

Feeling a bit relieved that Monte was safe for the time being, I tried to think. I needed a plan. For some reason my eyes went straight to the large tent in the center of the quadrangle and the activity surrounding it.

I looked closer at the old Model T and then at the dust-covered touring cars. One of the touring cars had American flags on both front fenders. I looked again at the Model T.

Then it hit me. I was standing across from the headquarters of the entire expedition!

The Dodge with the flags was Pershing's touring car and the Model T belonged to Floyd Gibbons, the reporter I had been assigned to by the *Chicago Tribune.* With him would be Robert Dunn of the *New York Tribune.* The two of them had been with the general since leaving Columbus weeks before. They would know what Pershing had in mind, what he planned to do with his supposed traitors.

"Can you get a message to someone for me?" I asked Darby.

The private thought for a moment, his eyes shifting left and right as if he were reading his orders off an unseen paper.

"I suppose that's alright. But I can't leave my post."

I pointed to the soldiers going in and out of the tent, no more than forty paces away. "Can't you wave for one of them to come over here?"

Darby shook his head. "No. Can't do that."

I rolled my eyes. "How about me. May I?"

Laughing derisively, Darby said, "Wave all you want. Them over there are all officers. Busy as bees. Look how they're running in and out of that tent. They won't pay you any mind. Or me either for that matter.

They're officers."

Immediately I thought of Gibbons and Dunn. But mostly I thought of Gibbons. He wasn't military and he sure as hell owed me for leaving me behind in Columbus. And sooner or later he or Dunn had to come out of that tent. And when they did I was going to get their attention one way or the other.

"Can I have visitors?" I asked.

Darby scratched the back of his neck. "My orders didn't say one way or the other. You expecting company?"

"Yes. There's a reporter from my paper that's with the general. I need to speak with him."

"I suppose it's alright, then," agreed Darby, still scratching his neck as if it somehow stimulated his brain. "Since he's with the general and all."

Darby had no sooner finished with his neck scratching than Dunn stepped into view followed by Gibbons. Both paused for a moment, lit up a couple of cigarettes, and then to my surprise, started directly toward my tent.

As they sauntered closer, Dunn, with his cigarette forked between his fingers, pointed at me. I could see them speaking to one another and then I heard both of them chuckle.

I swore that very instant that if I ever got the chance I would destroy the both of them. But at the moment, I knew I damn well needed them. Seething inside, I swallowed my pride and for the first time in my life experienced the revolting taste of utter humiliation.

As they neared I stood up straight and forced a smile. "Good day, gentlemen," I said, which was the best I could come up with under the circumstances.

Both men were smiling. Gibbons extended his hand. "Depends on how you look at it, Billy."

I shook Gibbon's hand and then Dunn's, glad that my grip was solid and did not slip. I looked them both in the eye trying to appear nonchalant. "How are the two of you? What's it been, six weeks? Seven? It's easy to lose track of time down here, isn't it?"

I could see that my demeanor caught them off guard and that buttressed my backbone considerably. "Hell of a war," I offered. "What's the latest from your end?"

Their snide grins drooped. "You know you're in a lot of trouble, don't you?" Gibbons asked.

I shook my head and waved a hand. "No, no. It's merely a misunderstanding. Not to worry."

"You better think again," Dunn said. "You don't know Black Jack Pershing like we do. The war is going to hell in a handbasket and he's pissed, really pissed. His aide-de-camp, Georgie Patton, is suggesting he put you and your friend in front of a firing squad. Shoot you for traitors to boost troop morale."

I shook my head again. Acting unconcerned for myself I asked, "What do you mean about the war? It's not going well?"

Both men took a drag on their cigarettes. Dunn offered one to me. I declined but the private accepted and all three men smoked for a few seconds before Gibbons spoke again.

"Well, for one, we've no idea where to find Pancho Villa. None of the Mexicans will help us, not even the Carrancistas. President Carranza keeps ordering us out of his country. Funston says war with the de facto government is all but inevitable."

Gibbons paused. As he took a turn on his smoke Dunn said, "This morning several hundred mounted Mexicans invaded Glenn Springs, Texas, and killed three troopers and a seven-year-old boy. Some of those Mexicans wore Carrancista uniforms.

"And there are all sorts of reports, rumors maybe, that tens of thousands of Carranza's soldiers are starting to move in our direction. Some claim one army is composed of fifty thousand Yaquis Indians. And all we have down here is ten thousand men, total."

Gibbons nodded. "We only have a few troops left in the states. And those are being deployed right now to Arizona, down in Douglas and Nogales. That means, outside of the one division that has to stay and guard Washington, D.C., we're flat out of soldiers. The regular army, and I mean every division we have, is down here or on the border. Even so, we're out numbered ten to one."

"You ever hear of the Federal Bureau of Investigation?" Dunn asked.

"No."

"It's new," continued Dunn. "Been around three or four years. It's kind of like the Pinkertons, only bigger. The bureau reported that a man named Luis de la Rosa is secretly plotting a greaser uprising in the Rio Grande Valley in Texas. And right now, we know that de la Rosa's guerrillas and Carrancista regulars are massing along the Texas border.

"The bureau also tells us there's another fella named Morin recruiting homegrown Texas Mexicans for an uprising that's supposed to stretch from San Antonio, Texas, all the way down to the Rio Grande. It's part of something called the Plan de San Diego."

Gibbons exhaled a long blast of smoke up into the fading sky. "You remember what I told you on the train down here, Billy, about the Plan de San Diego? How the Mexicans are hoping to kill every American male sixteen and over? How they plan to take back parts of Texas, Arizona, New Mexico?"

"I remember," I said, though I could hardly believe my ears. It all seemed so impossible.

"Turns out Carranza is behind this new version of the plan."

"You can bet the Krauts are in on it, too," offered Dunn. "The Germans have been trying to get us into a war with Mexico for at least a year."

Gibbons disgustedly shook his head. "And there're Japanese crawling all over Mexico, too. There's a Carrancista general named Esteban Fierros up near El Paso that has six of the slanty-eyed sons-of-bitches in his army. Army intelligence thinks they're going to handle the artillery. So, it turns out that both the Germans and the Japanese want a war between us and Mexico.

"But Pershing doesn't care about Japan or Germany. Mexico is all he thinks about.

And after all that's happened, he doesn't see much difference between the Carrancistas and Villistas. He wants to kick both their asses and take over all of northern Mexico. Only then, he says, will we be able to stabilize Mexico and stop the border raids."

Dunn glanced at Darby. "The general just got new orders, though. We're moving out in a few days. Lock, stock, and barrel. The whole army is pulling back, all the way to Colonia Dublan. Funston's orders. Funston says our supply lines and communication lines could be cut by the federales any minute. He wants us closer to the border.

"Pershing's mad as hell at Funston and at President Wilson. Instead of invading Chihuahua like he planned, now the general has to tuck tail and retreat all the way back to Dublan. As he sees it, we have to run from a ragtag Mexican army that he could easily whip."

I glanced from Gibbons to Dunn. "Why don't we just go all the way back to the border? Just go home?"

Gibbons laughed. "Because we're in a pickle. First President Wilson was totally against getting involved down here. Now, since we're being 'ordered' out by Carranza, Wilson knows we can't leave because we'd look weak to the Germans and Wilson figures that would be asking for trouble."

"And the people of Texas," said Dunn, "would be furious if we just up and left. There are raids across their border all the time now and have been for years. Only the rest of the country didn't know or care about that until Villa hit Columbus. Then it got a lot of press. Now our national pride's at stake. And that means votes, my friend. Votes are at stake."

"Well," said Darby, "it's fine with me if we leave. I've had a belly full of sweat and sand. And there's no women. A few days ago, some boys went to town looking to chase some tail and all they got was their throats cut."

"So what about me?" I asked.

"Who the hell knows," sighed Gibbons. "You can see the general has bigger fish to fry. But he won't forget about you. Not General Pershing. And even if he could, that blowhard Georgie Patton would never let him."

"But I'm a civilian," I protested weakly.

All three men laughed, puffed on their smokes, and then laughed some more.

"What's so funny?"

Darby grinned. "When we first left Columbus we had to use civilian drivers because the army didn't have any. Before they could drive for us the general had them dress in army green. No insignias but all of them put on the wool. And they had to have their own sidearms, to boot. Those were the general's orders even if they were civilians."

"And," said Dunn, "Floyd and me have our own Springfield rifles. We keep them with us all the time we're out in the field. We're expected to use them if there's a need. Black Jack Pershing's not worried about formalities. He tells us what we can report and what we can't. He doesn't give a tinker's damn about 'freedom of the press' and neither does President Wilson. Not in war, anyway. When they want a news blackout, that's sure as hell what they get."

"So you see, Billy," Gibbons said, suddenly serious, "your fate is entirely in the hands of the army of the United States. There are no civilians down here, only army rules and regulations.

"But I did hear you're going to get some kind of a trial, though."

"A trial?"

"Yeah. Lieutenant Patton volunteered to be prosecution. His tentmate, Lieutenant Johnson, will be your defense. The two of them went to West Point together."

"And who's the judge?"

"Right now, it's Pershing but he's likely to

bring in Major Howze and Colonel Dodd. That way it'll look more like a proper court-martial if you're found guilty of treason."

I thought for a moment trying to decide whether I was in real trouble or if Gibbons was merely amusing himself and lying to me. It sounded as if General Pershing was just looking for a dog to kick.

"What about the man I was with, Monte Segundo? Does he get a trial, too?"

Gibbons nodded as he inhaled and then blew smoke out his nostrils. "Same trial. They're trying the two of you together to save time. Called it 'co-conspirators' if I remember right."

I studied the faces of Gibbons and Dunn. Both seemed to be telling the truth. "And what about news coverage? Does this 'trial' make the papers back home?"

"Not a chance," muttered Dunn. "It's just one of a boatload of shady things going on down here. The public will never hear about you, I can promise you that."

Before I thought better of it, I blurted, "Just like they won't hear about the Apache scouts murdering Mexicans, right?"

Both reporters twitched, their eyes narrowing.

"What have you heard?" asked Gibbons.

"I'd watch what you say, Billy," chimed in

Darby. "Around here them scouts are known as *Pershing's Pets*. The general's mighty proud of how good they're working out. He swears by them."

"And they've gotten a huge amount of good press," agreed Dunn. "I wouldn't spread any rumors if I were you. Not about the scouts. It would only make matters worse for you."

I sighed, taking time to think. Gibbons and Dunn seemed well-informed on everything. But I was desperate to know how much they actually knew about Monte.

"What does the general know about Monte Segundo? What evidence do they have against him?"

Dunn dropped his cigarette and crushed it under his shoe. "For starters, he slugged a lieutenant in Columbus and then crossed the border without permission. Then he killed a Carrancista soldier in Las Palomas. Then it's reported, the two of you stole the Carrancistas' horses and joined up with the Villistas."

"Joined the Villistas?" I asked, dumbfounded. "Killed a man in Las Palomas? What are you talking about?"

Gibbons nodded in agreement. "Segundo killed a Carrancista soldier, an ally of ours, in that bar fight. That was confirmed by an

370

investigation right after the two of you left. And Lieutenant Shannon reported that he found this Segundo fella running with the Mexicans at Ojos Azules. The same place they found you."

Marco had told us that one of the Carrancistas in Las Palomas had been killed but at the time, we dismissed the story. Now, the fact that one of them had indeed died stunned me. "Is that it?" I asked, my head swimming. "Is that all they know of Mr. Segundo?"

"Is that it?" scoffed Gibbons. "What else do they need to know?"

"Is that it?" I repeated slowly. "Is that all?"

"As far as we know," answered Gibbons and then looked to Dunn and received a confirming nod.

"What more is there to tell?" Darby asked.

I thought about Monte. Neither Gibbons nor Dodd mentioned anything about Monte killing an Apache, which indicated he had not finished what he was determined to do. I hurriedly tried to imagine what he would be thinking, what he might be planning. I knew if there was a chance, even a small one, to get at the Apache Monte would take it regardless of the outcome. I also knew that I had to protect Monte Segundo from himself.

"Tell General Pershing," I said, "if he wants a trial he would be advised to double the guard around Monte Segundo."

"I told you he's got two already," Darby protested.

"Two is not enough, Private. You have no idea with whom you're dealing. If a Carrancista was killed in Las Palomas, it was solely because Monte hit him with his fist, hit him just once. I was there. I saw it. He took on five Mexicans bare-handed. Monte Segundo is a bull-of-the-woods lumberjack. He flung those Mexicans across the bar as if they were rag dolls. Believe me, double the guard."

That evening I was given a mess kit with cold beans and rice and warm water to drink. Darby was rotated out and another guard replaced him for the night watch. The entire evening a kerosene lantern illuminated my tent but even if it had been dark in the tent, I couldn't have slept. My mind, filled with unanswered questions, raced all night long.

Morning came with another round of army cuisine. I asked the night guard for coffee but my request was refused with a heavy dose of profanity that was followed by a vivid description of what lay in store for me after the trial.

By midmorning Darby returned and resumed his duty as guard. He glanced at me thoughtfully and then nodded a hello. I nodded in return, sensing a question in the private's eyes.

"Is that true," asked Darby, "what you said about your friend killing a man with a single punch?"

"It is. Like I said, he's a lumberjack from the north woods. He's that and more, much more."

Darby chewed the inside of his lip for a moment. "Well, I told them what you said. They doubled the guard."

"Good," I replied and breathed a sigh of relief. "That should keep Mr. Segundo out of trouble until we can straighten this out. I hope."

I had not paid much attention to the area around headquarters but when one of the touring cars drove up and stopped, I realized that both touring cars and the Model T had been missing since sunup. The car that pulled up and then stopped in front of the tent was a Dodge but not the one with the American flags in front. A single driver stepped out. He was tall, clean-shaven, and possessed a lean, athletic build. After surveying the quadrangle, he started for my tent.

As he got nearer, I could see he wore a sidearm but it was not the typical army issue pistol. His had bright white grips. The steel beneath those grips glistened like silver in the Mexican sun.

"That's Lieutenant Patton," whispered Darby, then came to attention.

I got off my cot and took two steps to the front of my tent.

Darby saluted and the lieutenant saluted in return but as he did so his eyes were riveted on me.

"Do you know who I am?" asked Patton, his tone that of someone conducting a cross-examination.

"Lieutenant Patton," I answered easily. "I assume you know who I am."

To my surprise, Patton grinned. He glanced at Darby and then back to me. "Son of a bitch. Now, I like that."

I blinked inquisitively but said nothing.

"I hear you know something about our Apache scouts," Patton said but this time his manner was relaxed. "Gibbons told me."

"I know a bit but as there is to be a trial, I'd rather not expound on the matter."

Patton grinned again. "Expound? Hell, you are a newspaperman, aren't you?"

"I am."

"Well, how about this. There's a scout

named Nonotolth. We call him First Sergeant Pony. He was supposed to deliver three Villista prisoners to me this morning, prisoners from the fight at Ojos Azules. He said all three got sick and died on the way. What do you think of that report, Mr. Cabott?"

I peered up into Patton's narrowed, scrutinizing eyes and said flatly, "May I speak off the record?"

Patton nodded. "You may."

"All right," I said. "Off the record, when Monte Segundo and I were riding south of La Quemada, we found what three of your Apache scouts had done to some Mexican wire cutters. It was gruesome. And at Ojos Azules, the only reason Monte Segundo was captured is because he stayed behind to help a woman that one of the scouts, the one called Norroso, had stabbed in the back even though she was unarmed. Her name is Rosa and if Monte hadn't stayed with her, she would have bled to death before they got her back to the hacienda.

"I understand you're in a delicate position here, but I'm telling you from firsthand knowledge that not all of Pershing's scouts are 'pets.' Some of them are wild beasts. I would venture to say those prisoners you were expecting are now dead, Lieutenant, but not from illness as the scouts claim. And I have no doubt they suffered horrible, lingering deaths."

"This woman that got stabbed," questioned Patton, "did anybody see that happen?"

"Only Monte. But there were two doctors at Ojos Azules. One of them will know about Rosa and her knife wound. Talk to them and they'll tell you I'm right. Talk to Rosa. And while you're at it, you might ask yourself what kind of man would use an unarmed woman as a human shield? And why would that man then go ahead and stab the woman even though Monte had already agreed to let him get away just so he could save Rosa?"

Patton mulled over what I had said, grunted, and then turned and walked away.

And that was the last visitor I had for the next several days. I did, however, get a glimpse of General Pershing from time to time. The only break in the monotony was provided by a three-day-old copy of the *El Paso Herald* given to me by Darby. I read every word of it including the advertisements. The story about the attack on Glenn Springs was on the front page along with a companion piece about a raid on Boquillas, Texas, where six hostages were taken.

Bridges all across south Texas were being guarded. Any suspicious Mexicans were being rounded up by the Texas Rangers. Anglo-Mexican tensions were near the breaking point.

Missing in the paper was any mention of Germany or the Allies fighting in Europe. The only remotely foreign story of interest was a small paragraph about a German named Einstein who had released to the world something labeled "General Theory of Relativity." And that tidbit of international trivia was of no interest to anyone, including me.

The people of Texas, or I should say the white people of Texas, were not concerned about a war thousands of miles away. They were living with the immediate threat of being invaded by a Mexican army or being murdered by Texas greasers as they executed their genocidal Plan de San Diego.

I was reading the paper for the fourth time trying to take my mind off the stifling heat when three Dodge touring cars roared into the quadrangle and then slid to a halt in a cloud of dust.

I hopped up from my cot to take a better look.

Darby swore and pointed. "What the hell?"

Even through the dust I could see bodies stretched out on the hood of each car. All three had been tied on with rope and all three were lashed face-up into the scorching sun.

A dozen soldiers stepped out of the touring cars. The Dodge in the lead was driven by none other than Lieutenant Patton and if ever a man could be accused of strutting like a rooster, that afternoon Lieutenant George S. Patton Jr. would have been found guilty on all counts.

Soldiers, including General Pershing, poured out of the headquarters tent. Then a swarm of other soldiers and war correspondents rushed in from all sides of the quadrangle. They crowded around the touring cars. Cheers erupted. Whoops and laughter mingled with the swirling dust.

Finally, an excited private broke away and ran over to Darby. "Patton killed Cárdenas, the head of the Dorados! Shot him with his old pearl-handled six-shooter!"

"Where at?" asked an awestruck Darby.

"A place called San Miguelito Ranch."

"It was just like an old-time gunfight. Face-to-face, it was. Horses charging, pistols blazing away. They're calling the lieutenant 'Blood and Guts Patton.' General Pershing's happy as a clam!"

The private ran off to spread the word as Darby and I continued watching the celebration.

At one point Patton stepped into his car and hoisted a saddle and sword inlaid with silver for everyone to see. The soldiers cheered again.

After several minutes, I saw Pershing reenter the tent and then the men began to break into smaller groups. Weaving between them, and receiving pats on his back, was Patton. Next to him was a shorter soldier, slight in build but with the same insignias on his uniform. Both were enthusiastically chatting back and forth while coming directly toward me. When the pair was ten paces away they stopped.

Patton took a step backward. "I backed up against this adobe wall," he explained to the other lieutenant. "I was trying to reload. Bullets slammed into that wall all around my head. I shoved in my last cartridge and then let him have it as fast as I could.

"It was a hell of a fight, Hughie. I haven't felt like this since I caught my first swordfish! Damn! You should've seen it."

The two started my way again and Patton continued. "The general says I can keep the saddle. He said I did more in a half a day than the Thirteenth Cavalry did in a week!

He dubbed me the 'Bandit.' "

The lieutenant Patton had referred to as Hughie smiled. "I think 'Blood and Guts' fits you better, Georgie. 'Blood and Guts Patton' has a good ring to it."

The two officers halted in front of me and for the first time made eye contact. "This is Lieutenant Johnson," said Patton, suddenly sober. "He's judge advocate in charge of court-martial proceedings. He'll be defending you and Mr. Segundo. I'll serve as the prosecution."

I glanced at Lieutenant Johnson and then studied Patton for a moment. I could see the obvious excitement in Patton's eyes. He had recently killed a man and had just remarked that it was like catching a fish. This man was a born fighter, a man who apparently relished the taste of battle. Lieutenant Hughie Johnson, however, seemed more of a politician. My eyes dropped and I took a closer look at Patton's pistol. It was not an automatic. When I recognized it as the same old-style pistol that Monte used I made a quick decision.

"If it's all the same to the two of you," I said cautiously, "I would like to have you, Lieutenant Patton, be in charge of defending Mr. Segundo and me."

"Me?" questioned Patton. "No, you need

the best damn defense you can get. That's Lieutenant Johnson, here. He's judge advocate for a reason."

I nodded politely to Johnson. "I am certain he is. However, Monte Segundo is a gunfighter, a rare breed in this modern day and age. A man of similar temperament would best be able to understand his motives for crossing into Mexico."

Seeing Patton's eyes flicker with a mixture of flattery and pride, I knew I had hit the right chord, a chord that harmonized with Lieutenant "Blood and Guts."

Johnson shrugged and looked up at Patton. "I have no objections as long as the general approves. And something tells me he will."

Patton grinned thoughtfully. "A gunfighter, you say?"

"Monte Segundo is an expert. He uses a Colt, a pistol similar to your own. Only his is not silver. It belonged to his father."

Patton grunted and rested a palm on his pearl grips. "Alright, by God. I'll be the defense."

CHAPTER 13

A few days after the Cárdenas shootout, the entire army began its retreat to Colonia Dublan. I was one of the last to leave San Antonio and had the honor of being transported to the new headquarters, riding a full day and sleepless night in the back of an empty hay wagon drawn by four plodding mules.

The following morning found me in another tent but still guarded by Private Darby. The only significant difference was that I was supplied with a wooden crate on top of which rested a metal washbasin and towel.

At sunup, another private appeared and emptied two canteens into the basin. Before leaving, he told Darby I was to be taken to headquarters in a half-hour.

Hearing the order, a stinging shock pulsed through me. Was this to be the trial, a court-martial if the proceeding even met that legal standard? After all, I was a civilian, a news correspondent at that. I wasn't supposed to be subject to military law. At least not a court-martial. But then, I was just guessing. I had no idea what a court-martial was or how they were conducted. And then, relaxing a bit, I recalled I hadn't spoken with Patton since the day he decided to serve as defense attorney.

No, I told myself as I washed my face and hands, I was only going to meet with Lieutenant Patton. We would review the facts, discuss the issues at hand, and then prepare a proper defense. That made sense to me and I began to calm.

"Big day for you, Cabott," Darby said.

I drug the towel down my face. I blinked as the rough cloth cleared my eyes. I focused on Darby. "What do you mean?"

"Your court-martial. You and your friend."

"Not today," I objected, tossing the towel on my cot. "It's too soon for that."

Darby confidently shook his head. "Nope. The general wants it over quick. Says too much delay is bad for morale."

"But we're not ready. I haven't even met with my attorney, at least not to explain what really happened."

"I don't think many of us care so much what happens to you, maybe just sentence you to a few years in jail. But I doubt there's a man in camp that wouldn't jump at the chance to be on the firing squad that shoots your friend. Word's got out he's a traitor. They say he went native and sided up with the Villistas. Even tried to kill one of our army scouts. Shot off his ear."

The part about the ear being shot off threw me for a second but there was no time to dwell on it. I wanted to set Darby straight but I knew there was no point. Using what remained of the half-hour, I sat on my cot trying to think as fast as I could. I was certain General Pershing would at least give me a chance to present the facts and when he did I needed to be ready. However, before I could organize a single thought my half-hour had evaporated.

"Time for the two of you to face the music," chirped Darby. "Front and center."

I came to my feet. My knees shook. It angered me. I swung my hands up in front of my face and glared at them the same as I had done at Ojos Azules. I reminded myself of the brutality I had witnessed and of the near-death experiences I had faced. This was just a legal proceeding.

My legs steadied. I thought of Monte and I began to smile. I had ridden with him, one of the bravest men on either side of the border. I was honored to be labeled as his friend and companion.

"Alright then," I said, stepping out of the tent and in front of Darby. "Let's get to it."

The trial was to be held at headquarters, which, I soon discovered, resided inside another large tent similar to the one in San Antonio but one stretched over a wooden foundation and plank floor. Two steps led up to the main entrance and as I approached them I could hear the rumbling of men's voices. Taking the first step, I got a glimpse of the courtroom.

Several folding camp chairs had been squared up with military precision into two sections with an aisle in between. Soldiers sat on every chair with their backs to me. In front of the chairs was a space of ten feet and then three oak desks shoved end to end to form what I assumed would serve as a makeshift judge's bench.

As I cleared the steps, heads turned. I looked past the probing stares to the front row and was relieved to see the broad shoulders of Monte Segundo sitting alone. I walked up the aisle intending to sit next to him, but was ordered to the right where I filled one of the chairs on the empty front row.

I looked across the aisle at Monte. He wore a faint smile. He nodded. "Glad to see the Apaches didn't get you."

I shrugged. "How about you? Did you get what you came for?"

Monte's eyes grew cold. "Not yet. Today maybe."

Before I could ask what he meant, the buzz of voices inside the tent suddenly ceased. I glanced up at the desks expecting to see General Pershing enter from the opposite end of the tent but there was no one. I then turned and looked over my shoulder.

Coming up the aisle, wearing a beautiful high-collared muslin blouse and floor-length blue plaid skirt, was Rosa. She held her head high and looked at no one. Following her and grinning like the cat that ate the canary was Lieutenant Patton.

Rosa must have been barefooted because the only sound in the tent came from the clicking heels of Patton's polished riding boots as the pair walked to the front row of chairs.

Patton pointed at a seat next to me and Rosa took it. He then sat down next to Monte. A moment passed and then the buzz of conversations resumed.

I could not take my eyes off Rosa. I was thrilled to see her, to see she was alive and well. "You're here!" I said, "You came!"

Rosa looked straight ahead. "I did not come. I was brought here from Cusi. By the lieutenant."

"To help Monte?"

"Yes."

Excitedly, I glanced over at Monte but his head was tilted to one side listening to something Patton was saying. It was if he didn't know Rosa was even present.

From behind, a booming voice ordered, "Attention!"

The soldiers sprang up as Monte, Rosa, and I came to our feet. General Pershing — followed by Colonel Dodd and Major Howze — strode down the aisle and then stood behind the desks, Pershing in the middle, Dodd on the right, and Howze on the left.

"At ease," said Pershing, "and be seated."

When our chairs were filled, the three senior officers took their seats.

I was immediately struck by the physical similarity in the three men, square-jawed, gray haired, and rigid. Howze was in his fifties but Dodd and Pershing were in their sixties. With their wiry builds, craggy faces, and mustaches, Dodd and Pershing could have passed for brothers, if not twins.

Pershing glared at Monte for several

seconds and then at me. He seemed to avoid looking at Rosa.

With a frown Pershing said, "We all know why we're here, so let's get started." Fixing his eyes on the back of the tent, Pershing continued. "Lieutenant Johnson, come forward and proceed with the prosecution."

Hughie Johnson, with a tablet and pencil in hand, came forward and stood to the side of the desks adjacent to Colonel Dodd. He checked his notes and then cleared his throat.

"Charges against one Monte Segundo, private in the National Guard, Company A of Sandpoint, Idaho, are to wit: disobeying direct orders, horse theft, murder, attempted murder, and treason.

"Charges against Billy Cabott, private citizen, horse theft, treason."

As the word *treason* registered in my brain, I felt the veins in my neck start to throb. My face flushed with heat but I did my damnedest not to show any emotion. Under no circumstance was I going to disappoint Monte, Rosa, or myself.

Johnson continued. "On eight, April, 1916, Monte Segundo struck Lieutenant John Forester and knocked him unconscious. Segundo then proceeded to cross the international border with Mexico.

Citizen Billy Cabott aligned himself with Segundo and crossed the border with him. In the village of Las Palomas, Segundo struck five allied Carrancista soldiers, killing one. Segundo and Cabott then stole several horses and proceeded deeper into Mexico.

"On five, May, 1916, Segundo was captured along with other Villistas at the battle of Ojos Azules. In the battle, Segundo fired at scout Private Norroso, wounding him in the right ear. Cabott separated from Segundo and surrendered at Ojos Azules before the battle."

Johnson lowered his tablet. The expression on the faces of the three presiding officers was that of grim indifference.

Pershing leered at Patton for a moment. "What does the defense have to say?"

Patton stood. "I'd like to call my first witness, sir."

"Proceed."

"I call Rosa del Carmen Fernandez Bustamonte," Patton said, indicating for Rosa to stand and face the officers.

"Miss Bustamonte, are you a Villista?"

"Yes."

"You are not a *soldadera,* a woman that serves the men that fight?"

"I am a captain in Villa's army," Rosa said

389

proudly.

The tent erupted in laughter. Pershing raised his hand and it stopped immediately.

Unmoved by the outburst, Patton continued. "How long have you known Private Segundo and Mr. Cabott?"

"Since Señor Segundo rescued me from the Carrancistas that had raped me many times. The ones in Las Palomas."

Patton paused knowingly. There was absolute silence until he spoke again. "And did, in fact, either Private Segundo or Mr. Cabott ever join the Villistas and fight against the United States?"

"Never."

Turning to Johnson, Patton asked confidently, "Would you care to cross-examine?"

Before Johnson could respond, Rosa thrust her arm behind her, gesturing toward the scar on her back. "What about what that Apache did to me?" she demanded as she pointed toward the rear of the courtroom.

Patton spun to face Rosa. Raising both palms, he strained to keep his voice low as he glanced nervously toward General Pershing. "I don't believe we need that testimony, Miss Bustamonte."

Rosa's eyes flared as she swung her arm back around. Making a fist, she pointed a finger at Patton and loosed a string of blistering Spanish that required no interpretation. When she was finished, she crossed her arms and plopped down in her seat.

Johnson raised his eyebrows for a moment, took a deep breath, and then sighed. "One question, Miss Bustamonte. Have you ever lied?"

Rosa huffed. "Of course, *gringo*! As have all of you!"

Shaking his head, Johnson said, "No further questions."

Patton took a moment to regain his composure. He managed a smile and then said, "I would like to call Monte Segundo to testify. And I would, at the same time, like to call scout Private Norroso, better known to us as B-15. Also, First Sergeant Nonotolth as interpreter."

The tent began to buzz again. Pershing spoke over the noise. "Is Private Norroso here? I won't have this proceeding postponed."

Patton took a step closer to Pershing. "I have him and the first sergeant right outside, sir."

Pershing flicked his hand as if shooing a fly. "Bring them in."

Patton waved. Two soldiers, each armed with a belted automatic pistol and knife, walked up the steps and into the tent. Both wore Apache moccasins. One was young with a military haircut. The older Indian had long unkempt hair that brushed his shoulders, and his face, except for a white scar running from the right side of his mouth to his ear, was the color of old saddle leather.

My eyes shifted from the Apache to Monte. Unashamed of my hypocrisy, I whispered another prayer, "God, don't let him do it. Don't let him do it."

The Apache passed within six feet of Monte and Monte did not pounce on him, did not break the Indian's neck before anyone could even react. No, Monte Segundo only stared at Norroso and allowed the murderer that had haunted him for a lifetime to breathe a bit longer.

The court quieted down as the Indians took their place in front of the desks, a mere three quick steps from Monte Segundo.

"Private Norroso," said Patton, indicating Monte, "is this the man that shot you?"

Nonotolth spoke to Norroso, interpreting.

"Him shoot," grunted Norroso.

"Mr. Segundo," said Patton, "did you shoot this man?"

"He was hiding behind a woman like the coward he is. So yes, I shot what I could see of him."

This time a chorus of angry voices erupted. Pershing let them go for a full minute while he conferred with Dodd and then with Howze.

Quieting the room, Pershing said, "Lieutenant Patton, you do know you're the defense and not the prosecution?"

Patton flashed his characteristic grin. "Yes, sir," he answered and then waited a few seconds before beginning again.

"Mr. Segundo, when was the first time you saw Scout Norroso?"

Monte's eyes were locked onto Norroso and Norroso's on Monte, both reflecting a mutual hatred. "That would have been 1886."

A rumble went through the court as Nonotolth interpreted for Norroso. Even Pershing's monolithic features reflected a hint of confusion.

Patton faced the desks. "This should be of particular interest to you Colonel Dodd, and to you General Pershing, since both of you were active that same year in the Geronimo campaign."

Waiting until Nonotolth had finished interpreting, Patton continued. "Tell the court, Mr. Segundo, about that time in 1886 when you first saw Norroso."

With unwavering eyes, Monte started his

story. "I was six years old. My pa was out tending our cows. I was at the house with Ma. The Apaches came out of nowhere. They killed Ma. Then they brought in Pa and tied him to our corral. They cut open his stomach. With Pa screaming, they pulled out his guts and stretched them across the sand, way out, while he watched. And, while I watched. One of the Apaches took me and threw me into a cactus patch to die slow like my pa. I felt like I was on fire from the pain. All the while, I heard my pa scream and moan.

"The Apache that threw me into the cactus, I got a good look at. A real close look. He had a scar on his face, only then it was raised up and purple because it was fresh.

"Except for a lifetime of nightmares, I'd forgotten about the whole murdering raid, all of it, until I saw a picture of two Apache scouts in a newspaper. Then it started coming back to me. It's only come back in bits and pieces but I remember enough to know who it was who did that to me."

Monte pointed. "The murdering Apache that threw me into the cactus was him, the one you call Norroso. He's older but he hasn't changed his look. And the scar cinches it if there was any doubt. Which there isn't."

Patton let Monte's words hang in the silence. It was a great deal to process and Lieutenant George Patton knew how to handle the minds of men.

"And this is why you came to Mexico?" questioned Patton. "Not to join the Villistas but to avenge the murder of your father and mother? For justice?"

Monte did not answer.

Norroso's eyes narrowed. He seemed to be seeing Monte for the first time, his coarse features reflecting a semblance of recognition.

Lieutenant Johnson was shaken but quickly regained his composure. "Even if all of that were true . . ." he objected but before he could finish he was interrupted by a soldier who bounded up the stairs and then hurried up the aisle. He stopped in front of Pershing and saluted. "Begging your pardon, sir."

"What is it?" demanded Pershing. "Can't you see what's going on here, Private?"

"Orders, sir, an urgent message from the Captain of the Guard."

"What message?"

"I'm to tell you a large group of Mexicans are gathering outside the front gate, sir. A very large group. Hundreds of them."

Pershing sprang to his feet. "Villistas or Carrancistas?"

"Neither, sir. And none seem to have any weapons. They appear to be peons. And they keep coming. From every direction. Men, women, children."

"What do they want?"

"That's the funny part. We've asked and they won't say. They're just there. Like they're waiting for something."

Easing himself back down into his chair, Pershing said guardedly, "Alright. Keep me posted. If anything changes let me know immediately."

The courier saluted and hurried away. Pershing looked to Howze. "What do you make of that?"

Howze thoughtfully leaned back in his chair. "Begging for food, maybe. Villa wreaked havoc in most of the villages around here. Likely they're just hungry."

Pershing turned to Dodd. "Colonel what's your take?"

Oddly, Dodd did not respond. He was staring hard at Monte.

Studying Dodd, Pershing followed his eyes. "What is it, Colonel?"

Dodd again ignored Pershing. Instead he asked, "Mr. Segundo, do you, by chance, have a middle name?"

Monte thought for a moment. "I do, sir, but I never use it."

"And what might that middle name be?"

"Dell, sir."

"Son of a bitch!" blurted Dodd. "Monte Dell Segundo!"

Dodd abruptly rose from his desk and went over to Norroso and Nonotolth. Forming a tight huddle, they spoke softly, their words rapid and unintelligible.

Finally, Dodd turned to face Monte. "Mr. Segundo. Your back, it is badly scarred, is it not?"

Monte looked to me. I understood that he was asking if I had told anyone of his scars. I shook my head, "No."

Then Monte looked at Rosa. She also shook her head, "No."

Everyone in the court waited to hear Monte's reply.

"It is."

Dodd put his hand to his forehead. "God Almighty! It is you."

"Him boy," Norroso said, pointing at Monte. "Same boy . . ."

At that moment, the courier came in again but before he saluted, Pershing growled, "What now?"

"Three thousand, sir. That's the estimate. And they're still coming. A priest seems to be leading them."

"Are you sure they're just peons? Could they be hiding weapons?"

"The best we can tell, sir, no weapons at all."

"Alright, alright. Find out what they want and report back!"

Pershing stood and spread his arms wide. "Colonel, what the hell is going on?"

Dodd looked at Pershing. "Remember, General, back in eighty-six? You and I and half the United States Cavalry were chasing after Geronimo and his band. He was hitting settlements all over northern Mexico, Arizona, and New Mexico. Back then we had no better luck catching him than we've had rounding up Villa.

"One day after a week of hard riding I was coming back across the border with my company. Near the Arizona–New Mexico line, we came across a settlement that had been burned and was still smoking. Our canteens were empty and we were trying to make the next water hole before dark, but I decided to stop and take a look.

"We found a woman a short distance behind a cabin with a pistol under her body. It was empty but there was blood near where the cabin door had been so we figured she at least hit one of the renegades before she died. We deduced from the wound in her temple that she had saved the last bullet for herself.

"Then we found a man, a man tortured to death just like Mr. Segundo described. But he was lashed to a snubbing post inside the corral, not to the fence rails of the corral."

Dodd paused, his eyes hollow as if once again witnessing the gruesome scene.

"And?" demanded Pershing.

"We had some Apache scouts with us," Dodd continued, "so I sent them out to search for sign while we buried the man and woman. I noticed one of the scouts circling around a cholla thicket but paid little attention to him.

"After we piled rocks on the graves we formed up and moved out. We had gone about half a mile when the sergeant in command of the scouts charged up to the head of the column at a dead run. He told me that back at the settlement he had watched one of his scouts work his way deep into a thicket of cholla, stare down at something for a long while, and then turn around and walk out. Just out of curiosity the sergeant decided to ask the scout what he had been doing in all those thorns. After a few more questions the Apache admitted to having seen a small boy lying in the cactus, a boy that was still alive. But the Apache told the sergeant there was too much cactus to bother getting him out and besides the boy was almost dead anyway.

"We wheeled around and in a matter of minutes were back at the settlement. The men found some hoes and an axe and tore into that thicket. By then it was after sundown, so we built some fires nearby and made some torches so we could see.

"Full of stickers, my men finally reached the boy and brought him out. The kid's back, arms, and legs were riddled with cactus needles, most of them buried an inch deep under his skin. He looked like a bleeding porcupine.

"We took him to the nearest town, which was mostly full of Mexicans, but no one knew too much about him. All we could learn was that the boy's father worked for an absentee rancher, worked as foreman.

"The boy hardly talked at all. And it turned out, he didn't remember anything. He didn't even know his own name.

"So, we just referred to the child as 'the son of the dead foreman' . . . only since Spanish was spoken so much in that area, it was usually *'el nino del segundo muerte.'* Or Americanized a bit, it became, *'del muerte segundo.'* Work that over a few more years as an orphan boy is shipped around from place to place without a proper name and you no doubt come up with Monte Dell Segundo."

Dodd paused and turned to Norroso. "And the Apache who saw that boy in the cholla and decided to leave him there . . . the Indian that had recently sustained a deep gash on his face . . . was Private Norroso."

In the hush that followed Dodd's revelation, every mind in the court was struggling to absorb the convoluted facts of the colonel's story. For me, the very fabric of reality was insanely distorted. My eyes would not focus. Instead, the vivid image of two tortured Mexicans flooded my thoughts, men that Norroso undoubtedly had helped kill. And yet, was Norroso, after the long, treacherous chase through Mexico, truly not the Apache in Monte's dreams? Was he, in fact, to be absolved of any guilt in the death of Monte's father and mother? How could such a man evade punishment at every turn? How could this be a court of justice if one such as he was to go free?

In seconds, Pershing's cold, heartless voice interrupted the silence and cut through the fog in my brain. When I glanced up, the general was on his feet, resting the knuckles of both fists on the polished oak desktop.

"The United States Army," Pershing was saying, "does not concern itself with hard-luck stories. The army lives by regulations and an unwavering obedience to orders. When it comes to discipline we go by the book and the cold hard facts. Nothing more. That's the only way to maintain an effecting fighting force and obedience to orders. Regulations are all that concern this court-martial."

Pershing cast his merciless eyes around the court and then settled on Patton. "Lieutenant Patton, it appears your defense of the traitor is finished, is it not?"

Patton clenched his teeth and then nodded. "Yes, sir. It would appear all the facts have been presented."

"Good," snapped Pershing. "Now let's get to the civilian."

The general glanced down at a pile of papers on his desk. He was reaching for them when he noticed the courier was again standing at attention at the back of the tent.

Pershing bristled with irritation. "What?"

Seemingly even more nervous than previously the courier said, "Sir, there's a Mexican priest here. I think he's the one in charge of all the peons. He says it's urgent that he meet with you. Extremely urgent, sir."

"He can wait."

"Begging your pardon, sir," said the courier. "We have been waiting. The priest and me. Just outside the tent, sir. He's been listening for the last several minutes. He says that if you don't want an all-out war with Mexico, that you should hear what he has to say before you . . . well, sir . . ."

The courier paused, his face flushing crimson with fear.

"Before I what?" boomed Pershing.

Swallowing hard, the courier said, "Before you sentence Monte Segundo, sir."

The veins on the general's neck bulged. "Bring that son-of-a . . ." growled Pershing but then caught himself. "Bring the priest up here."

The courier spun on his heels but the priest, dressed in a long black cassock and gripping a wooden staff topped with a silver cross, was already making his way up the steps. It was Marco.

Stepping around the courier and walking casually down the aisle, Marco smiled and nodded benevolently at the soldiers as he passed by them. Without hesitating he went directly to Pershing and stopped one step in front of his desk.

"It would be best, General, if we enjoyed some privacy."

Pershing sneered. "Well, at least you speak English."

Marco shrugged. "I also speak Greek, Latin, Spanish, French, and German. We may converse in any of those languages you wish, sir."

Pershing fumed, his square jaws clenching as he struggled to control himself. "What do you have to say that's so important? And what does it have to do with this trial?"

"What I have to say is not for everyone but it may very well prevent the death of thousands."

"That's easy to say," Pershing said. "Why should I waste my time listening to you?"

"Because, General, as you are well aware your army is slowly being surrounded as we speak. But what you may not be aware of, is that soon your lines of communication will be cut and there is, under the command of Esteban Fierros, a brigade of Carrancistas and guerrillas forming in La Jarita to invade Laredo, Texas. You may or may not know that Esteban Fierros also commands Luis de la Rosa, who is ready to activate the Plan de San Diego or that thirty thousand troops are amassing in Sonora and Chihuahua under the command of General González, and that there are fifty thousand Yaquis and Tarahumara Indians massing in the west to join the Carrancistas."

Marco paused. "Shall I continue, General? I assure you that I am prepared to go on if you wish."

Pershing's eyes flashed with rage but for a long count of ten he merely glared at Marco. Finally, he announced in a surprisingly calm voice, "Take Private Segundo and everyone else go outside for a smoke. Everyone but counsel and the civilian. The woman is free to go."

The court cleared quickly, leaving Marco standing in front of the three senior officers and Patton and Johnson within arm's reach. I sat alone only a few feet away.

"Who the hell are you?" snapped Pershing. "Who are you working for?"

"I assure you, General, I am but a simple priest. You may call me Father Marco or just Marco if you feel it more appropriate."

"If that's true," Dodd asked, "how is it you know so much?"

Marco chuckled. "You have spies in Mexico. Mexico has spies in the states. Germany has spies in both countries. Everyone talks, especially the Mexicans. It is a priest's job to listen. It is not so surprising that I know what I do."

Thoughtfully rubbing his chin, Pershing said, "Alright, you have five minutes. What's so urgent?"

Bowing slightly, Marco began, "I am a Spaniard and a priest. Carranza is against the church and Villa is against both the Spaniards and the church. I have nothing to gain regardless of who becomes president of Mexico. My calling is to care for the common people, the ones that die in the battles of both armies.

"The peons of Mexico are the descendants of Indians. Though they have forgotten much of their ancestry they have maintained many of their beliefs and superstitions. These peons include most of the soldiers that compose both Mexican armies, including many of the officers."

"What is your point?" Howze asked, his tone respectful.

"My point is that belief, whether in the Holy Faith or in superstition or rumor, is an extraordinarily powerful force. And at this time and place, a singular belief can change the course of history."

"Belief?" questioned Patton. "What kind of belief?"

"Belief, for instance, that the combined armies of Mexico allied with Texas militants can retake the Rio Grande Valley. Belief that after killing every white male living there, the Mexican army could proceed to recapture all of your southwestern states, all the land Mexico lost to the United States."

"That's ridiculous," Johnson said. "Mexico wouldn't stand a chance against us. Who could believe such nonsense?"

"Nonsense?" questioned Marco. "At the moment, your entire army is pigeon-holed here in Colonia Dublan. That fact is no secret, anyone can read about it your newspapers."

"True," Johnson said, "but we have thousands of men waiting in our National Guard. If you read our papers you and the Mexicans know that President Wilson has just called up the National Guards of Texas, New Mexico, and Arizona."

Cocking his head, Marco sighed as even Pershing squirmed a little. "My dear lieutenant, as I said, Germany has many spies in America and they in turn keep Carranza well-informed. Carranza is quite aware of the American army's opinion of the militia, that your so-called National Guard is completely inept."

Marco glanced at Pershing. "Am I incorrect, General?"

"Not about the guard," admitted Pershing. "But in the long run, Mexico still wouldn't stand a chance. We could train an army ten times the size of Mexico's."

"Perhaps," agreed Marco. "But Mexico is ready now with a force ten times the size of yours."

"Damn!" muttered Patton.

Pershing took a deep, resentful breath and let it out slowly. "So, what else do you have to say about belief?"

"Ah, yes. To recapture the southwest is only one form of belief. Superstition is another. In Mexico, superstition is deeply ingrained in the culture. It is the source of much anxiety as well as deep-seated fear."

"Like what?" asked Patton, his eyes narrowing with interest.

"For instance, the superstition that one must lock up your farm animals at night or *El Chupacabra* will slaughter them. The belief that stepping on a grave will summon the spirit of the dead person and it will harm you. That a full glass of water behind the door will ward off bad spirits. That on October thirty-first the spirits of the dead visit their families and literally eat and drink with them.

"These are the types of superstitions I speak of, the kind that almost all Mexicans believe in. These are but a few that invoke fear and awe."

"You've got two more minutes, Padre," Pershing grumbled. "So far this has been a waste of my time."

Marco flashed a patient smile. "One thing, however, that the Mexicans fear more than any superstition is an Apache. To a Mexican, the Apache is worse than any demon of their imagination. It has been so for three hundred years. But now they have heard of a white man, a white man who is so ferocious, so powerful, that he actually hunts the dreaded Apaches.

"This man is said to be a guardian of a secret land far to the north. For very mysterious reasons, this man left the snowy mountains and rode south through the deserts and recently entered Mexico through Las Palomas. There, to rescue a Yaquis princess, he killed five evil Carrancista soldiers. He did this while drinking from a bottle of tequila that he held in his left hand and, using only his right, vanquished the woman's captors without spilling a drop.

"From Las Palomas this man traveled to Boca Grande. It was here that he was first called *El Muerte* by the fearful peasants."

Marco paused to chuckle. He glanced at the faces around him but saw only blank stares. "Well, to a humble priest this proves that God has a sense of humor." Pausing again, Marco glanced around. *"El Muerte del Segundo?"*

"Go on," encouraged Patton. "We get the connection."

"*El Muerte*'s next stop," continued Marco, "was the village of Ojo Federico where, it is said, he killed an entire garrison of evil Carrancistas using only his pistol. Those men, you see, had molested a small boy's mother and thus were marked for death by *El Muerte.*

"After that day, everyone wondered where *El Muerte* would strike next, who he would mark for death and how they would die. The peons' questions were soon answered in the village of San Miguel. There *El Muerte* protected the entire village from marauding Villa bandits. He did this by using a rifle to shoot the bandits as he would flies on a wall. But he shot them from a distance of more than one thousand paces. He was so angry, however, that the bandits had tried to rob the poor people of San Miguel, that he was not satisfied with those he had killed during the day. *El Muerte* went out that night, caught a dozen more bandits, and hanged them high in the air between two trees, hanging them like a string of dead fish on a line.

"*El Muerte* could do this because he can track better than any Apache and can see in the darkest night like *el gato,* the cat. And he can detect north at all times, in any weather or time of day. Thus, he always knows where he is going and he never gets lost. For this reason, it is said that no one, not even the Apache, can hide from *El Muerte.*

"Even the vaunted Dorados fear him. That is why, though he was known to be an American, they let *El Muerte* pass by their Santa Rosalita hacienda unmolested.

"In La Quemada, *El Muerte* knew he was getting close to the Apaches he hunted so he had special moccasins made. These were made of the finest, softest leather in all of Mexico, just what he needed to sneak up on the hated Apaches.

"Most say *El Muerte* is a demon but they think he is a good demon. I tell them he is a Nephilim, an offspring of fallen angels. Even those that do not believe in such stories have no doubts that *El Muerte* is a ferocious killer of men, a man like none they have ever heard of."

"Just to be clear," Johnson said, guardedly, "you're saying that Monte Segundo is this *El Muerte?*"

"I am."

411

"That's a lot of bull, Padre," muttered Pershing. "And you know it."

Marco shrugged. "Of such 'bull' legends are made, General. What matters is the people believe the stories of *El Muerte.* And many of the Villista and Carrancista officers believe the reputation of *El Muerte* is justified."

"So," said Patton, a sly grin suddenly forming on his lips, "is it *El Muerte* those peons out front have come to see?"

"Yes. With a bit of help from Rosa and me, the word has spread that he is here."

"I still don't see the point," confessed Dodd.

"Yes, yes," agreed Marco. "Now to the point. It is a gamble to be sure but one that costs nothing to try."

"I'm listening," Pershing said.

Marco suddenly grew serious, the change in his demeanor was striking. "Your regular army is out of troops and cut off. Your National Guard, at least those in the southwest and eastern portion of your country, are known to be of little or no use. And even if they were somewhat useful, they could not organize in less than three months.

"Your only hope is to spread the word that you are about to call on an elite army of men hidden to all spies, a reserve that lives in the rugged mountains guarding the border of the far north. At the same time, you make it known that *El Muerte* is but one example of this army, this National Guard of the north. Make it known also that if this elite *'Guarda Nacional del Norte'* is summoned down from the mountains, they will come by the thousands and when they do, even the Apaches will run and hide."

"You're talking about a bluff," said Howze. "Is that all you've got?"

"North Idaho and Montana," replied Marco, "are still on the frontier. There is no reason for German spies to know anything about the National Guard in that region. I doubt, under the circumstances, they could convince the Mexicans that no such army exists. Even if they could, that would take quite some time.

"Enough Mexicans will believe the bluff, gentlemen. Not all but enough. And fear will follow belief."

Patton snapped his fingers and pointed at Marco. "Like Gideon and the three hundred."

"Precisely," Marco agreed.

"You mean the Bible story?" Dodd asked.

"Sure!" Patton said. "Old Gideon surrounded the Midianites' camp with just three hundred handpicked men. At a signal,

413

they blew their trumpets and lit up their torches. The soldiers in the valley below thought they were surrounded by thousands of Israelites and they stampeded in panic. It was an early use of diversion and deception, of mental warfare. We studied it at West Point. It's an intangible fact just like morale is an intangible."

Pershing rubbed the back of his neck. "This is thin, Padre. Mighty thin."

"Think of it this way, General," encouraged Patton. "Segundo is like Jesse James, Wes Hardin, and Wild Bill Hickok all rolled into one. Imagine what effect a reputation like that would have had back in the states a generation ago."

"What if they are like him," said Johnson, thoughtfully. "Those men up north, I mean. The National Guard. Most of them are probably hunters, miners, or lumberjacks, all as strong as an ox. Do we really know anything about that part of the country? Or what kind of men live up there?"

"I can't say that I do," Pershing said, glancing at Dodd.

Dodd shook his head and then Pershing looked to Howze.

"I certainly don't," Howze said. "It's so remote I doubt anyone does."

Pershing studied Marco for a moment.

"Tell me, Padre, just how much of your story is true?"

I felt like barging into the conversation and answering the general's question but then I thought it best to let Marco respond. My gut told me the officers were far more likely to believe a Catholic priest than a wayward newspaper reporter.

I was not to be disappointed, because Marco was quick to answer.

"You already know the truth of what happened in Las Palomas. With my own eyes, I saw the dead men of San Miguel, five of them, hanging like fish. No one knows how but he killed them all in the dark of night. And I know he shot several men that day at seven hundred meters.

"I also witnessed his ability to see in the dark and his unwavering ability to always know which direction is north. And there are hundreds of eyewitnesses at your front gate who saw the many men he killed in Ojo Federico as well the ones he killed in San Miguel."

"Son of a bitch!" exclaimed Patton. "He's like an Old West gunfighter and vigilante committee all rolled into one."

"I'll be damned!" agreed Dodd.

Placing his empty palm over his heart, Marco said slyly, "Belief, General, at times can be mightier than the sword."

A "humpf" escaped from Pershing's lips. Looking down, he rubbed his chin again, but this time for a full minute. There was another "humpf" and then he raised his head.

"And how would we go about this? For it to work, Segundo would have to cooperate."

"For his freedom," offered Marco, "I think he would."

A tense silence fell on the meeting.

"If he cooperates, John," Howze said to Pershing, "we can put him on a train at Columbus and have him out of the country before anyone's the wiser. The troops would never know what became of him. They would assume . . . well, most likely they would assume he was put in front of a firing squad."

It was then General Pershing realized I was still sitting nearby. His eyes bore into me like burning coals. "What about him, that damned reporter? All the ones I know have big mouths."

Everyone turned my way.

I didn't have to think. "I will not repeat anything I've heard. Nor will I report it."

"Why should we believe you?" drilled Johnson.

On impulse, I stood and faced them. I

took a deep breath to calm my nerves. "Because my name is not Billy Cabott," I said boldly. "It is William Cabott Weston III. And as a Weston, I give you my word that I will not report anything I have heard here today."

Johnson's eyelids peeled wide with surprise. "Weston? Are you related to William Weston?"

"He is my father."

Pershing cast a questioning glance at Johnson.

"Sir," said Johnson, "the Westons are a known family in Washington. Their shipping company is responsible for a good third of the supplies being transported to Britain and the allies."

Still staring at me, Pershing muttered disgustedly, "It figures."

Marco smiled at me and nodded his approval.

"Well," relented Pershing, "this whole thing sounds crazy. It goes against my grain, but it's worth a try."

"Sir," grinned Patton, "sometimes there's a very thin line that separates crazy from brilliant. I think it's a hell of a plan."

"Humpf. We'll see soon enough. Give Segundo back his weapons but make sure his pistol is empty. Gas up two of the Dodges.

Lieutenant Patton, you ride in the passenger seat of the lead car. I want Segundo in the back with a guard next to him. Everyone armed with pistols including the drivers.

"Lieutenant Johnson, you'll be in the passenger seat of the second car. Put . . . put Mr. Weston in the back. I want him out of here, too, and as far from Colonia Dublan as you can get him."

The situation was developing unexpectedly and very rapidly and I had to think fast. I had barely come to know Monte and Rosa, yet in some ways I felt I knew them better than they knew themselves. I also knew that I had to act quickly.

"The people are used to seeing the three of us together," I said. "It would have a greater impact if Rosa was present."

Surprisingly, Pershing didn't hesitate. "Alright, take the woman. Put her with Mr. Weston.

"Load them all up. Drive to the gate. Have Segundo make his appearance and say a few words. But just a few. And then drive like a bat out of hell to Columbus, no stops. Then get Segundo on the first train that comes through. East or west, doesn't matter. Just make sure he leaves Columbus."

CHAPTER 14

Marco and the officers quickly dispersed, leaving me alone with the empty desks and camp stools. I was beginning to think I had been forgotten when Private Darby bounded up the steps and stopped just inside the tent.

Waving at me he said, "Come on! The car's waiting."

Scrambling to my feet, I trotted across the wooden floor, down the steps, and into the glaring sunlight. Darby was standing next to a Dodge touring car that was surrounded three-deep by a semicircle of gawking soldiers. The car, as usual, had its canvas top folded down but unlike the shiny black ones I had seen at Pershing's headquarters, this Dodge was dull green in color. A driver was behind the steering wheel and Lieutenant Johnson was in the passenger seat ratcheting a bullet into the chamber of his Colt pistol.

Darby flung open the rear door. When he stepped back I saw Rosa, as beautiful as I had ever seen her, already seated. Composed, aloof, and holding the attention of every man present, she wore a faint smile of satisfaction.

Hearing the door slam shut behind me, I slid onto the seat next to Rosa, feeling the heat from the black leather upholstery burning its way through my pants and shirt.

The Dodge lunged and then hit the brakes. It lunged again and this time rolled slowly as the crowd of men split apart and cleared the way ahead.

Johnson holstered his Colt and then turned. "We're going to stop at the gate. Segundo will say a few words. You two sit tight."

"And then what?" Rosa asked, defiantly. *"Ley fuga?"*

It was only then I realized Rosa had no idea of what was happening. "No, Rosa. No one is to be shot. We're being set free. All three of us."

Rosa glared at Johnson, her skepticism plain to see. "It is a lie. As soon as we walk away they will shoot us and then say we were trying to escape. I am no fool."

Johnson shook his head. "What he says is true, Miss. When Segundo is finished speaking, you are free to go. And we're taking Segundo and . . . ah . . . Mr. Cabott, to the train station in Columbus."

Not allowing Rosa to respond, I asked, "Is Miss Bustamonte allowed to come with us to Columbus? She would like to at least say goodbye to Monte Segundo."

Johnson thought a moment. "Yes, she can come," he said and then turned back around.

Rosa raised an eyebrow. "You speak for me?"

I flinched, but only a little. "Have you talked to Monte?"

"Not since Ojos Azules. I did not see him until today."

"Then have you been able to thank him? For saving your life?"

Rosa's eyebrow relaxed. She took a deep breath and let it out slowly. Her eyes softened. "Why should I thank him? He would have done the same for any woman. You saw him in Ojo Federico. He did not know that woman. And he did not know me at Las Palomas."

"But he knows you now, Rosa. Think what he gave up to help you. He had come all this way to kill Norroso. But when he finally had the chance, he chose to help you instead. Don't you see that, Rosa?"

421

Turning her head away, Rosa fell silent.

We worked our way through the makeshift streets, swerving around hordes of meandering soldiers until we stopped at an intersection. In seconds, a black touring car with two American flags attached to opposite sides of the front window drove into the intersection from our left and then turned north to take the lead. Patton was the passenger. Monte and an armed guard were seated in the rear.

We followed Patton's Dodge with only a few feet between the rear and front bumpers until reaching the front gate, a mere gap in a barbed wire fence. The opening of the gate was blocked with a long beam of sun-bleached wood that soldiers raised and lowered by pressing down on one end. A platoon of riflemen lined the fence and guarded the gate. Ten paces beyond the gate stood Padre Marco with his staff. Behind him, in eerie silence, several thousand Mexicans were clustered shoulder to shoulder.

Before we came to a complete stop the gate beam started up. When it did, Marco and those directly behind him began to back up. Then the black Dodge rolled forward inch by inch. The steady popping of its engine, hardly noticeable inside the busy camp, now seemed almost deafening.

With only inches separating our touring cars, we followed the black Dodge for another fifty feet and then came to a gentle stop. Both engines were turned off.

Without any prompting that I could see, Monte stood. A dull buzz of muted voices rippled through the Mexicans as Monte looked them over. He spoke in English, his voice carrying over the crowd. As he did, Rosa interpreted.

"My father was an American and this day I will return to my home. But my mother was Mexican . . . and this day I say . . . this day I say, Viva Mexico!"

The crowd erupted with ecstatic *"Viva México,"* but in a matter of seconds switched to *"Viva El Muerte! Viva El Muerte!"*

Monte waved with his right hand. With his left, he gripped the back of the passenger seat. Still waving, the black Dodge eased forward, the chants of *"Viva El Muerte!"* growing ever louder. We followed immediately as both Rosa and I, caught up in the frenzy, began to wave as well. The exhilaration was intoxicating. Even Johnson and Patton started waving.

Amidst the uproar, I saw Marco and our eyes met. He smiled broadly, making the sign of the cross as we passed near him. For lack of a better response and out of utmost respect, I saluted him in return and then gave him a final wave goodbye.

In less than a minute we were through the crowd and picking up speed. I looked back and then got up on my knees facing the rear. Fascinated, I peered through the dust. The people were still celebrating. "Remarkable," I said. "Simply remarkable."

"There will be a grand fiesta tonight," Rosa said, raising her voice to compensate for the wind in our ears. "They will tell tales and make up songs. The legend will grow. For a while, my people will be happy."

I spun around and settled back into the seat. "I wish I could be there," I said and then noticed we had veered onto the main road and were already approaching thirty miles per hour. Patton's Dodge was only a few car-lengths in front of us and throwing up a cloud of fine sand and dust.

Johnson coughed and ordered the driver to back off. When we were able to see clearly, the driver accelerated just enough to maintain our distance.

The ride was surprisingly smooth, and except for an occasional jolt, which bounced us off our cushioned leather seats, we reached a steady clip that would see us barreling through the desert heat at nearly forty miles to the hour.

Speaking over the hissing wind and thundering Dodge engine, I asked Rosa, "What do you think Monte will do now?"

Rosa raised her voice. "I only know that he will not have his revenge."

"You mean justice," I said.

"Justice!" scoffed Rosa. "Justice is only revenge dressed in ribbons and bows. What he wants, what all people want, is revenge."

Having no logical rebuttal to Rosa's adamant declaration, I chose to ignore it. Instead, I offered, "I think Monte will look for the graves of his parents. Colonel Dodd practically told him the location, near the Mexican border where Arizona meets New Mexico. And when he gets in that area, he may see or hear things that bring back more memories. Or there could still be people living there who remember what happened and where."

Coursing through the dry air, my eyes began to sting. I rubbed them with my knuckles. Wiping the grit from my eyelids, I took a moment to consider what lay ahead for Monte.

Almost talking to myself I said, "I can't imagine how Monte feels now that he knows he was wrong about Norroso."

"He wasn't entirely wrong," Rosa said,

"Norroso is a bad man. He stabbed me. But he does know that the Apaches who killed his mother and father will forever go unpunished."

"Yes," I agreed. "But finding their graves might help put an end to it, an end to all he's been through. Don't you agree?"

Rosa thoughtfully tucked an unruly strand of hair back behind her ear. "Only the Holy Father knows such things. It would have been better if he never came to Mexico and his memories had stayed buried."

"You should go with him, Rosa," I said impulsively. "Go with him to find the graves."

Rosa thought for a moment, then somberly shook her head. "No. Graves are best visited alone."

"Alright," I conceded. "But I've seen him look at you, Rosa. And I've seen you look at him. You both try to hide it but neither one of you has to tell me how you feel."

"Has he said anything to you?" Rosa asked. "Has he said even one word to you?"

To that question, I had a ready answer. "Yes. The word he used was *beautiful.*"

"That is a word all men use," snapped Rosa. "It means nothing."

I raked my mind frantically, searching for anything romantic Monte might have said. I could think of nothing. I was out of ideas and left with nothing but total honesty. "There was only one other thing he said about you."

"What?" demanded Rosa.

"He said you were dangerous."

Rosa's eyes narrowed. Her lips tightened. In anticipation of a blistering string of epithets, I leaned away. She seemed to hold her breath for several seconds.

"Dangerous?" she repeated, but in a surprisingly mellow tone.

"Yes," I admitted, still holding my distance.

"We shall see," Rosa said, and then to my astonishment her face brightened with a genuine smile.

For the next two hours, nothing more was said. All anyone did was gaze out into the Mexican desert. The warm wind brushed over us and the steady vibration of the Dodge engine lulled us into a near hypnotic complacency.

The desert north of Colonia Dublan was just as bleak as I remembered, except now, being held up by scrawny wooden poles, a single black wire paralleled the road. I had every intention of breaking the monotony by counting those poles but I soon became so drowsy that I abandoned the idea.

My mind drifted and then lazily came back to the wire. It no doubt was a telephone line that had been erected to keep General Pershing in contact with Columbus. He would certainly have called ahead to Camp Furlong and have guards waiting for us, waiting to take us to the train station and make certain we boarded. But, I wondered, would the train be headed east or west?

Monte would want to go west toward Arizona but I would be going east. In a matter of minutes, I would have to say goodbye to Rosa and Monte.

I thought of clean sheets and hot soothing baths, of nice restaurants and of my home on Carnegie Hill. And it was the thought of Carnegie Hill that snapped me out of my daydreaming.

I was suddenly alert and strangely ill at ease. I blinked. Focusing my eyes, I could see the outskirts of a small village. I leaned forward, close to Johnson's ear. "Is that Las Palomas?"

Johnson nodded and shifted his weight to sit more erect. "Yes. Another ten minutes and we'll be in Columbus."

Just then we passed by a thicket of mesquite that hugged the roadside to my right. I caught a glimpse of a burro-drawn cart parked in the shade. Under a large sombrero an ancient-looking Mexican sat on top of a pile of grain sacks. His eyes locked onto us as we sped by.

I thought nothing of it but soon caught sight of another cart waiting by the roadside. This one was much larger and had a bare-boned mule in the harness. A man and woman sat on the seat watching us approach. The rear of the cart was packed with jostling children of all ages.

Suddenly the woman pointed at our lead car and every child's head turned and continued to follow us as we passed.

I sat up trying to see ahead of Patton's car. Squinting against the wind, I saw a few more carts on both sides of the road in the distance. But beyond those few, a solid quarter mile of Mexicans lined our path all the way to Las Palomas.

"They seem to be waiting for something," I said to Johnson as we rushed by the string of carts.

Johnson uneasily looked left and right. "I agree. And I don't like the looks of it."

We began to slow our speed.

"The people are here to see *El Muerte*," Rosa said. "Anyone can see that."

Half turning, Johnson studied Rosa. "What makes you think that? We got here in just over two hours. How could they know *El Muerte* was coming?"

Rosa shook her head and pointed to the telephone line. "Our border guards would have to be told something. And our people have pigeons. And pigeons don't follow a road. They fly straight."

"Makes sense," Johnson replied. "But they're not cheering."

"Here on the border," Rosa said, "the people live close to your government. They have learned to be cautious. Now it is enough only to get a look at *El Muerte*. They have come to see. That is all."

Entering the crowded village, we slowed to only a few miles per hour as the villagers quickly cleared the street. Three and four deep, they backed up and wedged themselves against the dusty adobe walls, but not a single word was spoken. The only sound came from the hum of our engines and a pack of barking dogs nipping at our tires.

In seconds the village was behind us and the border gate directly ahead. We slowed again but before we came to a stop the Carrancista guards raised their green and white gate arm. At that same instant, the American red and white arm went up as well.

Ignoring the Mexican guards, we rolled across the border and halted a solid ten feet north of the line. A half-dozen soldiers saluted both lieutenants and then one rounded the lead car and handed a folded piece of paper to Patton. Another salute followed and we once again gained speed. The desert was exactly as it had been for the last eighty miles but the feel of the land instantly changed. I was safe and secure. There was no war nor were there warlords or roving bandits. For the first time in my life, I was profoundly thankful to simply be in America, to be an American citizen.

With a combination of gratitude and pride welling up inside me, I turned my attention toward Columbus. I could easily make out the water tower and the roof of the train station but the rest of the town was hidden behind a checkered sea of green and khaki army tents that had flooded both sides of the dirt road ahead of us.

I strained my eyes, looking for any Mexicans that might be alongside the road. I saw nothing but barren desert. Only then did I begin to wonder what message Patton had received at the guard station. Surely it had come from General Pershing. Were there new orders? Had the general changed his mind? Had war with Mexico already begun?

As we approached the army camp my last question was easily answered. Men were everywhere but most were working at their various tasks without the slightest hint of urgency. No one was the least bit excited nor was a single soul in any sort of hurry.

We drove through the middle of camp and straight to the train station where, to my surprise, a westbound train was ready and waiting along with a half-dozen guards with rifles on their shoulders.

The guards stood in formation at the bottom of the stairs that led up to the boarding platform. Behind them the train held steady, its steam engine chugging in anticipation. Further down the platform, dozens of other soldiers were carrying boxes or unloading grain sacks.

Across the road to the west, several officers stood on the porch of the Custom House watching us as our cars pulled up and stopped. Except for a growing crowd of Mexicans on the north side of the railroad tracks, nothing seemed out of the ordinary.

Johnson hopped out of our Dodge first. Indicating both Rosa and me, he said, "Stay close to me."

Rosa and I exited opposite sides of the Dodge and then stepped down onto the blistering sand. My back felt oddly cool and then I realized I had been sweating against the upholstery. I could feel my heart pumping.

"Is everything alright?" I asked Johnson as Rosa came up next to me.

"The general called ahead and had them hold the train. As far as I know, you'll be on it in a few minutes."

Patton, the driver, and the guard unloaded from the lead car a few feet in front of us, but Monte remained seated until the guards that were in formation marched forward and up to the edge of the Dodge. After the soldiers had positioned themselves on each side of the rear door Monte stepped out of the car. He paused and, for the first time since leaving Colonia Dublan, looked back at us.

I had to smile. If there ever was a man who took things in stride, it was Monte Segundo. If he was the least bit bothered by what had transpired at the court-martial, he hid it remarkably well.

"Let's go," Patton said. "The train is waiting."

With Patton in the lead and Monte bracketed by riflemen, the soldiers rumbled up the wooden stairs. As soon as they reached the platform, Rosa and I followed, with Johnson bringing up the rear.

In parade formation, we walked down the

planks to the second car behind the engine, an empty passenger car that had been added to a long line of freight and boxcars.

Opposite the front door of the passenger car, Patton stopped. He waved and the guards took several steps backward, allowing the five of us a modicum of privacy.

"You're cleared all the way to California if you want to go that far," Patton said.

Feeling emboldened by Monte's demeanor and knowing Lieutenant Johnson was familiar with the Weston name, I directed my question to him. "I believe General Pershing's orders concerning me were to merely get me out of Columbus, were they not?"

Johnson looked at Patton. Patton mulled over my question for several seconds. "That's right."

"That being the case, I must say that I have no desire to see any more desert. It is time I return to my family. Not hearing from me in quite some time, they will be worried. I will wait for an eastbound train."

"Suit yourself," Patton replied.

Monte put out his hand. "Billy," he said, smiling, "you'll do."

I shook Monte's hand, feeling the hardened calluses and the enormous strength in it. "Monte," I began and then paused, searching for words, ". . . I owe you an immense debt of gratitude."

I let go of Monte's hand and took Rosa's and shook it as well. "And you, Rosa, thank you for putting up with me . . . and teaching me. I owe you, also. I have learned so much from both of you."

Rosa glanced down at my handshake, eyeing the gesture with a mixture of suspicion and curiosity.

Patton shook hands with Monte. Grinning broadly, Patton said, "I never met a gunfighter before. It's been a pleasure."

Monte looked down at Rosa and when he did I held my breath.

"Things didn't turn out the way I figured," Monte said. "So, parts of me are still missing."

Rosa looked up at Monte. "And part of me has been lost in the revolution."

"Come with me," Monte said, evenly.

Cocking her head to one side, Rosa asked, "Are you asking?"

Monte's instant reply was dead serious, "You bet I am!"

I expected Rosa to at least smile but instead she gazed deeply into Monte's eyes. A moment later she turned and gracefully went up the steps and into the waiting passenger car.

I watched Rosa take a seat inside the train and was about to offer Monte my congratulations, when I noticed he was removing cartridges from his pistol belt.

Unholstering his Colt, Monte said flatly, "I left Norroso alone at the trial because I knew that was my only chance of getting out of there alive."

Patton nodded his agreement as Monte flipped open the loading gate of his pistol and began shoving cartridges into the cylinders.

"And because I think I owed you that for helping me," said Monte, as he filled the fifth chamber. Snapping the loading gate shut, he looked up at Patton. "But if I ever see him again, I'll kill him."

"I hope you do." A half-smile creased Patton's lips. "And you may yet get your chance. During the trial, I thought it best not to bring it up, but in the melee afterwards I told General Pershing about Norroso stabbing Miss Bustamonte."

Patton grinned at me. "I didn't tell him *how* I knew, only that I had it on good authority." Turning his attention back to Monte, Patton continued. "The general ordered Shannon and Norroso to report right away for questioning, but Norroso got wind of it somehow. He and two other scouts took off on horseback. Norroso's a deserter now and my guess is all three of them will head for the Sierra Madres. I've heard there are bands of wild Apaches still up in those mountains."

Monte Segundo eyed Patton for a moment and then holstered his Colt and saluted. Johnson's return salute was more of an involuntary reflex, but George Patton stood tall, saluting sharply and with utmost respect.

Monte turned and stepped up into the train.

Patton then waved at the conductor. The train jolted and the wheels began to roll. Inside the passenger car, Monte took a seat next to Rosa. He leaned forward and looked at me through the window.

Monte Segundo was not the type to wave. Instead, he merely gave me a simple nod as the westbound train began to pick up speed.

The three of us stood there watching. As the freight cars started rolling past, Johnson shook his head. "Norroso stabbed that woman?"

"I got hold of one of the doctors that treated her after Ojos Azules," admitted Patton. "He said the cut in her back was too wide for a bayonet. Knowing how the general feels about his scouts, I wasn't sure if I should bring it up in the court-martial. Maybe I would have if things hadn't gone the way they did. But it sure as hell worked out, didn't it? Like a damned storybook."

"Poor fella," sighed Johnson. "As tough as he is, you still have to feel a little sorry for him."

"Sorry?" questioned Patton. "For him?"

"Sure, Georgie. He's had a tough life. Orphaned like he was and then to have a lifetime of nightmares. And just when he thinks he has a chance to set things right and turn his world right-side up, he's knocked down again. He traveled all the way down here from Idaho and then rode hundreds of miles into Mexico, all the while convinced he had discovered the murderer of his parents. But all of it was for nothing. His mission, his quest to finally avenge his parents, turned out to be a monumental failure."

"The only thing I pity," retorted Patton as he took out the folded piece of paper given to him at the border, "is that the poor son-of-a-bitch doesn't know just how successful he was!"

Johnson unfolded the paper. As he read, I watched his heartfelt expression of sympathy warp into a mask of shock.

"I'll be damned!" Johnson blurted. "I'll

be double-damned!"

Perplexed, I asked, "May I inquire what it is you're reading?"

Patton answered, "What Hughie is reading says . . . 'From all quarters, evidence of immediate withdrawal. Communication intercepts confirm unilateral order to stand down in Mexico. Texas insurgents included in Carranza's stand down orders.' . . . That's what he's reading."

"Then it worked!" I exclaimed. "Marco was right! It actually worked!"

Palming his forehead, Johnson's eyes filled with bewilderment.

"The padre was only half-right," Johnson said. "He was right about preventing a war with Mexico. But that's only half of what this means. If war with Mexico has indeed been averted, America will now be free to join the Allies in Europe. And there's no doubt whatsoever that our entry into the war will tip the balance of power. When that occurs, the Allies will win that war and instead of Germany controlling Europe, it will be the Allies. This stand-down of Mexican forces will affect the entire world."

I ran those words over in my mind several times before I asked, "Then you're saying," I muttered slowly, "that Monte Segundo has changed the course of history."

Patton turned back and continued watching the train. "That, my friend, is exactly what Segundo did. Think of it. One man with a Colt six-shooter was able to change the world."

Folding his arms, still looking westward, Patton grinned and said to himself, "I like the sound of that. One man with a six-shooter. I like that a lot."

Johnson refolded the paper as Patton turned and focused his attention on me. "Mr. Weston, will you remain at the station until you can board an eastbound train?"

"Yes, sir. I will."

"Good. Then you are released on your own recognizance."

"Thank you, sir."

Spinning smoothly on their polished riding boots, the two lieutenants walked away from me, their heels thudding across the weathered planks and down the stairs. They crossed the road and disappeared into the Custom House.

Only when they were out of sight did I realize that I was standing in the afternoon sun. Still dazed by the news of the stand-down, I made my way to the shady side of the train station and took a seat on an empty crate next to the wall. The words *changed the world* kept echoing in my mind.

Attempting to grasp the stupendous significance of that phrase, my head continued to
buzz.

Monte Segundo, a lumberjack, an orphan
who didn't even know his own name, had
singlehandedly determined the outcome of
a World War and altered the fate of mankind.
More incredibly, he had accomplished that
monumental feat unintentionally. Unlike
Alexander the Great, Napoleon, and others
like them, Monte Segundo cared nothing
about power. He was not a pharaoh or king,
not a kaiser, general, or president. And yet,
concerning world events, he was in every
way their equal.

Other words echoed in my thoughts. "God
works in obscurity," Marco had said.

I chuckled weakly, profoundly aware that
if anyone was qualified to be described as
obscure, it was Monte Segundo, a lumberjack from the uninhabited north woods.

I also recalled Marco quoting, "God has
chosen the simple to confound the wise."

And that was when I began to think of
home.

At first, I was thrilled. I imagined my
friends and family gathered about me, eager
to hear my incredible story. What a tale I
had to tell, a saga of epic proportions that
would fascinate and astound everyone on

Carnegie Hill.

But the more I thought about my return to New York, the more I began to have doubts. How, I wondered, would I begin my story and what events would it be best to omit? The fight in Las Palomas would certainly be thrilling. My introduction to saddle sores would provide a round of hilarious laughter. But what then?

I would have to skip the abuses suffered by Rosa, the bloodshed and the torture. Certainly, the ears of my listeners would be far too delicate to hear of such brutality.

But what of my observations regarding the peons of Mexico, how they were mistreated by the wealthy *haciendados*? Would that hit too close to home?

And what would my elite company think of me if they were to discover that I had learned to have the utmost respect for a Catholic priest, a simple man of God? And what would they whisper to each other when I told them about Rosa, a lowly Mexican woman who fought in the revolution whom I now counted as a dear friend?

And as for Monte Segundo, could they accept my ardent declaration that a common laborer had done more to change the world than any ten of them combined?

I wrestled with my questions for over an

442

hour and then grew restless. I slid off the wooden crate and walked around the edge of the depot and into a setting sun, the last rays reflecting off twin ribbons of polished train track. It was a path of steel stretching all the way to the western horizon, a path I knew I was eventually destined to follow.

Watching the sun go down, I experienced a wave of sadness mingled with sentimental regret. I realized that William Cabott Weston III would never return to Carnegie Hill. That person had ceased to exist.

Standing there, a gentle breeze stirred the air, marking the end of the day. Soon an eastbound train would arrive and in a few short hours I would walk up the steps that led to my parents' mansion.

As the door opened I would smile and act as I always had, at least for the duration of the happy homecoming.

I would tell everyone a polite version of my days in Mexico. I would keep many secrets, stories that I would save for my grandchildren, and God willing, for my great-grandchildren.

But the most guarded secret would be that William Cabott Weston III disappeared somewhere south of the border and the man who returned merely to visit Carnegie Hill would forever view the world and everything in it through the eyes of Billy Cabott.

And so it has been since the spring of 1916.

ABOUT THE AUTHOR

Paul Cox was born in rural Arkansas. When he was ten years old, his family moved to California. There he had a successful athletic career, culminating in becoming an All American in the decathlon at Cal State Fullerton. After graduating from Cal State, Paul attended graduate school in San Francisco and, like Zane Grey, received his doctorate degree in dentistry. He presently lives in North Idaho. Paul is an avid outdoorsman and employs "boots on the ground" research and personal experience to infuse his stories with authenticity.